# BACHELOR SOUL:

## A RICH INDULGENCE BILLIONAIRE ROMANCE NOVEL

### REGINA MORRIS

## AUTHOR

Silkhaven Publishing, LLC
Join Regina Morris' mailing list for games, freebies, and fun at http://newsletter.reginamorris.com
Please visit author Regina Morris on her website http://www.reginamorris.com
Regina Morris enjoys connecting with fans on social media. Please find her at:
Facebook: http://www.facebook.com/ ReginaAnnMorris (@ReginaMorris)
Twitter: http://www.twitter.com/ReginaMorris (@ReginaMorris)
Pinterest: http://www. pinterest.com/ReginaAnnMorris

Billionaire Scott Holister's ambition is to become a senior partner at his law firm. His track record is good and he has seniority at the firm, but he doesn't have the appropriate corporate image. He needs a house, an attitude adjustment, and, most importantly, a wife.

He finds a woman interested in dating him—not his wallet—but the woman he is falling in love with is a waitress at a local diner, who has mistaken him for being a homeless man after he has a mishap wile jobbing in the park.

When the restaurant she works at caters the Christmas party held by Scott's law firm, passions explode as they discover who they are and what truly matters.

Silkhaven Publishing, LLC

ISBN: 978–1–948997–56–0 (EPub Ebook)

ISBN: 978–1–948997–57–7 (MOBI Ebook)

ISBN: 978–1–948997–58–4 (Paperback)

Library of Congress Control Number: 2021915031

and do not participate in or encourage electronic piracy of copyrighted materials.

# CONTENTS

*M*onday—again. Just like clockwork. Same office, same coworkers, same everything. Scott gazed through the picture window at the adjacent skyscraper facing him. It'd be a beautiful view if the building wasn't in the way.

Something or someone was *always* in the way.

A soft knock sounded on the door and then Beverly, his assistant, entered. She closed the office door and walked to a coat rack where she placed her bag and coat.

He needed a distraction, so he asked, "You like your birthday present?" He eyed the handbag she now placed under the rack.

"Quality and good taste." She beamed a beautiful smile at him. "Thanks so much for the gift."

The bag, and a spa day, were the least he could do. She had eyed that bag for weeks, and had even hinted on at least one occasion how much she loved it. It was their usual gift-giving routine, especially on Mother's Day, her birthday, Christmas, and even Secretary's Day. Beverly always acted surprised when she'd open the gift, even though she always knew what it would be.

Beverly leaned heavily on her cane—which always made him remember that she was older than his own mother—and she walked to the window and stood next to him. He studied her wisdom-creased face, the one that had always been there for him since he was a child, and knew that one day she'd retire. Probably one day soon.

"You've seemed distracted lately." She removed her glasses and studied him in a way that always made him self-conscious.

He could never get anything past her. "It's nothing." He crossed the room and made his way around his desk where he plopped his bottom into the cushy, leather chair. It squeaked in protest as he turned and faced her. Raising his arms, he stretched his lean body and felt his spine pop in an incredibly pleasing way. His head shifted from side to side, popping his neck and causing some tension to leave his body.

His latest case file stared back at him from the computer screen. It was a small intellectual property case, one too small for a lawyer of his caliber, but an important client nonetheless. He only wished the man wasn't guilty as hell. He thumbed his fingers on the wood desk and let out a slow sigh.

Beverly's footsteps shuffled along the carpet. "I picked up your dry cleaning this morning." She glanced at the coat rack where she had placed the items. Her gaze focused on the plastic wrap of the garments with a skeptical eye. "The ink stain didn't come out of your light gray suit."

Wasn't that the purpose of dry cleaning? To clean your clothes? Scott waved his hand dismissively, knowing it was useless to get upset. "Write up a complaint." His gaze traveled to the ceiling and he closed his eyes while the tension began building once again. "And find me another dry cleaner."

She made her way to the couch and put on her glasses. Before she took a seat, she sniffed the air. "Italian?"

He opened his eyes to see her start tidying up the office. "I ordered in."

She picked up an empty food container and walked it to the coffee bar, placing the plate in the tiny sink. Before returning and taking her seat, she bent down and picked up something from the couch. "I know I'm not your mother…"

There was a 'but' coming. Nothing good ever came from that sentence, but the woman did raise him and was closer to him than his own mother. His expression soured and he stared at her. "But…"

With a raised eyebrow, she held up an earring

and gave him an all-knowing smirk that didn't hold an ounce of amusement.

"Like I said, I ordered Italian. The cute delivery woman from Giovanni's usually works on Thursdays, and she's always flirting with me." He let out a sigh and confessed, "Flirting with my position of being a lawyer at least. Besides, I was bored."

"This is beneath you," she said with a saddened tone, tossing the jewelry on the table and scanning for more bling in the cushions. "It's always been beneath you. And you tend to slip into this regressive behavior every time you undergo a breakup. Although, it's taking you a lot longer this time to snap out of it." She studied him, sizing him up, and finally said, "I hope you gave that delivery woman one hell of a tip."

"No harm was done." He gave Beverly, his childhood nanny-now assistant, a wry smile. She was the mother he'd never really had, one who'd taught him how to ride a bike, took him to the doctor's when he was sick, and made sure he had someone to talk to when he was down.

His parents had been right. You never let good help go. Thankfully, Bev had adjusted to all of his life changes. Of course, he paid her well, especially after her husband died and left her with little to live on.

"This firm is very distinguished. You'd never catch a *senior* partner acting like this."

No. Of course you wouldn't. "The senior partners are old, married geezers who cling to a title that I want, but can't have until one of them steps down." Beverly knew that he wanted to be a senior more than anything else in the world.

"Look at you." Her face held motherly concern. "You have everything you need, have led a life of privilege, and doors just open for you. And yet, you always want the next big thing."

"Some people say that aiming higher in life is a good quality."

"Your parade of women and living in that condo of yours… it's like you're back in college." Her hand went to her hip in a motherly way. Her eyes narrowed as she studied his hair. "You even need a haircut, which I'll schedule for next week."

His hand raked through his long and thick mane of hair. Nothing needed changing except his title at the firm.

"You need to have patience if you're going to climb the corporate ladder here. Do you know what you are?"

He was sure she'd tell him.

"You're a snob."

His gaze darted over and he blurted out, "I am not a snob."

"You can't relate to people. You only interact with them, especially clients, since you don't make any real connections." She pointed at him in a 'you need to grow up' way. "You'd have more patience if you could relate to people. You don't see them as anything other than inferiors or obstacles in your way. And you know what?"

He let out a sigh and gazed past her. She gave him this speech at least once a year. She should wrap it up and send it to him as a Christmas present.

Although, she had never called him a snob before.

That one really hurt.

"You'll find a good woman someday. And when you do," she pointed at the earring on the table, "you'll regret these... dalliances."

Her face hardened, and it was the look she gave him when she meant business, like the time she'd caught him drawing a picture for his mother on the dining room wall in permanent marker while in kindergarten. He hated when Beverly stared at him like this.

"I relate to people all the time," he said, defiantly. "But, if you remember, my last serious relationship didn't date me—she dated my wallet." The air grew stale in the room and he tugged at the knot in his tie. "Fourteen years I've given this company." He stood and made his way around his desk. "Fourteen long and hard years. And for what?" he asked, his voice rising in pitch and giving away his frustration.

"A partnership in a prestigious law firm," Beverly said. "A windowed office on the eighteenth floor overlooking Chicago. A hefty salary that most people only dream about." She then shrugged. "Not that the money means that much to you."

"It's the title. The prestige." His heart thumped so loudly in his chest that he thought it would explode. "I deserve to be…" he grabbed a sheet of paper from the desk and pointed to the top, "I deserve to have my name on this letterhead."

Her eyes rolled as though tired of hearing the same rant once again. "Patience is a virtue which you've never learned." She took a deep breath and said in a defeated tone, "That one is on me."

She picked up the table from the coffee table and took a seat on the couch. "By the way, I sent Tate flowers for you." Her voice sounded crisp and professional as she tapped away on the device—as if the mother/son chat were over. "Tate's wife sounded very appreciative."

Leonard Tate. Senior partner, cancer patient, and holding onto life by a thread.

Scott returned to his desk and thought of the old man as shame came over him. The man had a family and a wife who needed him. He deserved better than the lousy hand he was given. Scott didn't want to get promoted because of Tate's loss, he just wanted to be appreciated for the work he had done. "Thanks for taking care of the flowers. I've been preoccupied and had meant to send them earlier."

"I know you care about Mr. Tate and would have sent flowers eventually." Her eyes narrowed, and she added, "I understand you've contacted other agencies."

He paused and stared at her. Did she really have eyes in the back of her head? He had been so careful to keep his job search a secret. But, like everything else in his life, Beverly was either one step ahead of him or he'd break down and share everything with her—that is, if she wasn't plotting for world domination with him. "It's not a crime to keep my options open." His jaw tensed and he pushed aside his laptop, its keypad worn from use to the point that the letters 'e' and 'i' were no longer visible.

"You've been depressed for weeks." Her gaze traveled across the office at the fine furniture, grand desk, and the view out the window before resting on him and capturing his stare with caring, loving eyes. "What can I do to make things better?"

Gone were the days where she could take him out for ice cream or bake some brownies to make him feel better. His problems lived outside her realm of control, and had for years.

"I'm the best lawyer this firm has. I've brought in more clients in the last two years alone than anyone else ever has." He had given up countless weekends, missed too many holidays, and his vacation time always stacked up to the point where he tended to give some of it away to help others in the firm deal with long-term illnesses. Was it too much to ask that his efforts be recognized?

"You are the best lawyer this company has ever had." Bev nodded in agreement. Of course, she always believed he was the best at anything he did—even when he was consistently picked last for childhood sports teams or games.

He had left his last company for lack of advancement; he could do so again. "If a change doesn't happen..." he said, reaching deep into what he knew the next move would have to be, "I'll have to take a position elsewhere."

*Caroline Wenzel entered her efficiency apartment and the smell of last night's dinner wafted toward her. She meant to clean up last night, but fell asleep hunting down Algebra problems on the web. Then, again this morning, she had promised to clean, but was running late for work.

There was never enough time to get everything done.

She glanced at the mile-high stack of dishes near the sink, only to find a fat roach resting on a plate with food residue.

Not now. Not now. Not now.

She removed her shoe and left the outer door open, knowing that if she turned any apartment lights on, the bug would scatter—probably finding her later while she was in bed asleep or in the shower defenseless.

She crept closer to the sink and was happy to find the can of Raid still sitting out after last night's ant infestation.

Raid, then shoe. She could do this.

She shook the metal can, happy to find the container still contained some juice. "You're going down, Mr. Cockroach."

God, the size was big enough to slip a saddle onto.

She took a deep breath and held the can close to the bug.

In a chemical fume cloud resembling a nuclear bomb, she drenched the bug until it lay belly-up in a pool of insecticide, its antennae still twitching.

She took a few steps back when she began coughing, which allowed her to view the devastation surrounding her.

If her apartment were Oscar's trashcan, the Grouch would be happy to have her as a roommate.

God, she'd be happy to have him as a room-mate. Any roommate. She'd save on half the rent then.

She tossed the empty can and her purse onto the table before turning on her computer. While it hummed to life, she removed her CTA nametag. Picking up the evening shift at the Chicago Transit Authority helped with the bills, but the job stole her evenings and gave her clothing a pungent subway-station stench.

She waved her hand in front of her nose. Subway station, raid can, and dirty dishes. Not pleasant. The door remained open and the apartment was airing out, soon the stench would be gone.

The heater had been turned off to save money while she was away, and the place was freezing, so she turned it back on. She kept her jacket on but rolled up the sleeves as best she could so her coat wouldn't get dirty as she cleaned.

Work, cleaning, and more work. She needed to make sure to toss in some sleep in the mix somehow.

She barely had time to sit with her grandmother for dinner before her shift had started tonight. And, she wouldn't be able to visit with her again until after her shift at the diner tomorrow.

She let out a heavy sigh. No. She'd have to visit her grandmother the day *after* that. She had picked up some tutoring assignments for tomorrow.

A prickling sensation pulled at her eyelids, making her want to close them and go to bed. She had no time.

The trash can stood overflowing, so she cinched up the plastic bag and pulled it from the container. She placed the bag by the door before putting a new bag in the can.

The computer beeped, and she knew her third part-time job awaited her—not that she wanted to sift through Algebra questions left by high schoolers on her tutoring board. God, she felt too tired to do math problems tonight.

Her stomach twisted, and she put her hand against her nose. The mix of the trash can smell with the rest of her apartment was enough to make her throw up, even with the front door still open to air the place out. If she didn't clean up soon, more roaches would camp out on her floor and start demanding wake-up calls and room service.

"Nicely done," a voice rang in from the hallway. Caroline recognized the voice immediately and cringed. Dealing with the cockroach and math was welcoming compared to a conversation with Vince, her landlord and neighboring Neanderthal man.

In her best frosty, leave me the hell alone voice, she said, "Thanks, but I'm very busy."

He took a step into the apartment, tracking in mud on her concrete floor. His unshaven face held a seductive smile, his shifty-eyes were half-hidden behind greasy, unwashed bangs, and his jeans were two inches from falling off his hips. "Do you need some help? I could..."

"No." She stood and walked to the door. The scent of beer became stronger with each step. "I'm fine."

"You sure are. But I could lend a hand with..." His gaze darted to her chest which caused the heebie-jeebies to race up her spine. Why were only men with IQs in their teens or whom hygiene was a foreign word interested in her?

"That's thoughtful of you Vince, but it's late and I have to do math tutoring tonight."

"How is my computer working out for you?" He pointed to the computer on the table, the borrowed, old Dell laptop he held over her head.

"I appreciate the loan." Overall, Vince wasn't a horrible man, just intrusive and single-minded on sex. He existed as the anti-ruler to which she judged all men, which was why she had sworn off of seeing anyone for the unforeseeable future.

"If you need anything else…"

"Goodnight." She managed to get him out and closed the door, making sure to lock and deadbolt it. Raid fumes were better than the alcohol-soaked, smooth talk from him.

No matter how tired she was, no matter how stressed life got, no matter how lonely she felt…she had to remember that she had a roof over her head, food in her stomach, and decent jobs to work. She was one of the lucky in the world to have so much.

She glanced over at the dead roach and the messy kitchen. She knew her life would be better one day, she just had to put in the time and energy to make it happen.

She stretched to wake up and then walked to the sink to take care of her murder victim.

## 2

_C_aroline stifled a yawn and shuffled over to the "to go" area of the restaurant. She placed the five bags on the counter, their receipts safely stapled to each and ready for pick-up. The delivery bags lay on the opposite counter, waiting for one of the two distribution people to handle them. Quite a few orders had come in this morning.

At least she wasn't on delivery duty this week, unless she needed to repay some favors and switch shifts with another waitress.

"Can I get a refill?"

The mature, manly voice came from behind her. She'd recognize its low and comforting sound anywhere.

She picked up the orange carafe filled with the morning's hot decaf and refilled her customer's mug. The older gentleman, wearing khaki pants and a button-down shirt was one of her regulars—and someone Caroline had considered a blessing to have in her life.

She suspected the retired man was used to a certain work dress code and didn't own any jeans. Like many of their generation, his late wife had probably done all the shopping and caring for the house and kids. He always came in, whether it was a workday or the weekend, many times telling stories about the grandchildren he rarely got to see.

She would be opening up a floodgate, but she asked, "How are you today, Mr. Sweeney?"

The white-haired man put his hand on his waist. "My hips have been acting up. This unseasonably cold weather, with all the rain we've been having, plays havoc with my joints."

A smile quickly spread across her face. Who still used the word 'havoc'? She suspected that the widower had no other place to go and simply enjoyed the hot meals of the restaurant. Bored, retired, and lonely. She may be one of the only friendly faces he had in his life.

"I'm sorry to hear that, Mr. Sweeney." She let the words trail off and began her nodding routine so she'd appear as if she were intensely listening. The man could talk for hours. When she had first started working at the café, she would lose track of time and not get her morning chores done.

"I said, what's with the lovely flowers?" Mr.

Sweeney asked louder, pointing at the beautiful bouquet of roses at the end of the counter. "Is it your birthday?"

She stared at the red, pink, and yellow atrocity that had arrived at six o'clock sharp. "You should know better, Mr. Sweeney. If flowers arrive around here, they're not for me."

"Maria?"

"Of course."

He shook his head. "A woman as pretty as you should have a husband and a slew of kids by now. I can't believe you haven't dated anyone seriously since you found your college boyfriend cheating on you all those years ago." He shook his head. "And to think you were with him for eight years—and no ring."

A heaviness settled in the pit of her stomach. She really needed to stop talking about her private life with her customers. Of course, Mr. Sweeney was a special case.

"I've been out a few times," she lied. "I'm just super busy."

"You're too sweet of a girl to work so much and not have a man in your life." His eyes were filled with fatherly sincerity and concern. "I honestly don't know what's wrong with the young men today." His eyes studied her face. "If I were forty years younger..."

"You would sweep me off my feet," she said,

smiling a true smile that she felt in her heart. Men like Sweeney were a lost breed, and she knew it firsthand. She placed her hand atop his. "I'll find a man one day. I'm focusing on my grandmother right now."

"Your time will come." Mr. Sweeney eyed the beautiful roses. "If I know Maria, she'll probably cut the flower stems short and set them out in those little bud vases you have. You know, like she did for Valentine's Day."

Caroline hadn't been here last Valentine's Day, but it gave her a good indication of how long Mr. Sweeney had been alone. Too long.

He grabbed his hat and coat and then gestured around the room before beginning his way to the door. "Those flowers would brighten up the place."

She gave him a sad smile. He'd be back again with the dinner crowd, asking for the senior discount on whatever special they offered. She hoped he had people to see and things to do—happy, exciting things. "That's a good idea about the flowers, Mr. Sweeney. Have a good day."

Caroline took his empty breakfast plate and then peeked at the wall clock. The time was 6:40 a.m. She had already been here for nearly an hour, setting up the place and getting the coffee started with the other two waitresses who bothered to show up on time.

The jingle of the bells above the door caught her attention, and she turned to see Maria racing in.

"Sorry I'm late." She dashed behind the counter and tossed her purse out of sight. "Did the boss notice?"

Caroline studied Maria's uniform. A spaghetti stain from yesterday's lunch rush was there. She then glanced at Maria's unkempt hair. Apparently, the woman hadn't gone home again last night, and Caroline knew what that meant.

At least someone was enjoying herself.

"Mr. Boss Man notices everything, but he hasn't been out on the floor in a while, so he won't know how late you are this morning. Besides," she said, her hands indicating the coffee, the dining room setup, and the huge to-go order on the counter, "Me and the other waitresses took care of everything."

"Thanks, hon. I owe you one."

Caroline straightened a stack of menus on the counter. "More like two or three."

"At least there's no crowd yet." She fastened her apron snuggly around her waist and noticed the stain on her uniform. She plucked a napkin from the container and tried to make herself more presentable. "I see I missed Mr. Sweeney this morning. How's he doing?"

"The same as usual."

Maria eyes widened and she stepped toward the roses. "Flowers?" Her hand searched for a card.

"They're for you."

She read the card, her lips twisting as she did so. "I wasn't planning on seeing this man again." She placed the card in the trash and then cupped one of the flowers in her hand. She bent down and sniffed the open bud.

"You know whose day would be brighten up with this bouquet?" Before Caroline could answer she said, "your grandma."

A warmth spread across Caroline and she smiled at the thought. "It's sweet that you'd think of her."

"I'm serious. You should take them to her. Brighten up her little room at the center she's at." Maria placed her hand on Caroline's shoulder. "How is she doing?"

"She's settled in now." Caroline felt the pain of loss for putting her grandmother in a memory care facility and forced a smile on her face. "I feel bad that I can't meet her needs anymore, but she seems to like the place I found for her. It's the third facility she's been in over the last year. I hope this one sticks."

"Does she know that you quit college?"

Caroline hated lies, and keeping something from her grandmother made her sick to her stomach, especially since her grandmother had been really excited for her when she started studying at the local college. Of course, it seemed like Caroline was on the 'ten year' plan with school. Her grandmother couldn't keep track of time though and always assumed she had just started studying.

"I haven't told her yet. I'm not even sure she'd understand what I'm saying at this point."

Of course, there were days now where she wasn't certain her grandmother even remembered who she was anymore. Her grandmother had always been so strong and courageous. There weren't a lot of women in their fifties who could take on raising their young grandchild.

She always wanted Caroline to succeed in life and had raised her since the age of ten to know that college was in her future. The woman had set aside a portion of her paycheck each month just to ensure that there'd be an education fund for Caroline.

Now that money was being used to secure her a decent elderly care center. But the money wasn't enough.

"I need to work at least another year to build up some extra cash for the new expense of her retirement home. Maybe by next fall, I can start taking classes again."

"All you've been talking about is wanting to finish your degree. And you're so close."

Caroline couldn't make eye contact with Maria. Getting her degree meant everything to her, and she didn't want to dwell on lost opportunities, especially since she only needed eighteen course hours to graduate. Quitting school had been the only option, though. What was she supposed to do? First it was the cost of her Grandmother's medications, then the full-time care, now she had to find her grandmother a suitable place to live.

Everything was so expensive, and time consuming. Doing courses part-time was all she could manage. Having a family and a life of her own? Forget it!

She walked to the paid bill on the counter and collected it and the soiled coffee cup. "Family always comes first. Besides, school can wait."

Caroline stared into Maria's compassionate eyes. "I just have to focus," she said. "No men, no school… just hard work for at least one more year." She took a deep breath knowing full well that it had been several months since her last date, and there wasn't a man on her horizon anytime soon. She had already worked six months since dropping out of school and had lost touch with all her fellow classmates. She really needed to put in another two or three years to make ends meet.

"Then what?"

Caroline shook her head. Just managing day to day was a struggle. "I can't think that far into the future."

"If you keep putting your life on hold, you'll miss out on the best things in life."

*S*cott opened the sunroof of his Tesla and enjoyed the crisp morning air as it tousled his long blond hair. He glanced into the rearview mirror and studied his reflection. Beverly was right. He really did need a haircut. Another half inch and he'd look too unprofessional to appear in court.

But he'd worry about that later. Today was the first warm day of spring and he could smell the sunshine as it heated up the Earth and melted away the last remnants of snow. The harsh season had kept him away from the park. Feeling cooped up from nature and feeling the pressure at work were tearing away at him. He needed se personal time to think, and his favorite hiking path was perfect for the job.

He brushed his hand through his tresses and noted how good it felt to get an early start on his morning. A brisk hike to start the day, then returning some phone calls to law agencies that had contacted him back, and then off to work at the Tate Law firm.

Finding a new job, and keeping it secret, while working proved more difficult than he had expected. Thank goodness for cell phones. He certainly couldn't take such personal calls on an office line, especially since the Tate Law firm, in general, had treated him well.

Thinking of the four men that ran the law firm,

he counted up their collective years of experience. It totaled over two-hundred years. Each were gray-haired old men, with creased facial wrinkles and age spots. Scott had worked at another law firm earlier in his career, but had really enjoyed the time he spent at his current job.

He'd hate to see it all end.

He drove out of his neighborhood and traveled a short distance down the interstate. He easily drove down the highway since traffic was still light. Of course, it was only six o'clock in the morning and his Tesla navigation system had shown him the quickest way to reach his destination, free of any accidents and road jams.

"Show schedule," he said into his Bluetooth headset. His car's console divided in half with the map of his route now sharing space with his daily calendar. He programed the default to show a week's worth of data, and he noticed that Beverly had already scheduled a haircut for him.

Best employee ever.

"Show today," he said and the display changed. He touched the screen and the map disappeared and made the schedule larger and more easily read.

Today didn't seem too stressful. His only court appearance wasn't for several more hours, and case work filled his afternoon. A mountain of boring paperwork awaited him, and working quietly in his office would be the perfect time to fill Beverly in on his job search.

But first, his weekly run along Lake Potawatomi awaited him.

His calendar had a note section blinking telling him that something was due today. The highlighted color was pink, so one of the notes Beverly had made for him. "Show notes," he said into his Bluetooth.

The hidden message appeared. "Arrange date for Christmas party."

Scott felt his vegan breakfast smoothie threaten to come back up. That was certainly not a note he would have left for himself, although he had to agree that the task needed to be done.

He couldn't go to the damn office party stag, especially if that would factor in against him for a Senior Partnership. He just didn't have anyone to take, and it wasn't like he wanted his old nanny to fix him up. He had already been through her nieces and daughters of old friends, all with bad results.

God. Women only wanted one thing. Did a single woman ever offer to go dutch on a date? Did they ever suggest a quick meal instead of the five-star restaurants he always took them too?

No. Never.

Glitz. Glamour. Gold-diggers.

That was all he was able to attract.

Shit.

The old adage that behind every good man was a good woman usually held true, especially at work. All of the bigwigs had statuesque wives who bolstered their egos and careers. However, having a gold-digger on his arm would be better than showing up alone to the holiday party.

He knew that his coworker and resident asshole Ralph would bring a date.

He always had a floozy on his arm.

God, he hated competing with—of all people —Ralph.

Scott parked his car at the north entrance to the park and grabbed his cell phone. His running suit didn't have a large enough pocket for the phone, so he slipped it into his sports sock that had a built-in slot in the calf.

He took a deep breath of morning air and cleared his head, promising himself that he would find someone to take to the stupid party.

## 3

_C_aroline opened the empty dispenser and pushed the stack of napkins in, only to catch her fingers on the corners of the metal tin, again.

Her body tightened, and she threw the container onto the counter. "Son of a—" She caught herself and turned away from the nearby customer.

"Honey, you need to calm down."

Maria was right. Caroline took a deep breath and allowed her shoulders to relax. She shook out her finger and glanced around the dining hall. Apparently, no customers had heard, or at the very least, they weren't upset by the noise.

Getting angry wouldn't solve her problems.

Glancing at the tables, she saw the bud vases on each one, courtesy of Maria's unwanted bouquet, some sharp scissors, and a good thirty minutes of thorn avoidance. She had to admit, they did freshen up the place and make the restaurant look cheerier.

And she needed some happiness. Her rent was due, and she wasn't sure how she would make ends meet this month. Happy customers tipped better. And she needed some big tips.

God. It was always something. And today she could barely keep her eyes open.

She forced a smile. "I'm fine." She picked up the napkin holder. She dusted it off with a rag from her apron pocket and placed it on a nearby table where customers were eating. "Enjoy your meal."

Maria grabbed Caroline's hands and shook her from her rigid stance. "You seemed fine when I got here this morning, but now you're an agitated mess. You doing okay?"

Was she okay? She had stayed up until two o'clock tutoring a kid from Hawaii whose time was four hours behind hers. Getting up and at work before six o'clock was draining her. Spending the last forty minutes serving a rude customer who didn't leave a tip irritated her. It irritated her more than she'd like to admit.

Plus, she hadn't seen her grandmother in the last two days. If she really were going through Alzheimer's and starting to forget people, she needed Caroline there as often as possible to keep her in the present. She looked at the bud vases on the table. A year ago, her grandmother would have loved such a gesture as a bouquet of flowers. Now, Caroline was too busy to even take a bunch of roses to her—not that her grandmother would even notice them.

"You're too young to be shouldering so many troubles and responsibilities." Maria studied Caroline, eyeing her from head to toe. "You know what you need?"

A good night's sleep? The winning lottery numbers? She settled on, and said, "A fairy godmother?"

A smirk appeared on Maria's face. "Well, sure. A supportive fairy godmother would help, but I'm talking about something that could actually happen —a good one-night stand. When was the last time you even went out with a man?"

Caroline rolled her eyes and her body slumped in defeat. The last three men she had dated belonged to the 'losers and liars' club. "A man isn't going to solve my problems, only complicate them."

"I'm not talking about a relationship. Goodness knows you don't have time for that."

That was true. Other than Mr. Sweeney, the only man she ever interacted with was Vince.

Maybe she should just move.

Or rob a bank.

Maria's eyebrow rose. "You're thinking about it. I can tell."

"What?"

"A good one-night stand," she said, shaking her hips. "You know, relieve some tension. When was the last time you had a man in your bed?"

Years. But Maria didn't need to know that Caroline's one-and-only real boyfriend had been when she was just eighteen. They dated for years until she discovered him cheating. Now, at twenty-eight, she wondered if she could even remember how to please a lover.

"You need a real man." Maria flexed her arms and took in a deep breath. "Someone with a gorgeous build, who will pack your night with so much passion that you won't have a moment to think about your problems.

"Sorry to disappoint you, but"—Caroline glanced around the room—"there doesn't appear to be a line of men forming who want to take out a tired, in-debt waitress who'll be thirty soon with her biological clock ticking."

Maria's eyebrow rose and she placed one hand on her hip. "Well, not with that attitude."

Caroline pointed to her hairline. "My roots are down to my ears, I've packed on weight since my grandmother's health declined, and I don't even notice men anymore."

"Excuses."

"They're not excuses, just the facts." Caroline pointed to her friend's slim waist. "You're tall with a willowy build. You even have soft brown eyes and a sun-kissed tan. My skin is pasty white like a vampire's."

"Because you never go out." Maria's eyes squinted as she studied her. "You're beautiful, your hair needs some work, but you're curvy in all the right places, and have alabaster skin that poetry is written about. Men would kill to be with you."

Caroline couldn't help but let out a slight chuckle. "Yeah, everyone wants to be with this." Her hand made a Vanna White gesture over her body. "Which is why every man that comes into the diner hits on you."

"Honey, they notice me because I give off the vibe that I enjoy a man's attention. You give them half a scowl or a fake smile as you refill their coffee."

True, but Caroline didn't need to... She didn't want to... Hell, she couldn't afford to be friendly and happy just to attract a date. Pretending to be perky for bigger tips was one thing, and she didn't like the men it attracted.

"I think I should just focus on my grandmother for now, go back to school eventually, and then maybe find a man much later, in the future."

"Or, you can relieve your tension with the next man who walks in here." Maria turned and stared at the door expectantly. "The next man, Caroline. I swear. He's the one."

Caroline shivered. She had never been one to have a one-night stand, all though, the idea of no strings attached had always appealed to her. No strings meant no lies. "With my luck, the next man through that door will be a ninety-year-old man. I've seen too many of them lately at my grandmother's home."

"Or the perfect man to rock your world."

"I don't need…"

The door chimed, causing both of them to stare at the diner's entrance.

It wasn't as though Caroline had sworn an oath to the crazy plan, but her heart still raced. Just because she wasn't going to jump in the sack with the next man, didn't mean that she couldn't. What if a Helmsworth brother were to walk in?

Wait, she was pretty sure all the Helmsworth men were married.

God, even her fantasies were flawed.

Well, it didn't matter. She wasn't going to do anything foolish.

Caroline instantly plastered a fake smile on her face to greet the patron and repeated the greeting she was instructed to say to all customers who walked in. "Welcome to the Patio."

She was supposed to add, "*please* have a seat anywhere" but the man who walked in was not a family man. He wasn't coming from church with a wife and several kids. He was alone, which was not their usual customer type.

The man was tall and lean, with a chiseled jaw

that could cut glass. He had a rugged handsomeness in an outdoorsman kind of way. His torn clothes were dirty, and he looked to be down on his luck. He also appeared hurt and in need of help.

"Okay, we'll go with the *second* man who walks through the door." Maria's lips turned thin, and her eyes squinted as she glared at the customer. "The bums wander in and have to be chased away, but they always come back." She stood straighter and eyed the man. "I'll take care of this one."

Caroline stared at the limping man. He was covered in mud, but she could make out blond hair and soft, compassionate eyes. "What makes you think he's a bum?"

"There are plenty of them from the nearby park. Trust me. I know."

He maybe looked homeless in his wet and dirty tracksuit. He didn't look thin or gaunt, but what if Maria was right? What if he hadn't eaten in a day or two? "What if he's hungry?"

"And how is he going to pay for his food?" Maria grimaced in a way that showed an ugly side to her, one that Caroline rarely got to see. It wasn't a look she liked.

Maria shook her head. "He can't stay."

Caroline stared at the man's face that was smeared with mud, then looked at his dirty and torn clothes, noticing the limp that caused him to favor his right foot. "He needs help." She put her hand on her co-worker's shoulder. "I'll take care of him. You keep preparing for the lunch crowd."

"The next man, Caroline. We'll focus on the *next* man through that door."

Caroline turned away from her. "No man. We'll focus on *no* man."

---

*P*ain.

Each step shot lightning rods of agony through Scott's ankle and up his leg, each ricocheting back down again and torturing him.

Stupid, slippery rocks.

That was the last time he would hike down to the stream and try to step across. It had been a dumb idea, and one his inner voice should have warned him not to do, but...oh, no. It was such a pretty day with the sun shining and the crisp air. All winter, he had waited for a day like today, but he was foolish enough to push the limits of Mother Nature's generosity.

His car was a good five miles away, and his clothes were not only drenched but also muddy and torn. And that stench? Ugh! Pond water. His clothes were sticking to his skin and the smell was enough to have him gag.

What had he been thinking? His cell phone safely

tucked into his hiking sock? Dead the second it hit the water.

A neon sign had caught his attention and he was lucky this restaurant, Encanto del Patio, was close by. He knew of the place. A Chicago landmark since the 1940s—at least, the original one on the outskirts of town was—and it had the best breakfast burritos in town. Buttery eggs, melted cheese, and way too many calories for a regular breakfast, but a delicious treat nonetheless.

The warm air of the restaurant had welcomed Scott the moment he entered, as did a little bell above the door, announcing his arrival. Also present was the greasy smell of bacon, a taboo food he rarely allowed himself to eat, but the aroma of which now caused his mouth to water.

The place was already pretty full of customers. He had never been in the place before since he preferred ordering their burritos for delivery for his early morning meetings. Judging by the stack of to-go orders on the counter, it seemed like a lot of people did.

His soaked sweatpants clung to him, and the wintry air outside had chilled him to the bone.

Coffee.

Hot, strong, and black would be perfect.

But all of his money was stored safely in his wallet under his seat in his car. From now on, he would have to make sure to carry at least one credit card with him at all times.

He took a step and immediately favored his right foot. The slick, checkerboard tile surface of the diner floor was harder to walk on than the dirt hiking trail he had just left.

"Welcome to the Patio." a voice sounded in the distance. He was too busy making sure his footing was sure to even look up.

Thankfully, a booth was just to the right of the door, so he hobbled over to it. His hands furniture-walked the back of the booth until he could carefully sit down. His butt sank into the worn seat's indent. He scooted across the Naugahyde and propped his throbbing left ankle up on the bench.

Was his ankle broken? Or was it just sprained?

An image of the cast he had worn on his right leg as a child came quickly to mind. He'd been all of ten years old—young and foolish—climbing a tree that was way too tall. A misplaced step, a broken tree branch, and a bad grip on the trunk had caused him to fall and break his leg. The weeks he'd spent in an itchy cast should have been enough to teach him not to take risks. But here he was again.

His ankle was already swollen. He pulled back his sock and touched the puffy, red skin disappearing into his shoe when a flowery scent wafted over.

It was light and pleasant, cutting through the smell of bacon and the lake water. He glanced at the small arrangement of flowers on the table, finding it hard to believe that such a tiny bouquet could make such an impact.

"Are you doing okay?"

The sweet, feminine voice caused him to glance up.

His heart skipped a beat. The woman standing in from of him was by far the prettiest woman he had ever laid eyes on.

Prettiest woman—by far!

The pink waitress uniform hugged her petite frame, giving her an hourglass figure accentuated by the white apron tied tightly around her tiny waist. The flowery scent grew in intensity with her arrival, and he inhaled deeply, enjoying the fragrance of her perfume.

His gaze lingered on her soft, delicate facial features. Button nose, rosy cheeks, and soft, kissable lips. Her blond hair was pulled back behind her ears with a small wisp of bangs brushing her brows and framing emerald green eyes that stared back at him.

"Are you okay?" she asked again, pointing at his ankle.

He didn't have time to be laid-up with an injury. Pain or no pain, he needed to be showered, dressed in a suit, and in court in three hours. But, for this moment in time, all he wanted to do was stay lost in her mesmerizing gaze.

"Do you need some ice?"

Her soft green eyes held concern.

"I fell on the path." He didn't exactly answer her question. His voice was barely audible, and he could hardly think straight. He cleared his throat, not just to give himself a moment to focus, but also to clear the frog in his throat that had him speaking in too high-pitched of a voice.

"It rained overnight, and that made everything a bit slippery." She turned her head and studied his foot. "Do you think you broke it?"

He glanced at his foot. "Probably just a sprain," he said in a deep, manly voice. He winced as he shifted his ankle, trying not to be a baby about it in front of her. "At least, I hope it's just something minor."

"Let me get you a bag of ice." She handed him a menu and walked back to the counter.

The kind woman with the ever-so-fine butt walked away, her hips swaying in her uniform. She was a combination of girl-next-door pretty and sex-goddess sexy, with curves in all the right places.

But her bright pink uniform said one thing to him—she was a common person. High school degreed, minimum wage earning, serving the public type of worker bee. The type that Beverly accused him of not connecting with—or at the very least treated like an inferior.

He was able to catch a profile of the waitress as she turned and walked behind the counter. Pert little nose, delicate jaw, and the type of hair that bobbed up and down as she walked.

He took in a deep breath. She was probably a high school drop out with kids by three baby-daddies. Someone that worked day and night and had no chance at getting ahead. A slice of the American population that wasn't within the one percent. Someone average...he gazed back at her. Someone average except in the beauty department. She was a champion racehorse—a well decorated one—where looks were considered.

But...he thought back to what Beverley had said.

An average person.

Bev had accused him of not being able to connect with a commoner, that he was a snob. He could prove Beverly wrong, and he always loved doing that —ever since he was a kid.

This waitress would easily fill the bill. Obviously, he didn't care about mixing with wait staff, but he didn't like being accused of being snooty. He also didn't like someone he cared about believing he had flaws.

A sting of pride hit him square in the chest and an idea formed in his mind. Not only would he easily connect with this waitress, he'd get her phone number and parade it in Beverly's face. That would certainly prove that he could connect to the average man—or in this case—woman on the street.

Of course, he wasn't wearing an impressive suit,

driving his expensive car, or even freshly washed. How could he impress the waitress enough to give him her phone number? He didn't even have cash on him for a hot cup of coffee to keep warm.

He glanced at the cost of a cup of coffee as his hand felt the slick plastic of the menu and he moved it aside. In a place like this, the coffee certainly would not be gourmet. At best, a standard Folgers generic blend. At worst, instant coffee.

He gritted his teeth. He couldn't even afford instant coffee right now. She probably wouldn't charge him for a bag of ice and therefore would have no idea he didn't have money on him.

What he really needed was a phone. One that worked. Wasn't there a mobile that was waterproof? He'd have to get Beverly to look into that for him.

Scott grabbed a napkin from the dispenser on the table to wipe the mud from his face and hands, noticing a slight cut on his hand, and a huge tear in his sweatshirt. Dragging himself out and climbing through a thicket of bushes had just been a bad idea.

There was a clock on the wall, and he noted the time. Just hours until he had to be presentable, and there was no way he'd be able to walk back to his car on the north side of the park.

He studied the room and found no pay phone along the walls, but hardly anyplace had pay phones these days. He couldn't even remember the last time he had seen one. Plus, he didn't have any change on him to make a call.

The waitress headed back with a plastic bag filled with what he assumed was ice. In her other hand, she held a cloth and a glass of water.

Perhaps he could convince her to allow him to use the diner's phone. All he had to do was lay on the charm, and women tended to do anything he wanted, especially once they found out what he did for a living and that he came from not-so-humble beginnings.

She set the items down on the table but showed him the bag. "This will help." She hovered the bag above his ankle. "Is it okay if I…"

His hand was already reaching for the offering when he realized she was willing to help, not just drop the bag off at the table and scoff at him when he didn't order any breakfast.

"Yes. Please."

He watched as she not only placed the ice carefully down but also gently folded the elastic band of his wet pants' leg up high enough so it wouldn't get in the way.

"A bruise has already started forming." She gingerly touched his ankle to indicate the size. "You were lucky to get here before your entire foot turned blue."

If it were a joke, he was in too much pain to laugh. But he did notice the slight smile on her face and how soft her fingers had felt as they touched his leg.

God, what would Beverly think if he showed up to the Christmas party with a waitress on his arm? Naturally, she wouldn't be in her uniform.

Of course, she wouldn't have anything to say to the people at the party. What would they talk about? What common interest could this waitress and the senior partners even share? This waitress didn't appear to have an advanced degree or an exciting career to bore the fat cats with.

His gaze traveled from her soft, blonde hair down her curvy body to her un-ringed finger. He watched as she gently shifted the bag atop his ankle. Her head turned slightly from one side to the other. "It's pretty swollen," she said.

"Hurts like…" He caught himself before he said the word *hell*. "…the dickens." He glanced up and noticed a red, lacy bra strap on her shoulder as she bent down. Shifting his gaze, her nametag caught his attention.

Caroline the waitress.

"Here," she said, handing him the cloth. "I figured you couldn't make it into the bathroom to rinse off. Did you fall asleep in the nearby park and the sprinklers get you this morning?"

The warmth of the washrag felt good on his bone-chilled fingers, and he wanted to wrap his entire body in it. "I was jogging."

He unfolded the cloth and wiped the mud from his face, enjoying the sensation, but only until a twinge of pain ran through him as he touched his chin.

"The creek bed got me this morning. I fell right in." He wiped the rest of the mud from his face and then tended to his hands.

"I'm not supposed to do this," she said, reaching into her apron pocket and taking out a small vial. "I have some Advil if you'd like a couple to help with that swelling."

An angel. She was definitely heaven-sent.

Caroline might be the kindest person he had talked to in a long time.

Maybe ever.

He studied her. Not just her appearance, but really considered who she was.

Who the hell was this nice?

She handed him two Advil. "I could call a shelter for you. I think there might be one nearby. They could come and take care of you."

A shelter?

He stared into her eyes once more. Reflecting back wasn't concern for a man who had fallen and needed a little help this morning. No, it was much more than that.

His stomach churned as he realized what he saw. Pity.

Pity for him.

Did this sweet little waitress actually think him a bum?

He rolled up his sleeve, only to realize that he had left his Rolex at home. "I'm not homeless. I just had an accident."

She moved the glass of water closer to him. "I'm not judging. A lot of homeless wander in. I'll let you stay as long as I can."

Just as he was about to correct her impression of him, the kitchen door opened, and a man in a white apron came out. His presence caused Caroline to quickly leave the Advil tablets on the table and dash away to another customer.

Scott figured the man was her boss—definitely the cook, maybe even the owner of the place. Since she now scurried from table to table, Scott figured the man scared her. The other waitress had now come out from behind the counter and was refilling coffee mugs in an effort to look busier.

The scene fascinated him.

These two women obviously needed their jobs and appeared hard-working. They understood the value of a dollar and how hard it was to earn.

Not like the women he usually took out, who had used him as a bank. His credit cards were so heavily worn, he was surprised the magnetic strips still worked.

He set the soiled towel down and took the pills,

disappointed that Caroline had abruptly left before he could ask about borrowing a phone.

Several more customers entered the restaurant, and Caroline greeted each one as she carried on with her work. Her voice had a beautiful pitch, and the greeting nearly sounded genuine.

He sat back and studied her as she did her work. She picked up the check from one table, cleaned off the surface, and prepared the area for the next customer who would use it. Her fingers were not manicured works of art. Instead, her nails were short. Her hair was pulled back and unfussy. Not that he knew what the latest styles were, but Caroline had an easy hairstyle that didn't look two-hours-in-a-beauty-salon perfect.

The way the strands curved around her heart-shaped face and drew attention to her sensuous mouth begging to be kissed made her even more attractive to him.

But, did she really think he was a homeless man? He took a good look at his torn clothing and the soiled cloth on the table. He certainly wasn't giving off the impression of a wealthy individual at the moment, but there was still no need to assume that he was penniless.

He paid his assistant more in a week than Caroline probably made in a month, and yet... she wasn't judging him.

She walked around and kept busy, all with...no,

wait. He leaned forward, the best he could, and watched her worker-bee little dance. She flitted from table to table, one cheerful greeting after another…but her words were hollow sounding.

And that wasn't a real smile on her face. Each time she turned from a table her smile would slightly disappear. She was faking her way through her day just to get by.

After all those years dating women where he had no idea who they really were, it seemed as if Caroline wore her feelings on her sleeve—that is, if anyone cared to notice.

For a beautiful blonde with such a striking face and sexy build, she looked sad to him. Did others see her true self, as well?

Now that the boss had returned to the kitchen, Caroline walked up to his table, and he averted his gaze so she wouldn't see him staring at her.

"Here you go, hon." She placed a hot cup of coffee and a slice of pie down on the table and flashed him what looked like a million-dollar smile.

The problem was, he had no money. And not being able to pay would only advance her belief that he was homeless. "I didn't order…"

"I know, but you look like you could use a hot cup and something in your belly." She glanced over her shoulder and then turned to make eye contact with him. "It's on the house," she whispered.

He couldn't remember if he had ever received

anything *on the house* before without already having paid for something, making a huge contribution to something, or because someone knew who he was and wanted something in return.

Who was this woman?

"My name is Scott, by the way," he said, desperate to make some sort of real connection with her.

Her smile was so bright, it even lit up her eyes. "It's nice to meet you, Scott. I'm Caroline."

There was no tell-tale sign that she recognized him or knew he was rich—worth millions, actually. Would it matter to her if she did know? Would she treat him differently?

"Thanks for all this," he said, pointing at the free food.

She gave him a nod. "Eat up. I'll be back to check on you in a bit."

Before she could leave, he asked, "Is there a phone I can use?"

She pointed to the counter. "It's probably too far for you to get to, though." She pulled her cell out of her pocket and unlocked it. "I doubt you'll run away. I'll be right back."

Her hand reached into her apron pocket again, this time taking out an order pad. She pulled off a sheet and jotted something down. "Here." She handed him the note.

'Ice and ibuprofen...' he read. Was she actually giving him advice on how to take care of himself? He scanned further down the note and noticed a name of a free clinic he could go to.

Really?

She even signed it 'Caroline' with a heart above the 'i'.

He found that even harder to believe than the free clinic.

He watched as she walked away, only to be stopped by the patrons at a table with a screaming baby.

Scott watched as she shifted from one foot to the other as she talked to the family, smiling and appearing as if the screaming child with its blood-curdling voice didn't affect her.

The baby dropped a rattle, and Caroline picked it up, wiped it with a napkin from the table, and handed it back to the child.

Cute and thoughtful.

He usually dated women who wore power suits, thick makeup, and pencil-thin high heels. Their hearts also tended to be as black as their leather briefcases.

Caroline wore comfortable Keds. She had also given him a cell phone to use, trusting that he wouldn't walk away with it. He glanced down at the mobile, not even recognizing the style and model. It was probably a pay-as-you-use-it type. Probably all she could afford.

He called his private doctor and then arranged

for a car to come and pick him up. If it weren't for the crowd now circling the building for breakfast, he would have stayed for a while and watched Caroline. But he was taking up one of her tables, and a waitress needed tips. Sitting there for free meant money from her pocket, and he didn't want to do that to her.

Besides, he had to be in court shortly.

---

*W*hy was the place so crowded?

Caroline barely had time to take care of one customer when a second, or even a third one, needed her for something. Today was like a church-had-just-ended Sunday brunch type of a feel to it, and it was only Thursday.

Caroline wanted to check on the man she had sat in the corner of the room. She couldn't sneak him anything else to eat, but she could at least refill his coffee.

She picked up the coffeepot and decided to head over. Now was her chance. She walked toward the table, only to be stopped.

"We're ready for the check," a man sitting at Maria's table told her.

She nodded. "Of course, sir. Right away." She took two steps in Maria's direction, only to be stopped for a refill of coffee and another order of extra tortillas. At least the food request had come from one of her tables.

Plastering a fake smile on her face, she side-stepped two tables, refilled another cup of coffee on a third, and had to pick up a plate of overcooked eggs that needed to go back to the kitchen at yet another.

By the time she was near the spot where the homeless man had sat, he was gone.

Her head spun in the direction of the door. The handsome man, who seemed uncomplicated and sweet, had left the restaurant.

Maria had mentioned having a one-night stand with the next man who walked through the door. After five husbands and fathers had walked through, she had lost track of who the next available man was.

Not that any of them were appealing. Not like the first one through the door, whose beautiful blue eyes still haunted her.

The mystery man had probably hobbled out to sit somewhere else, maybe even beg for money. God, she hoped no one in the diner had made him feel uncomfortable to where he'd felt obligated to leave. Some people hit rock bottom. If her grandmother's bills got the best of her, she might be the next one living on the street.

She walked over to collect her phone and the melting bag of ice. She then cleaned the table for the next group to have a seat. She picked up the now cooled rag he had used to wash his face and found a ten-dollar bill and a note lying beneath it.

She picked up the damp bill and then unfolded the note. Scott's name and a cell phone number were written on the inside.

Did Scott have money? She guessed he must have had enough to maintain a cell phone.

He certainly hadn't looked as if he had any means. Perhaps a friend had come to collect him and paid after seeing the empty cup of coffee?

She stared at the phone number. It was local.

Perhaps he wasn't homeless. Maybe he had just fallen in the park like he had said. Just because all the men in her life were liars didn't mean she couldn't trust him about the park.

A one-night stand.

No strings attached.

She snuck a peek at Maria as she rushed from table to table. Her friend never seemed uptight or worried about anything, and she dated men all the time without any ties to bind her.

Maybe she did need a one-night stand.

Either way, she pocketed the money and note, then she wiped down the table.

4

"So, it's just a sprain?"

Scott studied his swollen ankle as he carefully put his sock back on, stretching the fabric to its limit. He knew better than to put on the shoe.

"A really bad sprain." Dr. Ravi Amarro sat next to one of his best friends on the couch of his office at Grant Memorial. "You're lucky I wasn't on the golf course and could take your call."

"It's not Wednesday. Besides, you wouldn't be golfing without me." Scott rested his back against the green, paisley print of the couch. He still had time to make it to court, but he couldn't show up barefoot.

"Thanks for sending a driver with some cash to my rescue." It was the only way he could give Caroline a tip. The driver even had a notepad with him

51

and pen so he could leave her a note. Hopefully, she'd call him.

"I've used that service for years and have a credit card on file with them. Glad to have been able to help."

A knock sounded on the door, and Ravi crossed the room to answer it.

"Size fourteen, left foot," came a voice from outside in the corridor.

"I guess being the head of your department has its perks," Scott said after Ravi had closed the door and showed him the big black boot he carried.

"You'll need to wear this for a few weeks." Ravi glared at Scott. "No excuses. Don't make me call Bev and have her keep an eye on you."

Scott's fingers touched the prickly Velcro fasteners of the boot. "Classic black. It'll go with everything."

"You need to take care of this. I called in a prescription for some painkillers." Before Scott could complain, he added, "I'm glad you thought to ice your ankle immediately and to take some Advil."

"Caroline saw to everything."

An eyebrow rose.

Crap. Why did he have to say her name? He didn't want to mention the pretty waitress to anyone. Although, he hadn't stopped thinking about her since he left the money and note for her. Would she call him?

"Caroline? Wasn't there someone at your work you were dating?"

'Dating' was not the term he'd call it. Fucking after hours and buying her whatever she wanted was more appropriate. "That was Joanna from research."

Ravi shook his head. "No. Wasn't it Wendy or something like that?"

*Seriously?* "You're thinking of Gwen, and she was a while ago." Gwen was someone he could have had more of a relationship with, if she wasn't a lying whore. "She was the one who cheated on me." He then corrected himself. "Joanna cheated too."

A sick feeling rose in the pit of his stomach. How many of his past girlfriends had been just as bad? You pay for whatever they want and then they walk all over you.

Ravi snapped his fingers. "I'm thinking of Gwen. You would think I'd remember her name. After all, she came down to plastics a few years ago and got a set of double-Ds on your dime."

She was one of the few short-term relationships Scott did remember. Her body was smokin' hot, especially after the expensive plastic surgery. New pieces to match her plastic personality and heart, but the latter wasn't the hospital's doing. "Your staff does good work."

"Cheaters and gold-diggers. Seems like you have a type."

Did he really attract she-devils? They all had

model good looks, were great in bed, and knew how to spend his money. Now that he thought about it, a few of them *were* models. All had degrees or were attending college. Smart, educated, beautiful...why weren't he and his wallet enough for them?

"Will you be sending this Caroline woman in, as well?"

"What?"

Ravi puffed out his chest and glanced down. "For some work."

Caroline was already sexy and curvy. She didn't need any alterations. She even had a pert button nose.

"It's not likely I'll see her again. She's just a waitress at the restaurant I stopped at." *Only a waitress,* Scott thought. He had made a promise to himself not to date anyone who didn't have loftier goals in life than working a menial job. He wanted someone he could come home to and ask about her day, then listen to the fascinating story that followed, full of more than news of disgruntled customers and the possibility of a small pay raise to go with her minuscule check each week.

And yet, he couldn't get the sound of Caroline's voice out of his head. She'd taken good care of him and thought him homeless. She'd even touched his foot. What kind of a stranger took care of someone like that?

"Hmmm…" Ravi muttered. "Only a waitress, yet you got her name."

"It's nothing." When Ravi gave him a smirk, he added, "She was wearing a name tag. Plus…," he let out a snicker, "she thinks I'm homeless."

Ravi pointed at the torn and muddied outfit Scott wore. "Probably for good reason."

As Ravi helped him with the boot and showed him how to bind the Velcro, Scott thought back to Caroline. If she were studying to be a nurse or even a doctor…

Before he even realized it, he asked, "Would you ever consider seriously dating someone who worked for minimum wage?" Okay, it sounded stupid as it came out, so he quickly added, "I mean, would you date someone who worked for a living…at a job that was…?"

"What? Manually demanding?"

Was that the phrase he sought? No, deep down, Scott knew what he was asking. He had known Ravi a long time and knew the man wouldn't judge him. "Would you date someone who didn't have an education equal to your own?"

It sounded vain as he said it, but he had gone to the law school at the University of Chicago, one of the best in the nation. He always figured he'd end up with someone who at least had a bachelor's degree. A hard-working waitress probably didn't have an advanced education.

And yet, he left her his phone number and hoped she'd call him.

Ravi let out a sigh. "You know I'm not one to consider long-term relationships. Hell, my relationships have all been sheer torture in the past... You know that."

Scott certainly did. Ravi's ex-wife nearly took him for everything he had.

"But you," Ravi said, pointing at Scott, "you *are* the marrying kind."

"Fuck off. That's a terrible thing to say."

Ravi raised his hands in surrender. "Do you still want kids?"

Scott took a deep breath and felt the pulling of his heart, as though something had always been missing. "Not necessarily."

"Liar."

"Maybe." Scott rolled his eyes, knowing full well that rugrats were missing from his life. He didn't want them right now, but one day...

"I can't see myself ever taking the plunge again, but you, my friend, are meant to be the happy husband, father of four, white picket fence, daycare concerns type of guy. Perhaps you've just been dating the wrong women," Ravi said.

Scott wasn't sure of the assessment, but a part of him knew that he did want exactly what Ravi had described.

"We both judge books by their covers and are

always looking for the tall, lanky models who are more interested in our wallets than anything else. Maybe this waitress is just what you need."

"I feel as though we're from two different worlds."

Ravi leaned in. "That's what could make it exciting."

*C*ourt didn't take long, and Scott only had one appointment for the rest of the day. Unfortunately, the meeting felt more painful than his ankle.

"Naturally we used the same font... but our letters have more of a decorative swirl." Frank Rancini stabbed his finger on the conference room table. "Our logo is nothing like theirs."

Scott studied the image on the tablet. A circle half blue, half green, the initials LM—for Landsmark Leasing—in the center with the name spelled out at eleven o'clock circling the image in a field of dark blue. The logo for a competing company, Prince Housing, was a mirror image, with them owning the trademark.

"Mr. Rancini," Scott said, always preferring to use the last name when he needed his client to see reason, "The image, color background, lettering...," Scott's voice trailed off, "Prince Housing has had this image trademarked for over twenty-five years."

"They can go to hell!" Frank Rancini puffed up his chest, and his face turned crimson as he swore—not just stated—the reasons he used the logo and infringed upon the intellectual property of a much more prestigious leasing agency four times his company's size.

Scott had heard the fake reasoning for weeks, and it was becoming time to cut-bait and run. The reason Landmark Leasing's logo mirrored Prince Housing was simple. Frank Rancini stole the logo and built his business around third-party stake holders confusing him for a bigger fish in the pond. Pure and simple.

Scott nodded for a few minutes, allowing Mr. Rancini to—once again—admit that he lifted the logo straight from a competitor and wanted full rights to do so. Unfortunately, Scott knew it wouldn't matter in the end.

"My friend, Mr. Gilkrist, said you could help me; I expect you to do so." He studied Scott, and then scoffed. "Gilkrist said you were one of the best."

His gaze wandered over Scott's appearance, taking in his stance, his demeanor, and his five-thousand-dollar suit. Frank wore an off-the-rack suit that didn't fit him appropriately, didn't conduct fair business practices, and was an ass to deal with.

"I don't give a fuck if these logos look kind-of

similar," Frank said, doing air quotes over the word 'kind-of'. "I'm not rebranding my company image because the idiots of the world can't tell the difference between the letters LM and PH!"

If his gaze wasn't venomous before, it sure was now. "Just do your damn job and fix this, or maybe my friend Gilkrist should get me another lawyer to help me."

Mentioning senior partner Gilkrist, one of Scott's bosses, wasn't going to have Frank's proof of guilt disappear, or help him to win the case. Prince Housing held the national trademark of the logo, plain and simple.

"Mr. Rancini, I do believe Prince Housing has just cause to claim that you've been infringing upon their registered logo for the past..."

"I've been in business for eight years. And I'm not infringing upon anything." His fist beat on the table. "This logo has opened doors for me. I've been able to acquire housing, rental properties, ..." he said, beginning to count on his fingers.

Scott held up his hand and stopped him. "Like you just said, 'this logo opened doors.' The infringement is that you've modified a logo from a more successful competitor in order to build your business, getting clients to trust in your name based upon a confusion they may have from your branding."

Frank's body stiffened, his jaw hardening to

stone. "This is the first time anyone has ever said that the images were even similar..."

"I find that surprising." Scott's gaze slyly went to the clock on the wall behind Frank Rancini. His hour was nearly up, and Scott was done talking to the man.

"I encourage you to settle out of court. I'll have some papers drawn up for our next meeting."

"Settle? Haven't you been listening to a word I've been saying?"

No. Not really. Not for the last ten minutes anyway.

"If we go to court, I don't think you'd like the outcome." Scott stood—his ankle throbbing with pain and reminding him he needed pain killers—and buttoned the top button of his suit jacket. "I'll give you some time to think about what we've discussed, Mr. Rancini. Our next meeting is scheduled for next week." He gestured to the door and watched as Mr. Rancini's face grew redder and he shook his head in frustration.

"Gilkrist said you were the best." Mr. Rancini sneered as he stuffed his tablet and loose paperwork into a satchel. "I don't understand what I'm paying for if you're not going to help me save my business."

Pay? He was getting the special 'friends and family' discount, and then some. Gilkrist had put the case in his own 'special projects' folder, which usually meant that the case didn't bring in much revenue to the company other than paying for court fees and a small hourly fee.

Scott's stomach churned. At first, he was excited to be given this assignment. Any way to ingratiate him into Gilkrist's good graces was important. If they could settle out of court Mr. Rancini might be able to keep his business alive with just a branding adjustment. If they went to court and lost, the man could lose his properties. Why couldn't he see that?

Regardless, Scott had to get as much a favorable outcome as possible—no matter what.

Scott opened the door and waited for his client to leave the room. He then ushered the man to the elevator a few feet away, glad to be rid of him.

He hobbled around the secure surroundings of the hallway, down to his office, and put his foot up on a small stand near his desk.

A fellow lawyer, Ralph, poked his head into Scott's office. "Closed two more this morning." His judgment-filled eyes sized up Scott, and he looked at him as one would a lesser man. "I would have to say that I'm the senior partner of all the junior partners." A crazed grin spread across his face. "With Tate... not doing well, they'll be looking for me to take over that beautiful corner office."

The stereotypical stigma that lawyers were ambulance chasers and pariahs waiting for people's ill fortune had always irked Scott. But to hear such blatant disregard for someone's misfortune made his jaw tighten. The fact that Ralph was the nephew of Larimer, another senior partner in the firm, made him wish he had kept better company over the years. "You're an ass for even…"

"What? Getting my hopes up that an opportunity is about to drop in my lap?"

Scott glared at the man—his rival once a senior partner position opened—with his best get-the-hell-out-of-my-office face, but the man didn't get the hint so he decided to change the subject.

"Good for you on your win in court today. You really needed a win to boost your pathetic average." Scott glanced down at his computer, feigning a lack of interest. "I'm glad to see you're hitting mediocrity these days. Your uncle must be so proud of you."

Ralph stepped farther into the office. "Jealousy is an ugly color on you. Was your prom dress this shade?"

That was two more case wins for the man, and Scott hated his smugness. "Did you ever give the research team a gift for saving your ass last month when you botched the Goldman case?"

Ralph shrugged, just as he did for all of his failures when they were called out. "Unforeseen technicalities botched that."

Scott glided his hand through the air. "You're flying under everyone's radar on your cases. Good thing you have the big brass at the company watching out for you."

"It's called team effort."

Ralph showed up late to meetings, lost an average number of cases, and was the 'Frank Burns' of the office. Unfortunately, nepotism was his friend.

Scott picked up a pencil and notepad, leaned back in his soft leather chair, and pretended to write some notes. "Was one of the cases this morning the Hora vs. Deanda litigation?" He didn't wait for an answer and added, "My case. The one you stole from me."

"MacMillan hadn't made a final judgment on the team, and you know it. It's not my fault that Larimer thought I'd be the best man to win it."

A grin spread across Ralph's face. It was the 'I'm mom's favorite kid' look that Scott hated. If Ralph could chase ambulances, the ones carrying multi-millionaires, he would.

Actually, he wouldn't. He'd wait for his uncle to finish chasing them down and plop the case in Ralph's lap.

"And how are your cases coming along, Scott? What were you working on lately? Some sort of dispute over property lines or stolen cats?"

Now writing out his grocery list, Scott did his best to ignore the ass in the room. But the jerk seemed quite happy to plant himself and take up roots—walking in and actually sitting in one of Scott's guest chairs.

"How's the Landmark Leasing deal coming?"

"Jealous?" Scott asked, holding down his best poker face.

Ralph's eyes narrowed, and his face pinched. "You may think you have a golden ticket helping out Gilkrist's friend, but..."

"But what?" Scott leaned in, taking care not to move his ankle. "You're afraid that I'll win the entire chocolate factory with this ticket. And you?" He sized up the competition. "You're just a kid that got suckered into a river of chocolate and gets to go home with nothing."

Ralph picked up a slip of paper from the desk and quickly read it. "Who's Caroline?" He flipped the slip over once and scanned the front of it. "A waitress at the Patio," he said, obviously noting the servers name. An eyebrow rose. "Who signs her name with a heart over the 'i.'"

Scott reached across, hurting his ankle in the process, and plucked it from the man's hands. Before Ralph could say anything else, Scott cut him off. "You know where the door is. It's the big, brown thing that leads out into the hallway. Please close it on your way out."

Ralph stood and took several steps toward the door, walking past the leather chairs and the corner table for clients' use. "You mean this door, the one leading out of this non-corner, small office."

"The last time I checked, your office was four square feet smaller than mine."

Ralph's face twisted, and a sneer appeared on his face. "I've got more cases to win anyway. Wasting time in your space isn't bringing more money to this firm, although I do enjoy mixing with the riffraff occasionally."

He paused just before stepping out and inhaled deeply. "It smells in here anyway. What is that?" He sniffed the air a few more times. "Oh, I know. It's desperation."

An evil grin spread across his face. "My date to the Christmas party is going to blow you away, and she's someone who will completely impress the senior partners. She's bright, intelligent, works within our industry, ..."

Rage hit Scott, and he felt acid churning in his stomach. "Out!"

"Well, it'll be a race to the finish then. With me winning." Ralph opened the door and left.

Once alone, Scott threw the notepad down and swiveled in the chair to stare out his big picture window, only to see the damn skyscraper staring back at him. He knew Ralph would not give up, and now he had an impressive date to the party.

Shit. He'd like to bring Caroline. He took in a deep breath and felt the heaviness of the situation. If he brought Caroline, he'd have to impress the senior partners and board members in some other way. She wasn't a part of this industry. Didn't have a degree. Wasn't as boring as the others.

A knock sounded on the door, and Scott turned to find Bev peeking in, her gaze focusing on the floor.

"Is it safe to come in?"

After having ordered in food service the other day, he couldn't blame her.

"Come in."

She entered and closed the door behind her. "New cell phone. This one is waterproof. Same number, and all your info from the cloud has been switched over." She placed the phone on the desk and then walked around to stare at his foot. "How are you feeling?"

"I'm fine."

"Are you going to tell me how that happened?" She pointed at the foot, and the expression she wore told him that, other than the details, she already knew.

"Yes. I was careless," he said, knowing the right answer to give her.

"Uh-huh."

Scott's hands gestured in a twisting motion. "The path snaked around a stream, and there were slick rocks…you can figure out the rest."

She didn't even blink.

"And, you're right. I should be more careful."

He stared at her stoic face. He hated that expression.

"I *will* be more careful. Okay?"

Her lips pursed. She had heard him make such promises ever since he was a kid. She knew not to trust him.

"I like taking risks." The tone of his voice was soft, nearly apologetic, just like when he was a child.

"The doctor gave you only a walking boot? No sturdy cane?" She held up her own cane. Solid wood, a bit old fashioned, with little curly-ques burned into the length. A perfectly good walking device, albeit a bit feminine.

"I'm capable of walking without one. Thanks."

She shook her head. "I should have picked one up for you. Here." She handed him a small bag from Walgreens. "These pain killers are better than just taking Ibuprofen."

A cane and painkillers. Scott was decades younger than Beverly, but got a glimpse into her world of arthritic pain. At least his issues were only temporary since his ankle would heal.

He raked his hand through his hair to tame the Gumby hairstyle he knew he sported. His efforts probably just made things worse since Beverly seemed to study his wayward coif closer.

"Ever since you were a kid you've had lush hair," Bev said, studying his hairstyle. "I've scheduled a haircut for you for later today."

Yeah. It was about time for a cut. He was beginning to look unprofessional. Thank goodness she managed all the little details like this for him. He didn't even know his barber's phone number, and he'd been going to the guy for nearly twenty years.

She typed on her tablet, her fingernails clicking against the device and echoing in the room. "Is there anything else you need for me to do?"

He let out a heavy sigh, one that should have relaxed him but didn't. "When was it a crime to be a successful single?" Scott straightened his tie.

"Crime?" Beverly brushed the back of his jacket. "I doubt you'd go to trial for something like that."

"I'm being serious. 'Henderson and Jackson' are entertaining the idea of taking me on at their company with a five-year probationary period before making me a senior partner."

"'Henderson and Jackson?" Beverly took a deep breath and shook her head as if the idea were ridiculous. "That outfit is small. Two lawyers and a small office barely located on the good side of town."

"It's a growing business where I could advance quickly. But the five-year probationary period comes with some catches."

"Catches?"

Scott propped his foot better on the footstool. He winced while he did the adjustment. "Both those lawyers own a home within city limits. It gives clients the impression that the lawyers are a part of the community."

"Your townhome doesn't qualify?"

"Evidently not."

He didn't care if it was only eleven in the morning. He limped to the mini bar and poured himself a scotch. "And, evidently, the senior partner image they have in mind comes with a Mrs. Senior Partner."

"They want you married?"

"Archaic. Nearly barbarian ideals."

Bev stared off in the distance, her facial expression looked like she was doing a difficult math problem in her head. He knew that meant the wheels were turning and she was deep in thought. "Do you think being single is what's holding you back here?"

"Here?" The firm had made no demands on him. No expectations of any kind had been set. But he now thought about the four partners: Tate, MacMillan, Gilkrist, and Larimer. All were married men. Even the one senior partner who had left the firm before he got there had been married.

Scott wasn't going to accept that a ringless finger could hold him back. Mostly, because he had promised himself that he'd do anything to get to the position of senior partner, but not something as crazy as getting married.

He wasn't that desperate.

"I doubt my being single is standing in my way. I have Ralph to compete with, and I'd say he's the biggest issue. Larimer's damn nephew is always biting on my heels. When an opening for senior partner becomes available, it'd most likely go to him."

Beverly's expression changed, as though she became evenly more heavily focused with an evil plot brewing in her head. "When Tate's position opens, you'd need the backing of one of the other three senior partners to be presented to the board."

"I'd need the backing of two of them to win."

She took in a deep breath. "It's a sure thing that Larimer will back his nephew." She paced in front of his desk. "Gilkrist is a wild card, but I think MacMillan would favor you." She turned and faced him. "Is there a third player on this field?"

"I can't think of any other junior partner that would be considered. It's just Ralph that's in my way."

"Ralph's track record for courtroom wins isn't as impressive as yours." She turned and paced again, leaning heavily upon her cane. "And you certainly have brought in more clients over the years."

"True, but nepotism runs deep. Always has." He downed the scotch noting that the painkillers would have to wait.

"You're always bragging about how you're the best lawyer this firms got."

"You know I'm the best."

"So other than an uncle, what does Ralph have over you? Is he married and the owner of a house?"

He wasn't friends with Ralph, but the expression

'know your enemies' was something he believed in. "He rents a condo, just like me. The one thing he does well is he puts on a good show. He tends to find out what is expected and molds his weasel image into whatever is needed."

She circled him, her critical eyes studying him. "You're practically picture perfect. You just need some polishing up."

Beverly could always concoct some wild hair scheme. It was usually some 'I Love Lucy' skit that would later backfire on him. "What do you mean?"

"You should buy a house. You can always use it later as rental property."

He exhaled the breath he didn't know he was holding. "Easy enough. We can call some realtors."

"You need to be married."

He glared at her, a sinking feeling pulling at his chest. "No, not going to happen."

"Not really married, just present a woman who is perfect to the last detail to the board during the Christmas party. Hint that you're thinking of settling down with the woman, tell them about the house you just bought, and get them to believe you're the perfect lawyer, with the perfect image, that they need as their next senior partner."

Shit. He wasn't even dating anyone, and he didn't need some woman thinking he actually was thinking of getting engaged to her. Scott picked up a pencil from his desk and began nervously twirling it around his fingers. The caliber of women he dated wouldn't cut the mustard anyway. Oh, they'd be pretty enough, they'd be sexy enough, but they'd lack in so many other ways.

An image of Caroline appeared in his mind, and a smile crossed his face. She wasn't wearing a wedding band. She'd be someone different and fresh to take to a swanky holiday party.

She was prettier and sexier than anyone else he could even think of.

"You know Ralph will bring a model-perfect, fit for the company, date to the party. He's not a stupid man. His date will be some CEO of a company, legs 'till Tuesday, bombshell with a brain to impress anyone," Beverly said in a strong, influential tone as if trying to convince him that her half-baked plan would work.

"Ralph date a sexy CEO of a company?" Scott shook his head. That'd only be in Ralph's dreams.

"For this grand prize he will find somebody. You don't normally date executives either." Bev paused and then said, "usually." Her eyes narrowed and she studied him. "The woman you two take to that party could be a deciding factor."

"Eye candy shouldn't be any type of deciding factor." And that is what really bothered Scott. Ralph was crafty and he wouldn't put it past him to bring a bombshell, smart as hell, sexy woman to impress the bosses. The woman might be his cousin, but she'd still fit the bill.

A sudden bit of sadness filled him. The firm needed someone better as a senior partner than Ralph. If the man weren't Larimer's nephew—well, half-nephew on his half-brother's side—he probably would be on television commercials trying to secure new clients at a lesser firm.

Ralph got all the breaks.

Scott unconsciously tightened his grip on the pencil he held. It snapped in half, causing him to jump in his seat.

Making it to senior partner before fifty was a long shot for him. Ralph had a good five years more experience. If Ralph was being groomed to make Senior Partner, he'd be Scott's direct boss. God, he hoped it wouldn't come to that.

His phone buzzed, and his eyebrow rose when he read the number and recognized it as an internal one. He gave Bev a quick this-could-be-big glance before answering. "Hello?"

"Hello Mr. Hollister. MacMillan would like to talk to you today. He's leaving court right now and wants to have lunch with you at Basils restaurant right away."

Scott's gaze remained on Bev who was now leaning in and doing her best to hear some of the private conversation. "Absolutely. I'll be there," he said, his cracking voice surprising him.

Bev stood and took a step closer as he hung up the phone. The anticipation showed in her face to the point where she might explode.

"MacMillan wants to have lunch with me." Scott's heart raced. Getting a call from MacMillan was like the Hague calling you about your past war crimes, or someone saying they wanted to crown you king of the world. It could go either way.

Whichever it was, it was big news.

Very big.

He straightened his tie and took a good look at his suit. Why hadn't he worn his dark gray, double-breasted today? It was his power suit and made him look more intimidating in court.

And, dammit, his hair still needed to be cut.

"This is it." Bev's high-pitched voice, wide smile and toothy grin showed her excitement. "Tate must not be doing well." She looked upward as though remembering what an opening in the company really meant. She crossed herself and mumbled, "Not that we want him to die."

Beverly was borderline religious, and he liked that she saw this as a bitter sweet opportunity. He hated thinking of himself as a vulture, but an opportunity was presenting itself and someone was going to get Tate's position in the company. "He's a good man and served this company well." He didn't want to jinx anything, or get his hopes up. "We don't know for sure that this lunch is about me being offered the position."

Her shoulders sagged. "Really? We don't?"

Yeah, she was probably right. He just didn't want to get too excited about the meeting.

"I can start house hunting, and..." Her excited tone turned to a severe, 'we have to be careful' one. In a hushed tone, she said, "There are companies that hire out women."

He turned quickly to stare at her, his ankle complaining about the movement. "An escort service?"

"A professional date." She rolled her eyes and he could see the anxiety she had, mixed with hope, for him in the creased lines of her face. "Not that kind of a professional, but a business-savvy woman in a size four dress that can impress anyone."

He was still thinking about Caroline and perhaps of asking her to the company party. Certainly, she'd be better than any paid woman.

"Don't think of this as hiring an escort," Beverly said, correcting him. "Think of this more as hiring a PR expert," she said in an upbeat and positive way.

"Public Relations?"

Her hand went to her hip. "It's what you need, unless you're dating an heiress or some other ultra-impressive woman that I don't know about."

There was no-one. At least, not yet.

Beverly waved her hand dismissively in the air. "I'll make the arrangements. Then you'll hire her to be your date for the party. You'll want to make the best impression possible. I'll make some calls at lunch."

It seemed too phony, and too desperate. "Give me some time to think about it."

"You don't have that much time."

Her words were rushed and he could tell by her stiff body language that she wanted the details sorted out and taken care of. Once a plan had been created, she always needed the details done as soon as possible. It was one of her most desirable qualities that he liked about her, but not today.

"Let me at least meet MacMillan for lunch and see what is going on." He stood and struggled putting weight on his foot.

She helped steady him. "Fair enough. But I could research some nice neighborhoods for rental properties in the meantime."

House hunting was fine. Fake dating...he had to give it more thought. "All right. Look at houses." He tapped the breast pocket of his suit jacket to confirm he had his phone with him. "I'll text you the details in a bit."

"We'll need to move fast. You need a house and a sexy date. One that will turn heads and get you noticed."

He wanted to laugh. When did his sweet childhood nanny turn into a pimp?

She gestured to the sack of painkillers on his desk. "Take those now so they'll kick-in by the time you're having lunch."

He stared at the Walgreens bag. Pimp and drug dealer.

She held tightly on his arm to help him to the door. "I've been grooming you to be a senior partner since the day you made junior. We need to lock down this deal."

Scott didn't like the idea of being a vulture, but life happens. If Tate were to pass away the company would want to replace him. It was just standard business fare. Maybe Scott needed to be more aware of company politics, although Bev certainly had a handle on things.

The lunch with MacMillan was the first step, and he knew that in his heart he wanted Caroline at the party with him, but she wouldn't be his date.

# 5

"I just heard." Joanna's voice sounded an octave higher than normal—just slightly above her 'I'm lying to you range" but under her "how did you ever find out" one. The tone also matched her insincere puppy-dog eyes, the look she had given him the time he had caught her in bed with another man. "Are you all right?"

The slight sympathetic expression on her face seemed slimy to Scott—even in a pit of lawyers. Plus, she blocked his path down the hallway. He needed to get to lunch and, with his leg, needed more time to get there.

"Doing just fine." He enunciated each word through gritted teeth. Why had he been so stupid? Sleeping with someone in the research department? She had access to all his accounts and roamed freely among the company, hearing and carrying on gossip as if it were one of her daily tasks.

She moved her body to block his path even more, and then placed a hand on his shoulder. "We need to talk."

"We really don't." Scott repositioned the clunky boot he wore and tried to sidestep her, only to have her grip his arm even tighter.

"I'll help you."

She snaked her arm around his waist, her long nails slightly scratching his lower back.

God, he used to love her nails digging into his back.

A shiver ran up his spine, and he wiggled his way out of her deadly embrace. She wasn't worth the effort or his time. Not then, and certainly not now. "I can manage."

"Scott, the company party is only a couple of weeks away. I've already made some arrangements, but I thought…"

He spun around, nearly falling, and looked deeply into her snake eyes. "You thought what? That'd I'd forget what you did and take you?"

It surprised him how upset he still was about her deceit and infidelity. Their hookups had started out as just fun afternoon delights, but over the months had become more meaningful—especially after their summer vacation together.

Looking into her eyes, he knew he didn't miss

her, didn't want her back, and would never trust her again. The pain of being treated as a sap is what really stung. He had never been the best of men in the 'wine and dine' romance department, especially with all the one-nighters he had experienced, but his women always knew where they stood with him. He wasn't a cheater, never would be one, and would never condone being with someone who could treat him that way.

She stood taller and softened her expression, her doe-like eyes piercing him in a way that always used to work on him. "I went with you to the last Christmas party, and this year with the possibility of a big announcement I just thought...well, since we mean so much to each other."

"*Meant* so much to each other," he said, his tone frosty like her heart. "And you've moved up from grunt researcher in the company pool to a research director with my help." He looked at her pinstripe, Armani suit and whatever designer shoes she now wore. "From wearing off-the-rack to tailored, runway perfect outfits."

"My feelings for you are genuine." Her finger twirled around a lock of her hair—a black widow spider spinning her web for an unsuspecting next meal. "I'd like to be your date again this year."

"I already have a date," he lied. The words were barely out of his mouth when his mind raced to a vision of Caroline. Kind. Sweet. Caring. Exceptionally pretty. It'd be nice to get a fresh start with someone completely different.

She glared at him. "You can wipe that silly look off your face."

His grin widened into a full smile as he stared at Joanna. Whatever spell she thought she had on him, her magic had worn off. "I've moved on."

Her face hardened in a bitches-be-crazy way, resembling what could only be considered an evil, searing stare that bore into him. Scott's heart skipped a beat, and he backed up the best he could with his sore ankle to move away from her.

"Who is it?" She glared at him and took a step closer. "Who?" The tone of her voice deadly.

A one-hundred-eighty-degree turn like that usually caused emotional whiplash, but not with Joanna. Scott had never seen her like this. The little vein in her temple popped out and he could practically see it pulsing.

When he didn't answer, she narrowed her eyes and smiled a truly wicked grin. "It doesn't matter. You'll regret not taking me. I'll make sure of that."

The desperation in her voice spoke volumes to him. Surely gossip of him having lunch with one of the partners was already running its course through the building. The look in her eyes was one he had seen before—she wanted something from him and she was pissed that she would have to work for it.

If her schemes weren't clear before, they

certainly were now. "You just want to use me to get close to the partners. Being the girlfriend of a senior partner is exactly what you want."

"Girlfriend. Wife." She took a deep breath and moved in closer.

A deep, nagging thought occurred to him. "If I don't take you, how many of the junior partners are you willing to screw to get what you want?"

---

*S*cott finally made it out of the building, dignity intact and feeling pretty good about himself. The sting of Joanna's slap across his face was like a trophy to him, too bad the pain had already waned.

Scott hobbled from the building and onto the street in front of the office. The restaurant was close by, only half a block away. Should he take a cab? Uber his way over? Glancing the length of the street he figured, even with his ankle, he'd get there faster by foot.

It was an agonizing short walk, but he brushed the rain from his suit jacket and was thankful that he'd made it safely to the place before it began to pour. He stood under the protection of the restaurant's awning checking himself out in the reflection of the blackened glass door. His hair actually benefited from the slight downpour, and his suit wasn't worse-for-wear. The black boot he wore looked hideous, and it didn't match his loafer, but the medical shoe seemed rainproof enough and did help him put weight on his ankle.

Thank goodness for pain killers. He couldn't focus on his physical pain. Meeting with one of the partners of the firm was always nerve-racking. At least this was one of the three partners he kind of knew. MacMillan had mentored him when he was brought into the company nearly fifteen years ago. Other than holiday parties and the few large accounts they had worked on together now, they didn't exactly hang out together anymore.

In fact, the man didn't like many people. Social events? MacMillan usually avoided them, but there was always a reason behind everything the man did.

Scott entered the building and took the elevator to the thirtieth floor, where he found a dozen people waiting to be seated at the restaurant. He made his way to the hostess stand.

"I'm afraid I'm unable to seat you, sir," a woman wearing caked-on makeup, overly styled hair, and a blouse cut down to her navel spoke to the man in front of Scott in line. "I can have a table for you in the rear of the restaurant in about an hour."

Her palm rested on the wooden podium. It lay up and empty. The man wasn't picking up on her subtle cues for a bribe. The world worked on money, and Scott usually kept a twenty in his pocket whenever he went somewhere without a reservation.

The man then excused himself, allowing Scott to approach the gatekeeper.

"Good afternoon," she said with a lilt in her voice. "Do you have a reservation?"

She was cookie-cutter perfection and reminded him of his last four quasi girlfriends. Size four, plastered-on smile, tight hips, cruel heart.

"Mr. MacMillan's table," he said, knowing that the man preferred this restaurant for business meetings and figured she would know daddy big bucks.

Her fake smile broadened across her face and a glint of hope danced in her gaze, as though knowing that anyone who dined with MacMillan also had money. "Of course, sir." She unnecessarily bent down low to grab a menu from the hostess stand instead of taking one from the top of the counter behind her. Her dress hiked up, showing him her long legs and tight bottom. The show would normally be appreciated, and he wondered if she gave every wealthy customer—including MacMillan —the same view.

She stood and eyed him like a hefty cash cow that came in for milking. Her left, ringless hand touched the diamond necklace on her cleavage, showcasing her bare chest. She leaned in and stood close to him, his sense of smell picking up her designer perfume. "Please, follow me," she said in a breathy voice.

Scott clenched his jaw as he squeezed out a smile. This woman needed to work in advertising, in the subliminal images department.

She turned and made her way through the small hallway filled with various wine bottles. He refused to glance at her butt, even though she was strutting it as if a blue ribbon were wrapped around it.

With MacMillan's standing reservation, she knew exactly which private table with its killer view the man always sat at. Employees knew who he was and the type of clientele he dined with. Rich.

It made sense that MacMillan would be a regular at a swank place like this. Dim lighting, soft music playing in the background, and picture windows giving all tables a fabulous view of downtown Chicago gave the establishment its five-star rating and merited small, but expensive, entrees.

With each painful step, Scott reminded himself to breathe. Being called into MacMillan's office was a far cry from having lunch out with the man. He must have good news to share.

MacMillan sat sipping scotch, looking out at the rainy day. He was known for enjoying a drink in the afternoons, which was why Scott always gave him a fifty-year-old bottle of single malt every year for Christmas.

"Sir." The waitress waved her hand, suggesting that Scott take one of the seats at the table. She then took the linen napkin and placed it across Scott's lap, taking a little longer to place the cloth than necessary.

Scott grabbed the napkin from her.

"Would you care for a beverage?"

There was no choice. "Scotch. Neat."

When she left, the old man pointed out the window. "This town has changed so much since I moved here as a boy."

Scott rarely appreciated scenery but feigned interest now as he looked out the window. The Chicago skyline with its skyscrapers and the lake was postcard-perfect in front of them. The view was unobstructed and he could see for miles. "It's a beautiful town."

"Did I ever tell you that I came to Chicago with my newly widowed mother when I was only ten years old? We had no money back then."

Scott sensed the familiarity in the air and took in a deep breath. His old friend, his mentor, was now seated with him—not the big boss man whom everyone was scared of. His chest felt lighter and he shook his head. "I've never heard the story."

MacMillan gave a harrumph from the back of his throat before looking at his drink. The beverage must not have been his first of the afternoon.

The waitress reappeared and dropped off the drink. MacMillan paused while she did her job, but once she left, he said, "My mother was working two jobs, and we lived in this crappy apartment, struggling to make ends meet." His eyes seemed slightly glazed over, but not from the alcohol. This was a tender moment rarely shared by MacMillan. He held prestige and power, and seldom showed his vulnerable side.

It was a good sign that the meeting would go well.

Scott settled more comfortably in his chair. "I'm sorry to hear about your father, sir."

"Don't be," he said in a curt and rough voice. He downed his scotch in time to order another when the waitress brought Scott his. "He was an awful man, and my mother was better without him." He took in a deep breath and let it out slowly. "Times were tough, but she didn't need a man in her life that didn't appreciate her, that didn't stand up for her, that didn't put her before anything else." His voice drifted off as he strolled down memory lane.

"Sounds like she was a strong woman. Your childhood must have been difficult with her being a single mother."

MacMillan slowly nodded his head, so Scott added, "Money must have been tight."

"There is nothing wrong with coming from humble beginnings," MacMillan said, looking Scott sternly in the eyes.

Shit.

Scott's stomach somersaulted, and he felt that he had just overstepped.

"Having no money makes you work harder for what you have, and appreciate it all the more."

Scott sat straighter in the chair and wished they were still talking about the Chicago skyline. His family was rich, and he was one of the heirs to the Hollister Hotel fortune. It wasn't a secret, and MacMillan knew that Scott came from money.

"I met my wife while in law school," MacMillan added. "She worked so I could get my degree. The plan was for her to return to school, but responsibilities came up." He gave a slight eye roll, one that looked to have held years of disappointment. "You know I have three kids."

"Yes, sir."

"Three ungrateful children." MacMillan stared out the window, and Scott didn't know how to reply to that last comment since he had never met them and had never seen a picture of them on MacMillan's desk. Scott sipped his scotch slowly.

MacMillan talked about putting in the time and work to climb a company ladder and how important it was to have a plan in life.

"Do you have a plan, Scott?"

Scott wished the waitress would come by and take their food orders. Anything to stall so he could think of something intelligent to say. How was it that he had prepared talks like this for years in his head, combing out each comment in fine detail, and yet, when it was time to share his thoughts with the head honcho, he couldn't think of what to say?

"My plan is to become a senior partner in a successful law firm one day," Scott finally said, going for broke and getting right to the point.

MacMillan chuckled. "It may be old school, but the support of a good woman always helps if you have such lofty goals." He eyed Scott in a what-are-your-intentions-with-my-company sort of way.

"You're not married, are you?"

Scott swallowed the lump in his throat. This was exactly what he had feared. He didn't meet the corporate image. Didn't exactly fit in. Didn't fit the cookie-cutter mold. "No, sir. I'm not married."

MacMillan glanced away as if Scott had somehow become less desirable.

Wrong, wrong, wrong.

"But I'm seeing someone," Scott blurted out. He had to do something to get MacMillan back into his good graces, even if it were to make up a fake girlfriend.

"Is the relationship serious?"

Scott smiled as though proud to have his fake woman in his life. "I'd like to think so."

Okay, so he wasn't seeing anyone. Hadn't seen anyone in nearly a year. And, Beverly certainly didn't count, but she was the only woman in his life at the moment.

MacMillan shifted in his seat and his gaze studied Scott. "Is your lady supportive?"

For the next few minutes, Scott answered questions about loyalty and the caring nature of his fake woman. It wasn't until he shared a made-up story about her picking up a toy for a child dining next to them at a restaurant that he realized he was describing Caroline.

"She sounds like a keeper." MacMillan picked up his drink, his hand wrapped around the glass but his finger pointing at Scott. "You remind me of myself back in the day."

"I do?" It was probably the best compliment the man could have given him. Scott leaned in to hear more, but the waitress came to take their orders.

MacMillan glanced up at the woman. "Two of today's specials, please. Thank you."

Scott had no idea what the special of the day was, but he'd eat cooked shoe leather if the boss ordered it for him.

"I remind you of yourself when you were my age?" Scott wanted to stay on a good thread and keep the conversation going.

The man nodded slowly and sipped his drink. Finally, he said, "Tate's health is failing." His face pained, and a slight sniffle escaped. "He's in hospice care."

Scott knew the man was ill, but hospice? He had

no idea the man was so close to death. "I know the two of you are close. I'm sorry he's not doing well."

The man stared at him, his head slightly nodding. "I believe you really mean that." MacMillan's voice was soft and sincere as he looked away. "Larimer wants to seat his damned nephew in the opening senior partner position."

Scott held his breath. "I'm aware."

MacMillan shook his head. "Ralph's a good attorney, but I need someone stronger in the senior partner position." For a moment he studied Scott. It seemed like an eternity. "Our partner, Gilkrist, doesn't have anyone he's looking into, so it's up to me to offer another candidate for the board to vote on."

"Yes, sir."

This was it. This was the moment. Scott could feel it. His heart raced and he had to force himself not to grin from ear-to-ear. He took in a deep breath wanting to somehow preserve this moment, and yet, somehow jump to the end where MacMillan wanted to present Scott to the board.

MacMillan's deep blue eyes now glared at Scott. Gone was the softened expression of reminiscing and in its stead was a stern businessman. "How is the Landmark Leasing case going?"

It was the verbal dagger piercing Scott's hope. The topic change felt odd, if not disappointing. The case wasn't going well, and a heaviness settled in

Scott's stomach. Hopefully his future didn't depend upon this one case. "I'm suggesting that the case be mitigated out of court."

The short answer seemed the best one to give.

"The owner of that franchise is a good friend of Gilkrist's son. I chose you to work on it since it's somewhat high profile. Landmark Leasing owns franchises across the country, and it's a personal project for Gilkrist. I thought it'd be a way for you to shine."

So, MacMillan had suggested him for the job. Not surprising, but Scott had hoped that Gilkrist had picked him out of all the junior partners for the pet project. "Yes sir. I'm doing my best but I think drafting a settlement and avoiding a huge law suit by Prince Housing is the way to go."

A disappointing frown appeared on MacMillan's face, one that deflated Scott's hope. "I was hoping for a better outcome," MacMillan said, his voice soft and somber.

"I'm still hoping for that. But we'll have to see."

A moment of silence filled the air, and Scott's brow beaded with sweat.

MacMillan's eyebrow lifted under his whitened hairline and Scott took in the age of the man. In another fifteen years or so, another senior partner might be having the same discussion with someone over MacMillan's replacement. The corporate food-chain.

"Why don't you tell me why you would make a better senior partner than Ralph."

It was Scott's big chance; too bad his heart was beating so loudly and fast that all he wanted to do was throw up.

Scott cleared his throat as his mind raced with the success of all his old cases and tried to think of how to begin. He needed to say something impressive, but his prepared speech—the one he had been practicing for the last few years—seemed hollow and just wrong.

Working with MacMillan for over a decade, having been his mentee for years, and knowing his personal history, Scott knew how to proceed. He started by simply saying, "I believe in justice."

*C*aroline place the hot plates in front of her customers. "Is there anything else I can bring you?"

The woman's face pinched in disgust. "This isn't right."

Caroline didn't need one more thing to go wrong today. She took a deep breath, plastered a smile on her face, and dug out her order slip. "Enchilada plate number three?"

The customer pointed to the bowl of black beans

and then gestured across the entire plate. "I ordered refried beans and no cheese."

She so didn't. But Caroline grabbed the hot plate. "I'm sorry your meal isn't correct. I'll be right out with another one." Glancing at the table, she then asked, "Is everything else okay?"

"We need some tea refills. More lemons, too," one of her companions said.

"Of course. I'll be right back."

The customer didn't order refried instead of black beans, and she certainly didn't say 'no cheese' for her meal. Caroline walked back to the kitchen and asked a table runner to refill the teas.

The food smelled great, cheese and all. Being hungry and smelling food all day was torture, but at least she was being paid. Although, this was a table of five and not six. One more person would guarantee her a tip of fifteen percent. She'd be lucky to get even ten percent from them.

Her legs weakened under her and she was tired of walking the length of the dining hall, weaving in between crowded tables and carrying heavy trays. Glancing at her watch she realized she had three more hours left on her shift.

"Table six. Tan blazer." Maria said as she quickly passed by with her own tray of food.

Caroline wanted to resist, but her gaze darted over to where the man sat. Dark hair, strong build, and obviously here with co-workers talking about business. The man was on the phone and ignoring his lunch companions.

Handsome, self-absorbed, and rude.

Maria had spent the day pointing out good looking men to her. She was convinced that a one-night stand would lift Caroline's spirits. There was no way she was going to pick up some rude random guy, give him her number, and then... an icy chill ran up her spine. And not do that with him either.

She entered the kitchen and told the Expo, the person who guarantees the plates of food are done correctly, "I need this plate to have refried beans, no cheese."

He studied the plate. "This is a number three. Did the customer modify it?"

"It's not my fault. She changed her order."

He grabbed the plate from her hands and set it on a counter. Another order for number three was ready to go out, this one without cheese as well. "Here," he said, scooping refried beans on the plate. "We're too busy for me to have to fix every order that comes in here."

Every order?

Puh-lease.

This dish was only the second one from her that needed to be modified—and it truly wasn't her fault. She wondered how many other orders from the other waitresses were being returned.

Walking back to the main dining hall, a new bus

boy bumped into her. He nearly dropped the dirty plates he was bringing in to be washed. A glass filled with water spilled from his hands and crashed to the floor, smashing into pieces.

"Shit, Caroline."

"Code four," someone shouted, meaning that broken glass lay on the floor.

The bus boy set down the dishes and reached for the broom. "Watch where you're going."

"You bumped into me."

It didn't matter. She walked past him, picked up her next order from the window and walked back into the dining hall.

She just needed a break from all this. She needed to escape. Needed to…

Maria was now slyly pointing to a handsome man in a suit and mouthing the words, "this one."

No. That wasn't the one. If anything, the man she was interested in was Scott. She had thought of his blue eyes all day. She wondered how he was doing with his bad ankle. If he were homeless, which she didn't really believe, he would probably sleep in the park tonight. Alone on a park bench if he were lucky, on the hard ground if not. At least the forecast didn't call for rain tonight.

"Total ten at table seven. Am I right?" Maria said as she swerved past her, her eyebrows waggling suggestively.

Caroline didn't answer. But she did mentally

scribble a list of pros and cons for having a one-nighter. Sure, it'd feel good to be held by a man. She couldn't claim that she didn't enjoy having sex, at least, she remembered enjoying it all that time ago. But she didn't need the added turmoil in her life.

She placed the order down at her table and the customers seemed pleased that it had come out correctly. Her four tables now all had meals, all had more tea, and didn't need her for the next five minutes. She went back to the kitchen where it was quieter to gather her thoughts, that's when she heard her cell phone chirp. Glancing around, she didn't see her boss so she took a moment to visit the restroom.

A voicemail from Avalon had come in. Her heart raced and she just knew it had to be bad news. She hit the button to listen to the message.

'Hello, Ms. Wenzel. This is Ruth Rubinstein from Avalon. I'm the Resident Coordinator and I'd like to speak to you about your grandmother's care. Please call me back at..."

Caroline let the number trail off and she ended the call. She knew the number for Avalon by heart. She didn't know a Ruth Rubinstein from the place, and certainly didn't talk with the administrative staff often.

If her Grandmother had been sick, the nurse would have called. Or even a doctor. She swallowed the lump in her throat. Or an ER technician as they raced her Grandmother to the nearest hospital.

The bathroom felt warmer and she sprinkled some water on her face. There was no need to get excited over a call from an administrator. Especially since a call like this could mean only one thing. Tears began welling in Caroline's eyes and she could hardly breath.

Avalon was the third center she had put her grandmother into. The other two also had someone from their administrative offices call her. Each call was the same. Her grandmother's care had become too much for the center to deal with and they recommended a more suitable home for her.

First it was a retirement community, then it was a fully staffed nursing home. Now a memory care center was kicking her grandmother out. What level of care was next?

Caroline's eyes pinched shut, and a tear escaped. After filling out mountains of paperwork—enough to fill an old-style phonebook—she'd have to start anew, this time with her grandmother possibly becoming a ward of the state with Medicaid to care for her.

Her grandmother deserved better than that. All these shifting of care levels meant one thing, she was losing the woman one day at a time.

Caroline's hands shook as she put the phone back in her pocket.

If she couldn't pay to take care of her grand-mother, she'd become a ward of the state. Given whatever care could be offered. What if the next state-owned bed was not even in Chicago? What if her grandmother had to be moved miles away to the next available facility? She couldn't visit her as often as she did. Her grandmother would go deeper into her mind and get even more lost.

She felt Scott's note in her pocket next to her cell phone. She played with the tiny slip of paper, rolling it between her fingers. A one-night stand with Scott —his strong build and his beautiful, blue eyes...

She needed an escape.

A delicious, 'oh my god' type of escape that included her being in some strong, protective arms —even if it was just for one night.

Her core began to ache in a way it hadn't done in a long time. She hadn't had even so much as a hug in months, let alone something to clear away the cobwebs down there.

His number had several zeros and fives, easy to remember. Now that she had been staring at it for a minute...yeah, she had the damn thing memorized.

She heard Maria's words once again, 'Forget your troubles and give in to pleasure'. It sounded like a tagline for a commercial. A relaxing dip in Calgon bath salts, a fun vacation to the Hawaiian Islands, or even a fun trip to Disney World.

She couldn't afford any of those things, except the bath. She definitely couldn't afford a one-night stand if she got a disease. What if she got pregnant?

She felt the wind practically get knocked out of her. No. She couldn't afford a baby, she couldn't afford to be a single parent... Hell, she couldn't afford name-brand Cheerios right now.

But she couldn't afford to continue being so miserable.

*S*cott had a mountain of paperwork to sift through when he returned to his office, but after the successful meeting with MacMillan, the world could come crashing down, and he wouldn't care.

Senior Partner.

His grin spread from ear to ear.

He'd be able to pick his cases, delegating the less high-profile ones. Yeah... Ralph would have his fair share of the mundane assignments for a while. He'd see to that.

Scott sat in his plush, leather chair and stared out the window, propping his feet up on the desk and reclining back. The skyscraper across the way still blocked his perfect view and he realized Ralph was the one obstacle in his way.

Damn.

And his ankle was still killing him.

The painkiller worked, but he shouldn't have walked so much at lunch. He opened the Walgreens bag and took another pill. The pain wouldn't last long. Besides, he'd (hopefully) soon have that nice corner office—the one so big he could turn it into an apartment and charge rent.

"You're back."

Scott jumped at the sound of Bev's voice, his feet hitting the floor as he became unbalanced in the chair.

"Goddammit." He winced due to the pain.

It took no time for her to close the door. "You okay?"

He pressed his fingers against the plastic boot he wore and felt the sting of the sprain. "It's nothing."

She stood in front of him, wearing her we-need-to-strategize face, the expression that meant winning silver only meant you lost gold. "And?"

"MacMillan is on board with me becoming a full partner. Potentially, so is Gilkrist," he said, knowing exactly what she wanted to hear.

For several minutes, Beverly paced the room with both hands on her hips, moving her head in short little nods. With her hair pinned up, and her thin legs, she looked like a chicken pecking in the yard to him.

He hadn't thought of her like that since he was a kid and they'd had to strategize telling his parents something unsettling.

"Well, we knew we wouldn't sway Ralph's uncle," she said.

"Larimer will always pick Ralph over me. But, Gilkrist…" Scott paused and thought of the man. He was stern and strict, but had a level head and loved crunching numbers. "Gilkrist appreciates my track record."

"So, you'll give the escort service a call?" Bev pulled out the paper with the company info and handed it to him again. "She'll do anything to make you look good."

"Anything?" Scott's eyebrow rose. "What exactly…"

Bev nodded and took a seat, leaning slightly forward. "She'll schmooze the bigwigs, talk you up to the people that really matter, and she's a nice piece of eye candy to have on your arm."

Why did he suddenly feel dirtier than earlier on the trail when he'd fallen into the mud?

Shaking his head, he handed the white sheet of paper that was like a flag surrendering his manhood back to her. "I'm not quite that desperate yet."

"The party is in two weeks. Unless you're planning to go through your little black book of ex-girlfriends…" She placed her hand on her temple and he knew she couldn't think of anyone suitable from his backlist of babes. "Don't even think about taking that opportunist Joanna."

Beverly should know him better than that, and he gave her a pinched expression that said so.

"Sorry. I know that won't happen," she said. "I've already RSVP'd you with a date."

"You RSVP'd that I'd bring a date?" He had always brought a date to the party, so he couldn't exactly be upset.

Bev held out the paper for him to take it. "Either call the service or I will."

He sucked in a deep breath, feeling like his mother had just threatened him with not going to the prom if his chores weren't done. "I'll think about it," he said, taking the paper and placing it on the side of his desk where a pile of case files awaited his attention.

He gestured to the door. "I'll be catching up on some work the rest of the afternoon."

His cell phone buzzed, giving him an even better excuse to dismiss the woman he used to accidentally call Mom when he as a kid.

Bev pointed to the paper. "Call the woman today. She books up, and I told her we'd pay top dollar for good PR."

He wondered how much a top-dollar actress or prostitute went for.

The door had barely shut by the time Scott read the display on his phone. He didn't recognize the number, but only his inner circle had knowledge of his private line, so he answered it.

"Hello?"

The number was local. He sat straighter in the chair, his heart skipping a beat. Was it her?

"Hi. This is Caroline, the waitress from *The Patio* —the one who gave you a bag of ice for your foot. I'm not sure if you remember me or not. Is this a bad time to call?"

His heart raced. "Hello, Caroline. No, it's the perfect time to call."

## 6

*W*ednesday arrived quickly, perhaps too quickly.

Going out on a Wednesday night wasn't as good as a Friday or Saturday date-night, but Caroline worked both those days. Double shifts, too.

She also planned to visit her Grandmother—that is, if she could avoid Ms. Rubinstein. She had put off going to meet with the lady from Avalon and had already received a second phone call and an email.

She couldn't put off the inevitable, but wanted to postpone it as long as she could.

And a one-night stand was the perfect distraction.

Caroline had kept an eye on the clock all day. This was the first time she had worked the same shift as Maria since she had made a date with Scott.

The restaurant had been busy so she hadn't been able to discuss her decision with her best friend. Not that she needed Maria's approval. The woman definitely wanted her to 'get some', but Caroline knew she'd object to the man being Scott.

Maria had pointed out several men as good candidates and Scott was the only one she had declined, but he was the only one Caroline would even consider.

She had made a connection with him that day. She couldn't put her finger on it, but his smile and brilliant blue eyes had mesmerized her. Plus, hearing his sexy voice on the phone had given her the courage to ask for the date.

This was it.

She was going to have a one-night stand. Actually, an early-evening stand since she had to be at her second job in a few hours. Two of her local high school students were taking a big Algebra II test next week. Algebra II wasn't her best subject since it stretched her math capabilities to their maximum, but she could manage.

"Finally." Maria's voice rang of exhaustion as she pulled her till from the register so a second shift worker could take over. "I didn't think quitting time would ever get here." Maria locked the till and the two walked through the kitchen to the tiny employee room in the back.

Caroline glanced at the clock. With no time to

return home to change, she needed to prepare for her date at work. After counting out the money and checking the receipts for their boss, Caroline went to get her bag from the locker, but Maria arrived first.

"What's this?" She put her purse on her shoulders and then pulled a small backpack from the locker. "Did you bring your purse today, because this is all that's in here."

Caroline grabbed for the backpack. "Thanks."

Maria held onto the bag. She opened the zipper and peeked inside. "A change of clothes?" Her eyebrow rose as she noticed a makeup bag. "You going out tonight?"

"Uh-huh." Caroline felt a blush forming on her cheeks, and felt as if she had been caught doing something wrong, but Maria was the one who'd suggested the fling in the first place.

She took in a deep breath and her lips curled into an embarrassed smile. "I have a date tonight. A date that will last exactly one evening. Thanks to the long shift, I have to get ready here."

A diva-like smile spread across Maria's face. "Girl, this is your first date in…." She eyed Caroline suspiciously, as though Caroline were helpless on her own. "Let me help."

Caroline walked to the small employee bathroom. "It's just coffee. Maybe a light meal."

Maria followed her in. "You should skip to dessert."

Stripping down to her underwear, Caroline felt subconscious as she caught her reflection in the mirror. "A man hasn't seen me naked... well, too long to mention, and I have to look like this." She pinched a good inch on the side of her waist.

"Men like curves, especially when they're covered in red, lacy under things." Maria studied Caroline's matching bra and panties. "Hell, I didn't know you wore such sexy lingerie."

"I don't." Before Maria could ask, Caroline added, "This is the nicest pair of underwear I own, especially since they match."

"Well," Maria said, "it's a darling combo. I know where your mind is at this evening."

Caroline never wore the fancy undergarments since they were old and she had no need for such lacy things. The panties were tight, and half her butt cheeks hung out, but Maria didn't seem to think that was an issue.

Maria glanced down. "Did you shave your legs?"
Shit.

Feeling the slight prickle as she rubbed her legs together, she knew she couldn't do this. It was a sign.

She tossed the makeup bag on the counter. "I need to cancel."

"No, you don't. This is a one-nighter. Once your

clothes are off, he isn't going to stop because of prickly legs. Plus, you're never going to see him again."

A wicked smile—naughty and seductive—spread across Maria's face. "Was it the man the other day in the suit and cowboy hat?"

"What?"

"Mr. Coffee, just black?" she asked seductively, her eyebrows lifting in a question.

Butterflies formed in Caroline's stomach. "No. It's not him."

Maria's eyes narrowed. "You went for Mr. Big Tipper at the end of the bar, the one with the luscious hair." A moan sounded in the back of Maria's throat. "Good choice."

Caroline could barely remember what those men even looked like. They were no Scott.

She pulled out her comfy jeans and soft T-shirt. She never wore such things on a first date, but this wasn't a typical date. Scott may clean up well, but she didn't need a boyfriend—just a good time.

"I smell like the diner," she said to change the subject. It had been a while since she had released any tension and she didn't like the idea of smelling like bean enchiladas. She brought a bottle of perfume with her but doubted that mixing the two scents would be more pleasing. She hoped Scott got turned on by the smell of Mexican food.

She thought of Scott, of his six-foot-something height and large shoe size. If proportion sizes were what she suspected, Scott would be the best ticket for what she needed. Rock hard. Exceptionally built. Well skilled.

Her core moistened in anticipation, but then a small amount of guilt crawled into her thoughts and threatened to camp out, but she squashed it. She was going through with the evening, even if, in some small way, she thought she might be using him. She figured no man would object to being *used* for one night. Didn't most men dream of such a thing?

Her work uniform had tomatillo stains on it, so she folded the mess to the inside and placed the bundle carefully in her sack. The bag would likely reek of food later, but she never could get the greasy smell out of her hair or clothes anyway.

She glanced in the mirror again. Her hair was a mess. She undid the once tight pony tail that now hung loosely. That was a mistake. She had pinned it up after her shower this morning and the hairband had ebbed its way into her hair making it bend stupidly in the middle. The look resembled a style someone unable to handle a hair straightener might have. She grabbed the frizzy loose strands. "Up, or down?"

"Loose and sexy." Maria took the brush out of the bag. "In fact, make that your mantra for tonight," she said, halfway chuckling.

"Loose and sexy?"

"Just keep repeating it until you believe you're the sex goddess that you are."

Maria frowned as she combed Caroline's hair. Overall, she did what she could, but really, the hair was a lost cause. Caroline pulled out the richest shade of lipstick she owned and put it on.

"You got some eye shadow and mascara in there, too?" Maria put her hand into the bag and dug around. "Let me give you smoky eyes tonight."

"Smoky eyes?"

"Shut up. Just let me take care of you. Turn around." She took the eye brush from the bag and loaded it with powder, making sure Caroline turned from the mirror so that she would only focus on her. "You take this man to a hotel. Neutral ground. You understand me?"

Caroline closed her eyes and let Maria cake on the makeup. She had spent the morning cleaning her apartment, but still said, "Hotel. Got it."

"And you stay in charge."

"In charge." This was absolutely not the same talk her Grandmother had given her when going out on dates back in high school. Curfew, have the boys respect you, and don't do anything you'll regret were usually the first words her Grandmother would say.

Her Grandmother would be disappointed in her today. Caroline imagined her shaking her head and could even envision the disappointment that would be in her eyes.

"No rope, no handcuffs. You make sure you only drink from a properly sealed container. You don't want him drugging you."

The rock that sat in the pit of Caroline's stomach felt heavier. Bondage? Being drugged? She wasn't prepared to do this. "Maybe I should just cancel."

"I don't want to scare you. You just need to know how to take care of yourself." She reached into her pocket and pulled out a pocketknife. "Take this, just in case," she said, slipping it into the backpack.

Caroline couldn't breathe. A knife? What did Maria think was going to happen? "Do you really think I'll need that?"

"No. But better safe than sorry. Look up." Maria traced Caroline's lids with an eye pencil. "Don't get personal with him."

Caroline became too scared to move. The eye pencil traced around her eyes and could jab her any second. "How do I have sex with a man and *not* get personal?" She swallowed the lump in her throat and took in a deep breath.

"You don't ask about his past because then he'll use you as a therapist. You don't ask about his present because then he'll ask about yours and know your schedule and routine. He already knows where you work, no need in him finding out any other personal information. You don't need a stalker."

The word was terrifying. "A stalker?"

"It can happen. So, don't ask him where he lives or what his job is. None of that is important for a one-night stand." She then paused and said with emphasis, "And under no circumstances do you ask about his future. You mention that, and all of a sudden, they think they're in a long-term relationship."

A needy man wanting to spend the rest of his life with her was the last thing she wanted. She planned to play it cool and loose. "I won't ask him anything personal."

Maria studied the pencil in her hand. "Buy yourself some good, quality, liquid eyeliner. Pencils are only good for shading."

Caroline felt painted up and nervous, especially since she hadn't seen herself in a mirror. "Am I going to look like a whore?"

"I'm almost done. I don't suppose you have fake lashes in this bag."

"I don't have...just finish this up before I change my mind." She needed to forget about her grandmother, forget about her rut of a life, and forget about her morals—just for a few hours.

Maria put the makeup pencil back in the bag. "Okay, good." She pulled out a box of condoms. "I was just going to ask if you had protection."

Caroline took a deep breath. "I was once a girl scout. Always prepared."

A moment later, Caroline was allowed to check herself out in the mirror. Caked on makeup, bright red lipstick, and monstrous eyes. She looked as desperate as she felt.

———

"*I* do not believe that is a wise course of action at this time, Mr. Rancini." Scott sat squarely on the park bench and checked the time on his phone's clock. He had left his Rolex at home, as well as nice clothes—and possibly his sanity.

He listened to Frank arguing about the initial settlement paperwork, and was glad the man had called and not personally come by the office since Scott wasn't there. The man didn't need to complain to Gilkrist about Scott not finding time to talk with him.

Scott's team had drafted and sent the document over that morning, and Frank Rancini had practically memorized it in just the few short hours. The settlement was fair for someone who blatantly stole a company logo, not that his client was willing to see that.

Settling out of court was in the best interests of everyone. Why did Frank have to be an ass and press the issue? He wasn't going to win.

A group of skateboarders headed in Scott's direction, and they all had loud, boisterous voices that he was sure Frank could hear on his side of the line. Scott needed to get off the phone. Talking in a public place to a client was not professional. "I advise you to compile a list of changes for our next meeting… Yes, it's scheduled for Monday morning."

The man wouldn't stop complaining.

The noisy group of teenagers thankfully headed down another sidewalk and out of earshot, but Scott wanted to get the man off the phone—for many reasons.

He never gave his personal number out to clients, but since Landmark Leasing was a pet project of Gilkrist he figured there'd be no harm. He didn't expect the client to call him repeatedly whenever he felt like it.

He'd never give another client his number again.

Scott glanced at his phone's clock once more. If he hung up now, he'd have to bill Frank for fifteen minutes of time. He allowed the man to rattle on for another two minutes until the length of the call exceeded the sixteen-minute mark.

"We can discuss everything on Monday. Good-bye." And hello to billing the asshole for a full thirty minutes. Of course, the rate was the 'friends and family' one with a discount that would amount to nearly nothing, but it was the principle that mattered. Plus, it added to the document time that Gilkrist would see. Hopefully seeing how much time Scott gave this client would make the old man happy enough to select Scott over Ralph for the promotion.

Scott jotted down some notes and tucked the paperwork into the picnic basket he had brought. He left the bench and hobbled over to the Serenity Bridge. Leaning against the concrete structure and favoring his good foot, he took a deep breath of fresh air and felt the stress of dealing with Frank disappear from his body. He didn't need to have his stress linger into his date.

Many people walked or jogged by, enjoying the beautiful weather. He looked around once more for Caroline. She was late. He wouldn't blame her if she decided to skip the date entirely. She was coming out to the park to meet a homeless man for dinner— knowing she'd probably have to pay.

His clothes weren't pressed, his newly cut hair was somewhat unkempt, and he felt like a fool. Shopping yesterday at Goodwill to pick up some hand-me-down clothes and an old wicker basket made him feel like a goofball, but at the very least, he looked poor. Not homeless poor, but I'm-in-between-jobs kind of needy.

Taking a good look at himself, perhaps he was dressed too needy. He had always used private shoppers or had Bev buy his clothes for him. He couldn't ask her to buy items less than his usual standard, she'd get suspicious. Bev always said she donated his hand-me-downs to Goodwill, and it was the first place he had thought of, so it would have to do.

His fingers touched the fabric of his shirt. He had never spent so much time dressing down for a date in his life, but the clothes, although run down, were good enough. The evening was a risk—one he hoped would pay off. His clothes and the blanket he carried retained the scent of the store even after he expedited a dry cleaning job on them. The handpicked wildflowers finished the ensemble.

To top off the whole evening, he had bought two KFC chicken meals to put into the basket. He'd probably have heartburn all night, but at least it was a meal she would assume he could afford to treat her to.

If she were a gold digger, she's run for the hills. If she were a genuine, loving person who saw him for who he was, then maybe…

"Scott."

He turned and saw Caroline walking toward him. She was a vision.

A carefree feeling—soft and warm—enveloped him, and he felt a smile spread across his face. Her soft hair blowing in the breeze, sunglasses hiding her beautiful green eyes, and her ensemble of T-shirt and jeans radiated an easy-going sense of style and personality.

She walked up to him, and he shifted his stance, now holding the basket in his left hand. Should he lean in for a fake two-kiss on the cheeks greeting, the type he always hated? Shake her hand?

What he wanted to do was kiss her, but he thought it might be too forward.

Maybe just a hug.

His grip slipped on the basket, so he held it tighter. He wiped his other hand on the used pair of jeans he wore so it wouldn't be sweaty.

"I'm sorry I'm late. I had car trouble."

She was only five minutes late, not the typical *fashionably* twenty-plus minutes most of his women kept him waiting. Still, she looked a bit flustered. "Is everything all right?"

She shook her head. "Nothing to worry about. Just an old car."

She looked anxious, but more than this-is-a-first-date type of nervous. She probably didn't know what to expect from a date with someone down on his luck and, from what she suspected, someone who lived in the park.

He didn't exactly know how to play his part, and he chickened out on the hug. He handed her the flowers that were sticking out of the basket. "You look lovely."

She smiled and then held them up to her nose. "Wildflowers are my favorite," she said once she had taken a big whiff.

He wondered if she would have said roses were her favorite if he had handed her a dozen of them.

She was easy-going, so he suspected she would. She just seemed that type of woman.

"I thought we'd have a picnic in the park." Scott held up the basket and flashed his million-dollar smile that caused most women to swoon. He opened the basket and showed her the meal, the scent of fried chicken wafting toward them.

"What's this?" Caroline picked up the paperwork from the basket and glanced at the pages. "Looks important."

Scott retrieved the proprietary paperwork from her hands. "Work stuff. I don't want to talk about work especially since there is a free play on Performance Hill starting in a few minutes."

She looked in the direction of the hill as he put the paperwork back in the basket. "That's on the other side of the park."

"Just a ten-minute walk." Cheap food and free entertainment were the best he could come up with. Was he playing up the poor act too much?

She studied his swollen ankle, obviously noticing the walking cast he had. "How are you feeling?"

In truth, the pain killers were working but he really didn't want to walk across the park. Just getting here was enough of a hardship.

"We can drive." She pointed to where she had walked from and reached out to take his hand. "My car is right there. I think it will live for another short drive."

Thoughtful and considerate. He held her hand and hobbled off with her. When she placed her arm around his waist to help him, he over emphasized the amount of pain he was in just to remain close to her.

## 7

*W*hat was she doing?

Dinner in the park? Caroline didn't have time for a play. Her panties were scheduled to be off within the next thirty minutes with a hasty goodbye soon after that. Plus, she had to be online and tutoring math soon.

Her heart beat so fast that she could barely catch her breath.

Maybe wiping the makeup off before arriving at the park was a bad idea, but she'd rather wear no makeup than look like a whore—not that she'd ever complain to Maria. It had been sweet of her to help, and Maria's makeup job would have given the right signal to Scott, but it just looked awful on her.

She slyly gazed at Scott as she held him and helped him across the bridge. His hair was shorter, and the style didn't look Sport's Clips-hacked. It was a good style on him, an *expensive* style. She couldn't see his eyes, but his warm smile was obvious.

She didn't know what he did for a living, but he obviously had a job. The paperwork looked like something in marketing. But, she wasn't here to talk about work or to get to know Scott on any personal level. Tonight was about her.

Holding him tighter, his arm felt strong and muscular under his jacket. Muscular, strong,... good stamina. She could hardly stand the wait.

"Thanks for helping me." Scott beamed a smile and his boyish good looks tore into her. He was handsome in an old-timey Robert Redford type of way. God, she loved old movies. Scott could certainly play a leading man. Tall, handsome, winsome smile.

"I don't mind helping."

He leaned into her as they hobbled over a patch of grass to a nearby parking lot. First few warm days after a harsh winter or not, there weren't too many people at the park enjoying the crisp weather of the start of Spring. Her parking spot wasn't that far away, and she hoped he would be able to make it without too much effort or pain.

She opened the car door. Retirement brochures littered the passenger seat and the floor, as well as fast food containers. She had spent so much time cleaning her apartment, defumigating the stench out, and making it sexy-inviting with candles that she didn't give her car a moment's thought—not that she had time to clean it out as well. "I'm so sorry." She quickly straightened up the mess and tossed everything into the back seat. It wasn't as if Scott would be around for the long haul, but she still felt a tug of embarrassment at having him see her mess.

An all-night cleaning effort on her apartment and laundering her sheets would leave him with a better impression than the messy car anyway.

What was she thinking? She was about to have sex with the man. *That* would leave, hopefully, an ever-lasting impression that would supersede anything else. She focused her mind on sexy thoughts, trying to get herself into the right frame of mind.

Caroline got into her car and turned the key. The ignition did its best to start her ten-year-old, secondhand car, but it failed. It had been all she could afford as a college student—and all she'd be able to afford for several more years.

She let out a nervous chuckle. After all that effort to get Scott into the car just to have it die on her? God. How much worse could it get? She was a desperate (knocking on thirty) woman who had a dead car. Not a chariot that took a princess to a ball, but a clunker of a car that would take them back to a run-down apartment.

And they would definitely make it to her apartment. There was no way she was going to have sex in the back of her car. She couldn't afford a motel like Maria had suggested, and she figured Scott couldn't either. They weren't teenagers who had no place else to go. Besides, with Scott's bad leg there'd be no room to maneuver in her back seat.

Maneuver. She sucked in a deep breath and felt her core tighten. She really needed some 'maneuvers' and wanted to give both of them plenty of room to really enjoy their brief time together.

Sexy thoughts.

Just think of sexy thoughts.

"Do you need me to check the engine?" he asked.

"No." She removed the key and waited for the dashboard lights to turn off. She then jiggled the gear shift. "It's just temperamental."

She didn't need him worrying about her car.

Sexy thoughts.

Thinking of herself sprawled out naked in front of him brought up worries of being so bare in front of a perfect stranger. The scene also brought out the lectures from her grandmother on protection and finding a good man to marry. She needed to wipe those thoughts away. She had protection in her bag. What she needed to think about was Scott sprawled out naked on the bed. His masculine body hard and ready for her.

She squeezed her legs together, her core already on fire.

God, she needed this car to start.

Fortunately, it clunked to life after the second try.

"Your starter giving you problems?"

It was embarrassing enough driving around town in the old clunker, but having someone actually *in* the car with her was even worse. The inside smelled like a habit trail with a hygienically challenged hamster stuck in one of the tubes.

She gave him a wry smile and, as nonchalantly as she could, said, "It's been acting up lately." She pulled out of the parking spot and made her way onto the street.

"You may need a new alternator. Have you had the fan belt checked?"

Other than putting gas in it and making sure the oil was changed every three months—okay, she did it every six months—she didn't exactly know anything about car maintenance. In a dismissive tone, she said, "The check engine light has only been on for a week or so."

From the corner of her eye, she noticed his eyes widen in surprise. It was a look her grandmother would have given her, followed by a safety lecture about responsible car maintenance.

"I've already made an appointment to have it fixed," she said, lying.

He glanced out the window. "I'm not sure what play is being performed tonight, but the few people who are at the park seem to all be heading to the performance. Should be a nice night for a picnic."

The aroma of fried chicken filled the car and masked the habit trail scent, at least a little. She suspected that what little money Scott had, he had spent on dinner. And she was hungry. A picnic sounded wonderful, and the type of date she always enjoyed.

But she didn't want a boyfriend. Boyfriends ate picnics with you. They walked on sandy beaches with you. They held your hand and whispered loving phrases into your ear. Boyfriends worried about your car starting and asked you things like if your car needed maintenance done.

She definitely didn't want—or need—a boyfriend worried about her car. Next, he'd be worried about her safety, start caring for her, and then she'd be in relationship city until he decided to care about someone else.

No, thank you.

The road curved to the right towards Performance Hill, but if she went left, she'd hit the side street to the highway and could be at her apartment in ten minutes.

They could be naked in eleven.

"Scott?"

"Yes, Caroline?"

How was it that he could say her name and make

it sound like it was the most beautiful and dignified word in the world?

She slowed down the car, not knowing which way to turn. Her hand trembled a bit on the wheel and she mentally told herself to just turn toward the Hill and watch the play with him. An evening out with Scott wouldn't be as satisfying physically, but it was more in line with who she was. Afterall, not everyone could be a sex-goddess like Maria. Caroline couldn't just turn off and on emotions like her co-worker could.

His hand touched her shoulder. "What is it, love?"

Maybe it was the term of endearment, but it strengthened her resolve. She wasn't his *love*, or any other cutesy nickname. She was in control of this date, and if that meant no picnic in the park, no getting to know one another, and no relationship then so be it. She was a sex-goddess. She called the shots.

She stared into his blue depths, the type of eyes she could get lost in. But not this time.

"How about a picnic at my apartment?" she asked in her sexiest voice. Her heart pounded, and she felt the thumping in her chest against the seatbelt strap.

He sat straighter in his seat, his widened eyes showing what she hoped wasn't shock but excitement. "You want to eat in your apartment? Okay."

Her mantra for tonight was 'loose and sexy'.

Other women got theirs all the time. There was nothing wrong with getting a little for herself.

Her jaw tightened, and she gripped the steering wheel tighter as she turned down the street to her home. "We can eat afterwards."

---

*T*he date wasn't exactly going the way Scott had planned, but he wasn't going to complain. The situation did give him an eerie feeling though. She thought he had no money, couldn't afford expensive gifts, and probably could never take her on a nice vacation...and yet she wanted to progress the relationship farther? And this fast?

His gaze slyly shifted so he could get a good look at her. Simple clothes, simple hair, and simple if no makeup. He didn't think she'd expect elaborate expenses from him, but she did seem to be the kind of woman who would require a deeper knowledge of the person, quite possibly some feeling of a commitment, and more than likely a ten-date minimum before having him at her apartment.

Perhaps she just loved to have sex, and was quite good at it. He mentally took in her curves, which caused him to lick his lips and stare at her thighs. Maybe he was her nightly workout instead of heading off to a gym for the Stairmaster.

His thoughts focused on having her ride him

hard all night, and he shifted in his seat as his already hard member firmed up even more. He had thought of her for the last few days, and figured it would take a lot longer until he could wrap her sensuous legs around his waist.

But that would happen in only a few minutes.

A few glorious minutes.

The anticipation was killing him.

He shifted in his seat, but remained quiet as his hand draped around her shoulders.

She sat straighter in her seat due to his touch, and she hadn't made eye contact since suggesting her apartment. She seemed nervous, but he was sure he didn't have the wrong idea. He knew she fully intended to have sex with him on the first date, or she wouldn't have suggested that they eat 'afterwards'.

Tonight wouldn't be the first time a woman took him to his bed on the first date, but, usually, the woman he was with knew the amount of money he had and had been taken to a hotel suite courtesy of a stretch limo.

And, Caroline chauffeured. She seemed like the take-charge type of woman, which isn't what he had pegged her out to be. He liked her strength, and wondered if she also took full control in the bedroom, too.

They pulled into the apartment complex and drove through the tiny parking lot which faced the street, the car jostling whenever it hit a pot hole or large crack in the worn pavement. He counted two cars that looked dead or abandoned, and one that was spray painted with profanity.

Caroline pulled into a spot in front of some broken windows, the only spot that had some light since the other lampposts were broken and casting no light.

Was this neighborhood even safe? He scanned the area and knew this scene was right out of a horror movie. All that needed to happen was someone in the audience yelling for them not to get out of the car.

"This is it." She said as she turned off the engine.

Leave the car, and maybe be mugged, stabbed, or even worse. The god-awful smell of the car no longer seemed to smell all that bad. At least, he knew he was safe.

"You ready?" Caroline grabbed her bag and put it around her shoulders as she reached for the door handle.

Stay in the car and be safe. Leave the car and get laid.

He caught her smile in the corner of his eye. She lived here. How bad could the place be? There were no gang members standing in the parking lot and blocking his way. He smiled and his hand tapped the food basket. "I'm all set."

Ignoring the pain from his foot and taking long

strides, he constantly searched the shadows for any hidden dangers. It didn't take long for them to reach apartment 14A, which was on the ground floor.

No one was nearby, and his mind now returned to how he would strip Caroline down, race his tongue along every curve of her body, and plunge himself so deep within her that...God, he couldn't wait. He stood close behind her and kissed the nape of her neck as her fingers trembled and she scrambled to find the key to her apartment door. "Wrong key." She quickly found the other gold-colored one on her chain.

Scott continued kissing her soft neck, enjoying the smoothness of her skin and the scent of her perfume. His hands traveled down to her hips, and he held her close to his own warm and excited body.

She let out a slight gasp as his hardened member pushed firmly against her lower back, a promise of where the evening was headed.

A second later, she managed to open the door. The two nearly fell in, the basket of chicken and her bag dropping to the floor.

He closed the door, and she turned in his arms.

Cherry flavored lip-gloss and warm, full-bodied lips found his.

Fast, passionate, and on fire.

If it weren't for his sore foot, he would have picked her up and carried her to the nearest sofa or bed. As it was, they began tugging at each other's clothes between kisses, and he hobbled over to her bed.

Her T-shirt was the first item off, revealing a red, lacy bra. Next came her jeans, and he noticed that the panties matched.

Women always knew how to dress up their underwear.

And lace?

Oh, yeah. He was a fan.

His shirt was gone just as quickly, but not the blasted black boot he wore. He stood on his good leg and undid the Velcro, but had to sit down to remove the clunky monstrosity.

Women could strip and look sexy. He always managed to look like a dog struggling to get out of a stupid Christmas sweater with no opposable thumbs to help.

She stood in front of him, and for a moment, he thought he saw hesitation in her eyes. She mumbled something and then, with one quick motion, her hand disappeared behind her back as she undid her bra. The garment fell from her body, showing him two perfectly round breasts with perky nipples that begged to be touched.

She was practically naked and waiting for him. Why were there so many straps on the damn boot? He tugged at the contraption and ignored the pain from his ankle as he ripped it from his foot. In an altogether non-graceful manner, he managed to remove his jeans before the two of them collapsed on the bed together, the squeaky springs announcing the start of their passionate evening.

She closed her eyes as she kissed him, but he kept his open so he could see her. One hand moved to her chest and cupped a mound of rounded flesh as the other traveled south, nudging her bent legs to lay against the bedding, opening her most private flesh to him. His hands caressed her inner thigh as he ran kisses across her chest, down her abdomen, and farther to her core.

Snaps along the side fastened her underwear. That was new for him, but he absolutely loved the idea. A tug on each side and the panties slid off—her rosy-colored, flushed-with-passion, ready-for-him, moist folds open to him.

The scent of her arousal was strong, and he inhaled deeply as he took in the sight. So open. So ready. So wet.

He moved his hand across the silky skin of her leg. Allowed his fingers to dance along the inner curve of her thigh, the ridge of her hips, and finally to the smoothness of her backside.

Holding on to the firmness of her bottom, he gently laid his lips onto the flatness of her firm belly and began kissing a trail down.

Her legs splayed open. Slightly at first, but then she relaxed and allowed him to see and feel her most intimate parts.

Blonde curls. Trimmed and shaved. Nearly a heart-shaped mound waited his touch.

His finger moved across her slick core, disappearing into a lush cavern of desire, and causing her to moan. With each movement of his hand, her body responded, telling him how badly she wanted him.

Her skin was flushed, and her hips shifted, and she eagerly stroked his fingers.

Her nub was firm, a pebble sensitive and hard. He rolled his finger across it. Back and forth. Back and forth.

She rode his finger wanting more, so he dove in.

His hot breath hit her core, and a gasp escaped her throat. His tongue explored her, swirling around her nub. Her body tightened, and she began panting.

Her back arched, her hands gripping the sheets, and her hips bucked beneath him as he sucked and licked—teasing, taunting, and tasting her—until her beautiful release.

"Oh, God." Her voice sounded labored as she panted, her body now finally easing. "That was amazing."

Her eyes fluttered open, and a smile of contentment spread across her face.

"We've only just started, love." He grabbed his pants from the floor and pulled a condom from his wallet. He then knelt on the bed, pulled down his shorts, and allowed her to see the full length of him.

He tore the silver packet, pulled out the protection, and rolled it onto his throbbing cock.

She closed her eyes once again as he laid himself atop her. Her eyelids fluttered as he eased himself closer, and his breath feathered across her neck. He kissed her cheek, causing her to turn her head—her eyes still closed.

Her legs were still splayed for him, but they were tense. Her breasts moved up and down as she breathed faster, and her rigid body shook with a slight tremble, but he suspected it was from neither excitement nor anticipation.

Something was wrong.

He leaned over and tentatively kissed her lips, causing another tremor to wrack her.

Judging by how her body had reacted to him going down on her, this wasn't her first time with a man. She was so eager, so commanding—and now shrinking like a violet. She couldn't be this inexperienced. Could she?

The room's dim light reflected off a glistening tear at the corner of her closed eye. Was she crying?

"Caroline," he whispered. "Are you okay?"

She barely glanced at him. "I'm fine." She took a deep breath, stroked his arm in a near mechanical way, and gave him a smile that suggested she'd suffer through it.

It wasn't a look he had ever experienced before. And it wasn't one he liked.

"Something wrong?"

"Everything is fine." Her tone sounded choppy and short as she enunciated each word almost dismissively.

He knew better than to trust a woman who said the word *fine*. It meant anything but that.

His body was tense. He easily could have dismissed whatever the hell she was going through and plunged himself within her, getting the release he so desperately wanted. But, studying her face, he realized she was now mentally miles away.

"You went from hot to cold pretty damn quick." His eyes widened as he looked questioningly at her, but he got no reply. He took a deep breath, knowing that he couldn't continue, and lay next to her on the bed.

He didn't understand women.

Whatever he'd done had quashed the passion in her, but he had never had any complaints before.

There were always plenty of women eager for his bed. Why did a waitress... why did *Caroline* not want him?

Beneath her breath, nearly inaudible, he heard her say, "Loose and sexy. Loose and sexy."

"Why are you repeating those words?" He now realized that she had said those exact words while in the car, while getting undressed, and possibly even as they got into bed together.

She covered herself with the sheet and ran her finger across the underside of her eyes.

He had never made a woman cry before, and definitely not in bed.

He didn't like it.

"Nothing is going the way I planned. This isn't how I wanted the evening to work out." Her voice sounded defeated, as though she'd had a mission to accomplish and now had an epic failure on her hands.

Maybe she had lost a bet, and he was on the receiving end of some bad intentions.

He knew he should just leave. Drama was the last thing he wanted in his life, but his still stiff rod convinced him to at least hear the woman out.

He leaned on his elbow so he could face her. Hoping he wouldn't regret what he was about to say, he asked, "What's going on?"

"I can't do this." She sat up and tucked the sheet around her body. "Don't get me wrong. I've enjoyed our time together."

He licked his lips. "You've seemed to enjoy it very much so far."

She blushed, and her tell-all smile led him to believe she was uncomfortable talking about sex, or, perhaps, she was embarrassed about being with him. Either way, the rejection gave him an awkward feeling in the pit of his stomach.

"I've never had a man do that to me before."

His eyebrow rose. "You're kidding."

He studied her face. Her innocent expression was peppered with sex-kitten desire. It suited her well.

She shook her head. "I've only been with one man in my life. He never wanted to…you know."

"He was a fool." His hand caressed her leg through the sheet. "If you didn't want me to touch you that way, you should have said so. I never meant to make you feel uncomfortable."

"Oh, it was fantastic." She blushed. "Honestly, at first, I was surprised." She bit her lip and her lips curled up in a smile. "Curious what it would be like."

Her smile widened and her face became beet red.

"And you liked it."

She looked beautiful all flushed and innocent. He wanted to hear her moan some more, wanted to feel her writhe under him, wanted her to scream his name. "And because it was so enjoyable, you wanted me to stop?"

Her gaze dropped down to his member, still hard for her, and he was confused by her expression. Did she not want him?

"The only advice I ever got from my grandmother was, 'if you get into bed with a man, make sure you're both there for the same reason.'"

He still didn't understand.

"Because," she added, "if you're not there for the same reason one, if not both, of you will end up getting hurt."

That didn't make things clearer.

"So… I don't know what you're thinking… or expecting…" Her hand gestured between the two of them and her eyes glanced down at the bed and his hardness. "But we should both understand where this is heading."

Was this really the 'where is the relationship heading' talk? This conversation typically comes towards the end of a relationship.

Was *this* a relationship?

"What are you talking about?"

She gave him a shrug in defeat. "I've just never had a one-night stand before and, even though I enjoyed what we did, I just feel…" She choked on the last word and touched her chest. "My heart is racing so fast." She took a deep breath. "You want me, that's obvious to see," she said, again glancing down at him, "… I don't know what you want, and I'm just using you."

"You're using me?"

"For just a one-night stand."

"This is a one-night stand?" Women had always been eager to get into his bed—to somehow oil their traps for him so he'd buy them whatever they wanted. They tended to stay as long as the money lasted, or until he wised up.

Caroline was different, and a heaviness in his chest told him that he didn't like the idea of her being just a one-time experience.

He also didn't like the idea being considered a one-time, easy to dismiss and never seen again, type of a lover to her.

"I feel that I'm using you."

"It's okay if you are."

She let out a slight chuckle. "It really isn't. Think about it. Do you really want to be used and not have your feelings considered?"

Those words hit him hard. He had been used. Used many times. Women wanted his money and they got it by using him. He just had never thought of it that way before.

"I'd hate it if someone just used me for…"

Her voice trailed off, and he had to know. "For what?"

She bit her lip and sucked in a quick breath. "I've hit a low point in my life. I wanted to escape, even for just one night."

"I've had one-night stands before." His voice was soft and understanding. "They're exciting and fun, but they're never really satisfying. But you can escape for a few hours."

He hadn't been honest with her, and maybe she had picked up on that. "My full name is Scott Hollister." He held out his hand.

Chuckling again, she shook it. "It's a pleasure to meet you Scott Hollister."

"The pleasure is all mine."

She smiled, but other than that, she didn't react

to the name. She didn't recognize his family as being the Hollister Hotel magnates. Or, maybe money didn't matter to her. Now, glancing around the small apartment for the first time, he suspected that she didn't read financial trade magazines or travel much, nor was she concerned with anything other than marginally making a living.

Actually, he was surprised that she lived in such a place. Her apartment, although somewhat clean and tidy, was a dump.

She sat still and stared at him. Her face looked as if she were doing a complex math problem in her head. "Is this a one-time thing?"

"I wasn't putting an expiration date on it, if that's what you're asking," he said, knowing full well the truth of his statement. "Why did you want it to be?"

She glanced away as if embarrassed. "My friend, Maria, the other waitress at the diner...she suggested the idea of escaping into someone arms for a night." She bit her lip and twirled a loose strand of hair between her fingers. "She knows I'm not looking for a relationship."

"A one-nighter, no relationship." He wasn't sure why women always had to label everything.

In a soft voice, as though it were painful to admit, she said, "In my experience, men are abusive, they leave, or they cheat on you. It never ends well, and I just don't need the heartache."

That was her take on men and relationships? He

had always found women to be conceited, demanding, and unfaithful. He knew his own experiences weren't the best, but the tone of her voice made her experience seem so much worse than his. "Sounds like you've been hurt many times."

She stared at him, and he could see the depths of her soul.

"My father left when I was a child, my first stepfather was abusive, and the second one went to jail. The one boyfriend I had ended up sleeping with my best friend. The dates I've had over the last few years just wanted to get in my pants."

It was as if the air had gotten sucked out of the room and he found it difficult to breathe. From what he could tell, Caroline was a beautiful and caring woman. She was definitely complicated, more so than he'd suspected, and she didn't deserve to be treated poorly. "I'm not like most men."

She remained quiet for several minutes, so he asked, "Why don't we just enjoy being together and see what happens?"

Her eyes gazed at him for what felt like an eternity, but then lay next to him on the bed. "Your eyes are the most beautiful shade of blue, Scott Hollister."

Her eyes focused on his lips as she rested back on the bed, her head denting the pillow. His still overly excited state would have him jump all over her, but Caroline was different. She was a nice, take-her-home-to-meet-the-parents type of woman. He had never been with a woman like her before.

He waited for her to make the first move.

She lay there quietly, her eyes suggesting that she wanted more, but her body sending signals that she was too timid to do so.

At least, that's what he thought.

He didn't want to, but he said, "I can leave."

"I'd like for you to stay." Her eyes widened, and she touched his shoulder. "Just never lie to me."

Something in her shaky voice told him how much she was afraid to trust. Overly complicated or not, drama or not, he wanted to see where this relationship—or whatever they had—was going.

She now knew his real name. Clothes, picnic basic, and KFC meal aside, she could easily Google him. Know his entire story. He liked that she was open with him but suspected it could be because she didn't know the balance of his bank account. His chest felt heavy. He liked Caroline, wanted to see where this would go. He knew that if she asked a direct question, he would tell her. But for now, he could let her assume he was middle class. "I'll never lie to you."

Her smile—wide and relieved enough to cause a twinkle in her eyes—told him that she was reassured. He licked his lips. "Kiss me, Caroline."

She kissed him softly on the mouth.

He moved his lips slowly and gently to match her

pressure. With growing boldness, he deepened the kiss. After she'd placed her hand on his back and held him tighter against her own naked body, he slipped the sheet from between them and allowed his hand to slide down her back.

He cupped her firm bottom with his hand and rolled her over, nibbling her ear and whispering, "It'll be all right."

He seated himself at her core.

There was no more crying, but her eyes remained closed.

"Open your eyes," he whispered, his breath hot across her lips.

Her eyes flitted open. "Why?"

"Eyes are the windows to the soul, and I want to see yours." He slowly entered her slick folds, watching her eyes widen and her lips part on a gasp as she experienced him stretching her. "I'm going to make love to you all night."

---

$\mathcal{T}$he next day, Caroline entered the diner, a spring in her step and a tune—playful and light—playing in her head. It was a good day.

"All right," Maria said once Caroline had cheerfully tossed her purse in the employee locker and began humming the tune from her head. "Only one thing puts a smile that big on a woman's face."

Caroline could feel the heat of her cheeks as she blushed. "Last night was, by far, the best night I've ever had." Her voice was confident and resounding, and she knew the statement was true.

"I told you. You just needed a release." Maria led her into the empty dining room and adjusted her apron. She lifted an upturned chair from a table and placed it on the floor in preparation for opening the restaurant.

Caroline sniffed the air; the smell of breakfast

burritos filled the room. The cook had already placed a to-go order on the counter and had placed wrapped breakfast burritos in the bin near the cash register for the early morning crowd.

Maria opened the front door and turned on the 'OPEN' sign. "Now that your body is more relaxed, you can better focus on other things in your life."

All Caroline could think about was Scott and his passionate kisses. She had woken up before him this morning and all she could do is stare at his beautiful body. Strong arms. Chiseled jaw. Scruffy beard already starting. She hated waking him up after her shower so she could drop him off at the park on her way to work.

It didn't even matter that her car had trouble starting and nearly died twice just on the way to the park. The world could tumble down around her and she wouldn't care.

"Help me set up the tables and tell me all about it." Maria placed another chair on the floor and nodded to the other ones. "How was Mr. Big Tipper?"

Caroline began at the next table. "It wasn't Mr. Big Tipper."

Maria's eyebrow rose. "I thought you said it was?" When Caroline just flashed a smile at her, she added, "It wasn't a family man, was it?"

"No." Her stomach flipped at just the thought of being a home wrecker. "I'd never do that."

"Was it a customer here, or someone from one of your night jobs?"

She had canceled her tutoring sessions last night claiming to be sick so she could spend the night in Scott's arms. The loss of income would hurt later, but she honestly didn't care.

The door bells dinged announcing a patron. The man was dressed in a suit and tie.

Maria walked up to him. "Welcome to the Patio. Please have a seat anywhere."

"I'm picking up a to-go order."

Caroline walked behind the counter and picked up the only available bag. "Ralph Larimer?" she asked, fully expecting it to belong to the man.

He walked up to the cash register. "That's me."

Caroline read off the receipt to confirm the order, and the man scowled at her.

"I ordered the first meal with natural white cheddar cheese and the second one without any cheese. Can you get this redone... " He glanced at her name tag. "Caroline?"

"Yes. I'll take care of it." Both had regular cheddar on them. This wasn't the best way to start the work day. "I'm terribly sorry about that," Caroline said, taking the bag and confirming the mistake. "I'll have it redone immediately. It'll only be a minute."

The kitchen runner came from the kitchen and put five bags of food on the delivery counter. She knew the cook had only a few pickup meals left to do. Redoing Ralph's meal wouldn't take that long.

"How about a cup of coffee while you wait." Maria took out a cup and sat the man down at the counter while Caroline told the cook to expedite the meals.

"So?" Maria asked, as they restocked the napkin dispensers farther down on the counter. "You were about to explain that smile on your face."

"I was with Scott, the man from the other day with the twisted ankle."

Maria's face pinched, and she shook her head side to side. "No, honey. Not a homeless bum. God, he probably didn't even have good hygiene."

She was reminded of the smell of Scott's cologne as it mixed with his sweat and the scent of their lovemaking. It was an intoxicating, heady fragrance, and her sheets probably still smelled like him.

"Girl, with a figure like yours, you should be aiming for a man with a bankroll." The derisive snarl on her face told Caroline that Maria didn't agree with her choices.

"Money isn't everything. Besides, Scott isn't homeless." Caroline straightened a set of chairs at a nearby table. "Men with cell phones tend to have a way of paying bills. Besides, I saw some paperwork he had from work. He does some sort of marketing job. Although," she said with a sly smile, "I wasn't interested in talking to him about his job."

"Having a cell phone doesn't prove anything. Marketing sounds pretty good, although anyone can carry around paperwork and claim to have a job."

Caroline didn't like being interrogated, and she knew Maria would give her issues about last night. "He used my phone while he was here. I did a google search on the two numbers he dialed, and one was to a car service."

"Any bum can call an Uber."

"She's right you know."

The sound came from behind them. The customer took a sip of his coffee and Caroline mentally reprimanded herself for talking about personal stuff in front of a customer. "I'm sorry but..."

"You know what? We could use a third person's opinion." Maria smiled at the man. "An objective opinion would be helpful. Especially from an attractive man such as yourself."

Was Maria actually hitting on him? Well, he was in a suit. Had money. Wasn't bad looking. Totally Maria's type.

The man looked up from his coffee and turned his body more toward them. He didn't look all that interested, but gave them a nod. He probably had nothing else to do while he waited for his meals.

"A man came in here the other day. All muddy. Torn clothing." Maria made a face and her hand waved in front of her body to indicate how much mud Scott had been covered in. She then described Scott's physical description but made him sound totally unattractive.

Nope. No way. This wasn't enough to spoil Caroline's good mood.

A ding sounded at the café door and a young man in bike shorts walked in.

"Hey Judson," Maria said.

"Good morning." The man nodded toward Ralph as he walked past on his way to the delivery orders. He inspected the bags and then picked them up. "You still good to cover my shift on the eighteenth?"

Caroline patted her notepad in her apron. "Already on my calendar. I'm off that day and can completely cover your deliveries. Not to worry."

"I owe you one."

Actually, she was paying him back for covering for her last week when she ran late to work from a morning tutoring session that went long. "Be careful out there."

Judson was barely out the door when Maria continued, "So *I* believe this man that Caroline is so hot over is a bum, but *she* believes Scott has a job and that I profiled him or something."

"You *did* profile him. And," Caroline added, "you profiled him *wrong*."

Ralph sat straighter in his chair as though the conversation piqued his interest. "The man's name is Scott?"

"Tall, blond, blue eyed...," Caroline said.

"And covered in mud and ripped clothing," Maria interrupted in a judgmental tone.

Caroline could not believe this was happening, but defended Scott by saying, "Fell while running, made a mess of himself and his clothes, and twisted his ankle in the process."

"Running while the rest of the world is at their jobs."

Maria's curt voice implied that as fact Scott probably wasn't employed. And she hadn't thought of that. Most people couldn't drive to a park and go running in the morning. Most had to get up and get ready for work. But that could mean that he had a flexible work schedule, or maybe worked only part-time.

Caroline then added, "And, if you must know, Scott didn't call an Uber. He dialed an actual car service that I hadn't heard of before. The website was really swanky." Now that she said it, her proof that he had some money seemed weak, but she didn't care.

"Uh, huh. What was the other phone number to?" Ralph said with an inquisitive tone.

"He dialed a doctor at Grant Memorial hospital."

"So?" Maria asked.

"It wasn't a free clinic. He called a doctor. Personally. He had the number memorized and got help for his ankle. You don't go to Grant Memorial unless you have money."

Maria's face twisted, clearly not believing she had misjudged the man. "He looked like he didn't have two dimes to rub together."

"Did this man Scott tell you he had a job?" Ralph asked.

"He didn't tell me exactly what he does, but I think it has to do with marketing."

"And why's that?" he asked.

"He had some paperwork about redoing a company logo. A contractor or builder logo? I don't know, but it looked vaguely familiar."

"That's very interesting," Ralph said. "What if you're wrong? What if Maria is right and this guy Scott has lied to you?"

Caroline's posture straightened and, even though this customer was a complete stranger, he had found her one button. "I don't like it when a man I'm dating lies to me. If I caught Scott in a lie...," she took a breath to calm herself, "I'd tear him a new one. I wouldn't care who was around, he'd get an earful from me."

Ralph's lips cured up into a smile.

"You don't believe me?" she challenged.

"A little thing like you? Causing a scene?"

"Oh, I would." She pointed a finger at Maria. "You've seen me get upset before."

Maria gave her a reassuring nod. "It doesn't

happen often, but my girl can put a man in his place when needed."

"Good for you, Caroline," he said, his smile widening. "I'm glad you can take care of yourself. Especially if he's down on his luck and taking advantage of you."

"I don't care if I make more money than the man I'm dating. It makes me independent." Caroline wiped her brow and really didn't want to share any more with a total stranger. "Let me check on…" Looking up, she noticed the runner coming out of the kitchen with the two new meals. She walked over and inspected the bags. "Looks like they got them right this time."

"My girlfriend and I thank you." Ralph pulled out his wallet and dropped a credit card on the counter. The credit machine was self-serve, and the man could easily have done the swipe himself, but Caroline picked up the plastic and ran the charge.

Suits didn't mean larger tips, just pickier customers.

Of course, the meal was done wrong and it was a pick up order.

When he filled out the tip amount, and she noted how generous the man was, she felt very fortunate.

Caroline grabbed a coupon from under the counter and signed her name to the voucher. "Again, I'm sorry we messed up your order. You can get 5% off if you spend over twenty dollars with us on your next meal." She stapled the receipt and coupon on the bag.

"Thanks Caroline." He read the coupon and his lips curled up into a smile. "Caroline with a heart over the 'i'. I appreciate the discount."

He was about to stand, but then the expression on his face seemed pensive. He pointed to the exit where Judson had left a few minutes ago. "Talking about the eighteenth and deliveries, that reminds me that my company is having a breakfast meeting that day."

"Breakfast burritos go well with office meetings," Maria said in a flat tone. She had stopped smiling the second Ralph had mentioned a girlfriend, but Caroline didn't think the man noticed.

"We do deliveries to offices. Well, *I'll* be doing the morning deliveries that day."

Ralph reached for a menu. "Great. This one for delivery to a law firm. I need to bring refreshments to the meeting and you can definitely help me out Caroline."

She helped him place a sizeable order and wrote down the address, time, and took the payment. He got up from the stool once they were done and added, "I hope this guy Scott works out for you."

The second he left, and they were alone once more, Maria started in again. "I told you not to ask personal questions when you were with Scott, but my guess is that you did. And, I'm guessing—because

I know you—you got to know the man. Did he even talk about this so called marketing job?"

Caroline felt giddy. She couldn't remember the last time she'd felt as if she didn't have a care in the world. "We didn't exactly talk about our occupations, but he did pay for dinner."

"I hope you had him pay for the hotel, too."

Stopping dead in her tracks, Caroline mumbled a dismissive, "Uh-huh."

Maria walked over, closing the gap between them. "Don't tell me *you* paid for the hotel."

"We went to my place." Her voice was soft, like a child being caught doing something wrong by their overprotective mother.

"Your place?" Maria's voice went up an octave and her hands rested on her hips; she had never looked so stern before. "That's even worse. Now the man knows where you live."

"You worry too much."

"Experience, honey. There's been a lot of water crossing under my bridge. Hopefully, he understands that it's a one-nighter and not to come back around."

The words cut deeply. Scott was not a man that a woman could use as a one-nighter. His loving caresses, his soft lips, his firm body, and his rock-hard rod that had been up four times... Her core moistened at just the thought of him and their time together. Four times. She had never had that many lovemaking sessions in one evening before. The man had stamina.

Maria walked behind the counter and asked, "Are you going to see Scott again?"

Not that Maria needed to know, but Caroline answered, "He said he'd call me."

"They all say that. Don't get your hopes up."

True. But she honestly believed Scott would. "He made me breakfast in bed before I dropped him off. I mean, honestly, breakfast in bed," she said. "There may be something special here."

"Was his cooking at least good, or can I make fun of him for that?"

"All I had was cereal and some questionable milk." But it had been delivered to her in bed this morning with a side of kisses and a promise to talk later. She hoped she could trust him.

The barista called Scott's name and he wandered through the crowded Starbucks to the counter to claim his morning dose of caffeine. He sat down at the small table in the corner of the room, his hot cup of coffee in his hands. He was no one's puppet, and certainly hated being at a client's beck-and-call, but, at the moment, he needed to win the Landmark Leasing case.

Even if it meant having an impromptu meeting

with an ass for a client before heading into the office. It wasn't the best way to start a day, especially after such a wonderful night, but the case was important.

Studying Frank, he noticed the man seemed upset—and not in an 'I'm entitled to do what I want and the world won't bend to my needs' sort of way.

"I need to fill you in on a few more details of my business," Frank said.

There was no 'thanks for meeting with me at the last minute' gesture, not that Scott expected one. He plastered on an expression of concern and leaned in, as if Frank were his only client and anything relating to the case was super critical. "What couldn't wait until you received the paperwork from my office?"

Frank pulled a sour face and said, "I haven't been completely honest with you about Landmark Leasing."

"How so?" Scott didn't like the sound of this and his stomach churned. It was never good when a client came out with last minute details.

"You asked if there had been any legal actions against my company in the past."

A deep heaviness filled Scott's stomach and a headache was starting to form. "Any past legal actions against your company that can be used to create a case around your business practices would be important for us to know."

Actually, getting this information from the client

was critical, but the research team needed to also do their job and confirm these types of details. Even without a confession from the client, his team should have discovered them. But Joanna worked in that department. He had noticed that research for his cases had become less timely since their breakup.

"None of them had to do with my company's branding, so I didn't think they were all that important."

'None of them'? Scott set down his coffee and glanced around the room. There was only a small amount of privacy in the room and he didn't like where this was headed. "What do you mean?"

"A woman with nothing better to do, from one of the apartment rentals, is suing me for sexual harassment."

Damn.

Not that a sexual harassment suit—one that hasn't gone to trial and can't have a negative impact on any legal matters yet—would affect an intellectual property case.

"A female renter," Scott said, correcting the man, "has recently filed a suit against you." He could guess the answer but still asked, "Is there just cause for this complaint?"

Frank's mouth curled into a guilty smile and his hands went up in a 'little ol' me?' type of way. "That bitch says…"

"That woman," Scott insisted, his voice louder and more dominating than Frank's.

His head shook from side-to-side. "That *woman* claims that when I brought my crew in to fix some plumbing issues that I groped her."

"Did you?" Scott asked, doing his best to keep his expression straight and even. "I need you to be honest since Prince Housing could use this suit to defame your character if our case goes to trial."

"I mean...she was..."

"Mr. Rancini," Scott looked around the room once more. The place was getting crowded and this meeting was not going to be quick and painless. "We should meet in private to discuss this. Please contact my office to set up a meeting."

"Should I bring the paperwork from..."

"Naturally. You should bring all the information you have regarding this harassment issue to our meeting."

"And the other ones?"

Scott's headache grew. He swallowed the lump in his throat and closed his eyes briefly to gain composure. "What *other* ones?"

"In the last five years I've had three similar issues filed, but the," his eyebrow rose, "the *women* never went through with going to court."

Scott could hear the implied 'bitches' remark. "They all dropped their charges?" When Frank nodded, Scott asked, "And all of these women reside in property that you own?"

"Yes."

He needed to be very clear. "None of these allegations went to court or were mitigated?"

The expression on Frank's face told Scott that the man didn't understand what 'mitigated' meant. "Did these accusations remain just that, accusations with no legal follow-up?"

Frank stood straighter in his seat, his hand waving dismissively in the air. "I took care of everything. I didn't even need a lawyer."

A shiver ran up Scott's spine. He didn't know what 'took care' meant and was afraid to ask. "Please call my office and arrange another meeting. I can't stress enough the importance of settling this issue out of court and my team is drafting the next set of paperwork as we speak. They should be delivered to you shortly."

"I'm not giving up my logo."

"Mr. Rancini, if the other party presses the issue, their lawyers may insist that Landmark Leasing not operate in this state. That would be the best-case scenario. Paying for damages, even to the point of losing your business completely could be a possibility."

Scott stood. He was done with this man and his lack of character. "Good day, Mr. Rancini."

Walking through the now crowded Starbucks,

Scott was glad to be leaving. He had asked the man repeatedly for any past litigations against his company and the man had looked him in the face and lied to him. True, none of the others went to trial, but that didn't mean that the plaintiff couldn't try to leverage them.

And, there had been several sexual harassment issues against the man, including a new one? It's one thing if you're accidentally accused of being an ass and treating women poorly, but if many women make the claim, there was probably some truth in the matter.

Scott believed the man would treat women poorly. He was just the type. The kind that took what was his, never called the women back, and couldn't even remember their names. He, and his type, were what gave men, and dating in general, a bad name.

Getting in his car, Scott left the parking lot and headed into work. Not soon after getting on the highway, he spotted a Goodwill store. His body reacted and his cock began to get hard—all just from seeing the Goodwill logo on the sign.

Shit. He had it bad for Caroline.

He quickly glanced down on the car's clock. He had time.

He needed more clothes if he were to take Caroline out again. He may be stretching the truth by the outfits, but he did tell Caroline his name. He was not as bad as Mr. Rancini, but he couldn't shake the slimy feeling he had with working with Frank and his Neanderthal views of women. Scott would never treat a woman so poorly.

Then, his thoughts drifted to the delivery woman in his office last week. What was *her* name. A list of names ran through his head as he parked. He was sure it started with either a 'b' or a 'd'.

Why did it matter? He took a deep breath and tried to shake the sick feeling welling in his stomach. His nooner with what's-her-name was different. That woman knew it was just an afternoon fling with no strings attached. He treated her well and certainly didn't hold the woman's rent over her head. He had no upper hand, no position of authority over her. It was nothing similar.

He thought about Caroline and her wise words. Both parties need to be in the bed for the same reason.

He and the delivery woman were on the same page.

Although, he did give her a hundred-dollar tip.

Like a hooker.

He wanted to throw up.

Taking a deep breath, he wandered into the store. The delivery woman wasn't expecting money, other than the payment for the food. She wasn't there to… he thought about what happened in that office. It wasn't the first time he had had a woman pleasure him behind locked doors of where he worked. His reputation of being a womanizer was well known among his coworkers.

Many thought of him as a male whore, actually.

Not very 'senior partnerish' to a couple of old men who had been married for decades who would be deciding if he got the promotion or not. Scott's stomach turned and he felt the slime of guilt spreading across his body. His way of life was going to hold him back from getting what he truly wanted in life.

Ralph would probably get the promotion even though his reputation was not quite squeaky clean, but clean enough.

Damn it.

Scott walked down the aisle of button-down shirts, leaning heavily on the shopping cart to support himself and keep as much weight off his ankle as possible. He needed to make a change.

Several shirts his size were placed in the cart, and they were literally 'off the rack' and poor quality, not his usual selections from *Jos. A Bank Clothier*. Next, he headed to the belt section. A leather belt would be good to complete his ensemble. Maybe some ordinary jeans as well.

He gathered his selections and walked to the counter to pay, feeling way over dressed in his two thousand dollar suit. Forty-three dollars, including tax, got him another five outfits to wear while out with Caroline. The clothing was cheap, and looked the part. They would easily fool her while their relationship grew and he knew he could trust her.

*"Never lie to me."*

Caroline's words echoed in Scott's mind as he loaded his car's small trunk with his bags.

Was he playing her? Was he as bad as the Franks of the world?

He had told Caroline his full name but had led her to believe that he was poor. Of course, he'd paid for dinner, gotten himself home this morning, and, sort of, between kissing her goodbye, had indicated that he needed to go to work.

So why was he back at this Goodwill store buying more clothes? Why did he feel the need to lie to her?

And it wasn't as though he had parked his Tesla outside the store. A quick stop at a car rental place currently had him driving a KIA Sportage.

A frickin' KIA Sportage.

He was in over his head.

The company Christmas party was days away and he wanted to invite Caroline to it. But she'd never understand why he lied to her. He didn't want to continue deceiving her, but he needed to ease out of this lie gracefully.

Some of the clothes he bought were nicer than the first set he had purchased. Maybe if he slowly started wearing nicer clothing, maybe taking her to nicer restaurants, perhaps he could build up to the fact that he was rich.

His phone buzzed, and when he realized it was Caroline, his heart fluttered. He couldn't remember the last time, if ever, that his heart fluttered.

"Hey, love." His voice sounded more excited than he had intended. "I was going to call you later."

"Did you get to work on time, or did I keep you too long?" Her voice sounded playful.

"I made it in." It was still early, and he actually hoped she was calling him for a nooner at her place but suspected she was at work. "You working now?"

"Yes. But I'm getting off early."

He heard the pause in her voice—and an unasked question.

Just thinking about her this morning already had him half-hard. Hearing her voice was nearly completing his stiffness. "I can be at your apartment by two o'clock. When are you off work?" He got into his car and started the engine.

"Unfortunately, I have some errands to run…and a job to get to tonight."

He shifted in his car seat, his pants tight in the crotch. "The diner open late?"

"No. Job number two."

Her answer struck him oddly for a moment. He had never known a person to work two jobs before although, certainly, people did.

"Super waitress by day, and something else by night? Where do you work?"

"At the glamorous transit authority."

He winced. TSA sounded awful, even for a second job that may be part-time. He avoided public transportation as much as possible, and couldn't imagine having to work at one of the smelly stations. "I'd like to see you today."

"Well, that's why I'm calling."

Again, he heard an unasked question and suspected that she didn't like to ask for help.

"Let me guess. It's your car, and you need a ride somewhere." He glanced at the car's clock. If he were smart, he'd be back at the office kissing the bosses butt and side-blocking Ralph's play for making partner.

He wasn't that smart.

His damsel was in distress, and he didn't often get the chance to play the hero.

"Do you have a car? And can you…"

All he needed to do was change his clothes. It'd be gross to wear what he just bought without proper laundering, but he couldn't show up in his expensive suit. "I can free up my schedule. I'll pick you up at the restaurant in ten minutes."

## 9

*S*cott's car pulled into the parking lot of the restaurant and Caroline couldn't help but smile. She stood from the front booth of the restaurant, the one that gave the best view of the parking lot, and walked to the door. She hadn't seen him since he had left her bedroom this morning. Even though she had been the one to call him, the fact that there wasn't a 'two day' waiting period before someone called, or even a 'why hasn't he called me' moment pleased her. She hated playing games, which was why she had sworn off all men.

All men, except for the Prince Charmings in life. Scott was kind, sweet, had a great body,... yeah, a fantastic body. He had come out of the woodwork. It just goes to prove, once you stop looking for something it naturally appears.

She felt a bubble of excitement within her as she

made her way to the car door. Scott had exited the car, ran around, and was opening it for her—smiling at her as though this unexpected errand had become the highlight of his day.

She kissed his cheek. "Thank you." Opening the door may have been an old-timey, chivalrous gesture, and maybe some women's libbers would hate the idea, but Caroline found it charming.

She sighed and felt the corners of her mouth curl upward.

Her Prince Charming.

She sat in the car and watched in the rear-view mirror as he walked around the car and then got in. The scent of his masculine cologne filling the small space and reminding her of last night.

His grin widened once he got in. "Where are we off to?"

It was too early in the relationship to explain everything about her family and issues, but she needed to see her Grandmother today and her car had overheated. "I have a meeting with an administrator at Avalon Memory Care Facility." When his eyebrow raised, she added, "It's off highway 290, heading east."

He pulled onto the main street and toward the highway. There were no questions asked, no refusal to help, and no passive-aggressive comments about her interrupting his day—only an eager determination to help her.

How rare.

"It's good to see you," he said, one hand reaching across the front seat to hold hers as the other steered the car.

"I'm glad you could come by." She held his hand and he squeezed it softly. How was it that she could find someone so quickly who was so helpful, sexy, and trustworthy?

She stared at his strong jawline and handsome features, remembering how his eyes pinched shut as he had climaxed repeatedly last night, how his breath hitched each time, and how he would hold her so tightly as he released into her.

Her core—which blissfully remained flushed from so much activity last night—flooded with desire for him, her body aching for the next time they could be together.

But it was more than just the pleasure she felt when she was with him. Last night she shined as a sex-goddess to Scott, and he couldn't get enough of her—nibbling and suckling every inch of her body as she in turn intimately pleased him. Her ex-boyfriend had always made sex about him and his needs, to the point where he'd wake her up in the middle of the night and five minutes later he would be satisfied, with her staying up and feeling empty.

She never knew sex could feel this good.

Scott pulled off the highway when they reached their exit and she directed him through a small residential area, telling him it was a short cut and an easier way to reach their destination. He followed her instructions with no hesitation.

"Keep driving straight, then turn right at the stop sign." She then added, "It will be in a while, after we pass the elementary school."

Her gaze wandered out the window and she took in the sights of the beautiful, brick homes which lined the street. Her dream to live in a red-bricked, two story home with lush gardens and large back-yard was always present in the back of her mind. One day, maybe. But no time soon.

"These homes are gorgeous," he said, pointing out one and then another commenting on the style and design of the home.

"I love this neighborhood." She enjoyed driving through the place, and on occasion, she'd jog around the homes after visiting with her grandmother. She pointed up ahead. "I especially love the red brick house at the end of this street on the large corner lot. There's a porch swing and all it needs is a white picket fence."

They drove up to the home and a "for sale" sign was in the yard. He slowed down and parked in front of it.

It was for sale? Not that she could afford it, but a girl could always dream. "It must have just been listed."

Scott let out a whistle. "That's a beaut!"

"There's sometimes an older woman rocking in the chair and two young children playing in the yard with a dog." She rolled the window down and looked up to the second story. "Awnings, a chimney... quite a Norman Rockwell picture moment."

"It really is." He got out of the car and went to the for-sale sign. Home information pamphlets lay inside a clear plastic tube, protected from any rain. He took two and returned to the car.

She took the paper from his hand. Finally, a glimpse into what she considered to be the best home in all of Chicago. "Over six-thousand square feet, five bedrooms," she read, "three and a half baths... three living rooms!" She leaned back in her seat and shook her head. "Hardwood flooring, crown molding..."

"Built not too long ago. Nice home theater, too." He folded his copy, leaned forward, and placed it in his jeans pocket. "Don't forget the three-car garage," he said, as he resumed driving and she continued to read.

"Great school district." She set the paper on her lap and let out a sigh. "I can't believe it's for sale. I hope the person who buys the place enjoys many years there."

"I'm sure they will," Scott said.

Once the house had disappeared in her side mirror, she turned and studied Scott. He had an old-timey charm about him. A 'let's slow down and take in the sights' type of personality. Most men had high-stress jobs and no time for anything or anyone. Maybe dating someone with only a part time job was the way to go, or someone between jobs.

Of course, she didn't know that he *was* in between jobs. She didn't know much of anything like that about the man. Understanding that Maria would scold her later, she didn't care. "Do you have to hurry back to work?"

He shook his head. "My boss is reasonable and my hours flexible."

She had never heard of a job where things were that good. All of her jobs had virtual time cards you had to punch into when the clock started. "What do you do?"

Stopping at the stop sign, he put on his right blinker and checked the street. "I work at a law firm."

Not quite what she was expecting, but good solid work and a nice surprise. For a brief moment her thoughts designed him as a stern but fair lawyer. Expensive suit. Tie. Commanding in the courtroom.

But it didn't matter what he did. His job was probably not that glamorous. And, who was she to judge? She smelled like burritos most of the time. "Do you work in the mailroom?"

Scott leaned forward and searched for Avalon, his head paneling from side-to-side. "No." He pointed at the building which lay on the right side of the street. "Is this it?"

The sign 'Avalon Memory Care' stood at the side of the street mostly hidden by overgrown bushes. She pointed toward the building. "Just park anywhere."

Do you want me to come in or should I wait?"

A smile quickly spread across her face. She hadn't expected him to be such a gentleman. "I'm here to visit my grandmother." She wasn't sure if she should go into details or not but said, "Sure, come in."

_S_cott followed Caroline up the flowered walk to the wooden door. The place resembled a home, but the sign "Avalon Memory Care" told him otherwise. Caroline punched in a code to get through the locked door. She didn't need to look up the number, she had it memorized.

She had come here before, perhaps often.

The place looked like a ski lodge. Dark wooden beams across the ceiling, a stone fireplace, and a row of leather recliners in front of a giant television screen gave the place a warm feeling. The three large, solid wood tables in the back suggested that as many twenty-four people could dine at one time. The place was single story, and hallways stretched out in three directions where he could make out doors to what he figured were bedrooms.

Caroline walked past a room with a large window and Scott followed her. Peeking into the tiny space, he saw two desks and a woman sitting at a computer in a nurse's uniform. There were two more caregivers on the floor, one sitting on a leather chair talking to an elderly man, the other behind a counter in a kitchen.

"Hello Caroline," the man from the kitchen said. "It's been a few days."

Caroline's smile greeted the man. She gazed around the room. "Is my grandmother in her room?"

"She had a busy day today. Got her nails done after she was showered. The day wore her out and she's been napping on and off for the past hour."

"Thanks, George."

George nodded at Scott and then glanced back to Caroline.

"This is my friend, Scott. He gave me a ride today."

Holding up his gloved hand, Scott suspected that George would have reached out his hand to shake Scott's, but he was preparing food. "Nice to meet you."

"Likewise." The place had a slight smell of cooked eggs and Ben Gay, not a winning combination. Scott counted the people in the room. A handful of residents were about, some sitting at the tables having coffee, others asleep in recliners. The home was small, and he didn't see any visitors other than Caroline. Perhaps most of them came by after work or on weekends, either way, the place was quiet with the only exception the television being on and running an old episode of 'Gilligan's Island.'

The place gave him the willies.

Caroline touched his arm and led him down a short hallway off the kitchen. "My grandmother is in room number six."

The door was open, and she didn't knock before she led him in. At first, he thought they might be disturbing her grandmother, or at the very least disrupting her privacy. But that wasn't the case. There, on the bed, lay a tiny elderly woman, her tiny frame comfortably tucked under the covers. Her eyes, the only sign of life the woman had, were open and she was staring at Caroline.

"Hi," Caroline said, her voice upbeat and cheery. She stopped a few feet shy of the bed, her feet not touching a rubber mat that ran its length. She hit a button on a cord that ran up the headboard and was attached to the mat.

"She's a fall risk and this is an alarm," she said, directing her statement towards him but not taking her eyes off her grandmother. "How are you today?"

The old woman's eyes focused on Caroline. "I want to leave."

Wiping her Grandmother's temple and stroking her hair, Caroline said, "But you are home."

"No!"

The woman's features hardened and her thin lips pursed. The small amount of white hair on her head was thin and her scalp showed through, her cheeks were hollow, and her paper-like skin lay tight against her scrawny neck showing the sinews of her throat. Scott had always thought that ostriches looked like disappointed, little old women—and this was a case in point.

"I want to go."

Caroline smiled and ignored the remark. "Do you know who I am?" She moved so that her face was directly in front of her grandmother. "Do I look familiar?"

Her grandmother's eyes focused on her face. "You're my mother. Take me home. Now."

"Is that anyway to talk to your mother." Caroline turned toward Scott, her eyes wide as though suppressing tears. "Last week I was her sister. She doesn't realize that I had to sell her home to help pay for this place, she said, whispering so only Scott would hear.

Looking past her, her grandmother said in a sad, pleading tone, "Please take me home."

"We'll go home in a little while." Turning back to her grandmother, she again stroked the woman's hair. "The kids are still in school, so we girls can make a day of it. Won't that be fun? It'll be just the two of us. What do you want to do? A picnic in the park?"

The grandmother stared at the wall. "It's raining."

Scott knew that wasn't true. The beautiful day outside said otherwise. When was the last time this woman went into the sunshine? Did you get taken out on strolls via a wheelchair? Or did her entire existence remain within the four walls of her room, and the rooms outside near the kitchen?

"Oh, yes. The rain." Caroline moved her face once again directly in front of the woman so she would look back at her. "I know what we'll do. I still have some sugar cookies left. We'll take our tea and the cookies out to the veranda so we can hear the rain as it hits the tin roof."

The grandmother's eyes softened and she yawned.

"Won't that be fun? We can take our books out there and read later this afternoon. How does that sound?"

She smiled and nodded, a glint of life appearing in her eyes. "Can we go?"

"First, you look tired, so you can take a nap and then we'll spend all afternoon together." Caroline tucked the woman more securely in the bed, leaned over, and kissed her grandmother. "You've always been such a good daughter. I love you so much and you make me proud each day."

The grandmother's smile widened and she slowly closed her eyes. After a minute of calmness, she nodded off to sleep.

Caroline stepped off the mat and reactivated the alarm. She turned, wiping a tear from her eyes and was met by Scott's embrace.

"You're a good granddaughter." His arms caressed her back and he felt her tremble as she sniffled. He had never taken care of an elderly loved one, and never thought of how difficult the end could be on someone.

"I just try to give her some good thoughts and to brighten her day if I can." She took a deep breath and composed herself. "Some people say that playing along is like 'green lighting' someone. You know, where you give into their world and enable them to drift—basically, keeping them crazy." She half-way turned toward her grandmother. "I think it's more humane to give her something nice to think about."

He leaned back so he could see her face. He had never thought about the caretaking of the elderly. Never gave it a second thought. Poor Caroline lived in this world every day. She understood what it was like and how best to navigate the situation.

"Well, for the record," he said, wiping away a tear, "I like sugar cookies, too."

Holding her hand, he led her from the room. She left the door open and he noticed most of the doors down the hallway were open. He figured they were closed when the residents were out in the main area, closed if they were in their rooms. The exact opposite of what you would expect, but it made complete sense.

"I hope I don't look like my great-grandmother. I've heard stories about how terrible she was." Caroline blew her grandmother a kiss and then looked Scott square in the eye. "From what my grandmother told me, the woman was overly stern and never told her daughter that she loved her."

"Like I said, you're a good granddaughter. She's lucky to have you."

"Ms. Wenzel? I'm Ms. Rubinstein. Can we talk for a moment?"

Caroline's wiped her eyes. "I need to take care of a few things." She pointed to the leather seats which faced a large television in theater-style rows. "It shouldn't take long. Feel free to sit and watch the television while you wait. It shouldn't take long."

Caroline left with the woman and Scott got the impression that she was being served up some bad news. Her grandmother, although old and mentally unsure of her surroundings, seemed fine—at least not in a 'we need to talk' desperate needs type of situation.

The room had a few more residents, with two of them actively watching the end of "Gilligan's Island." Scott had no interest in watching it, plus he didn't want to disturb the two elderly gentlemen. He had no experience talking to elderly people who needed to live in a memory care center, and thought he'd lack the patience to carry on a conversation like Caroline had just done.

She was amazing. The first time he laid eyes on her he would never have guessed the struggles she was facing. More than one job? That was nightmare enough. But taking care of someone with dementia, or whatever she suffered from? He knew he couldn't do it.

He stood behind the row of recliners, not really sure where to go. The television station must be showing a marathon, because another episode of "Gilligan's Island" came on the screen. This one in black and white. He had watched a few episodes as a kid, but they had always been in color.

The song jingle continued, and he wondered if the Skipper really was a mighty sailing man since his tiny ship was lost.

Great. Now he'd have that silly tune in his head all day. He wasn't even sure he even remembered the lyrics to the song, but sure enough, he began singing them in his head. He knew the castaways, even before the song had listed them.

"…a millionaire and his wife…"

Wait.

A millionaire and his wife?

Why wasn't it 'the millionaires'? Surely Lovey was considered a millionaire and not regulated to be just 'his wife'. Why wasn't she considered to be a millionaire?

She was a supportive woman, loving her husband, Thurston, due to who he was and not what he could afford to give her. Her husband always called her 'Lovey'.

'Lovey'?

That couldn't have been her name.

Did she have a real name?

The episode began and he remembered that she was Mrs. Howell.

*His* full name was Thurston Howell III. And all she got was a term of endearment?

How the heck did Scott remember all that? He hadn't thought of this show in years.

Scratching his head, he watched the show. Skipper, Professor, Ginger, Mary Ann, … wow, only half of them had first names. What kind of a name was Gilligan anyway?

He shook his head. Five minutes in this place and he felt he was losing his mind. Perhaps that was what made the show appealing, and why the place put it on for the residents. It was simple and, somewhat, engaging. It certainly had drawn him in, and he didn't particularly like the old show.

Needing to walk away from the television, he went to the kitchen area.

George was pleasant, but busy cooking, so Scott wandered to the front table where he saw a guest book. At the very least he could sign in and indicate that Caroline's grandmother had a visitor. The gesture seemed small, but he wanted to do something.

A feathered quill type of pen rested in a display case next to a bound visitor log. Not too many signatures were on today's listing, but he added his name at the bottom but didn't know the grandmother's full name. He indicated that he visited room number six, since that was her room and she didn't have a roommate.

Business cards lay in a holder near the book, so he picked one up. 'Avalon Memory Care' he read. Glancing at the bottom of the card was a blue and green circle.

His heart leapt in his throat, nearly choking him.

Eyes widened; his gaze darted to the details of the logo. "Landmark Leasing" with an "LM" in the center.

No. No. No.

Pamphlets lay on the desk, so he grabbed one and opened it. "A Landmark Leasing company property." The paperwork went on to describe the place and the host of services it provided.

He was dating a woman who had family living in one of Frank Rancini's properties.

Shit.

A sinking feeling hit his gut and he felt trapped. A conflict of interest now existed in a case he was in charge of. He couldn't be Frank Rancini's lawyer without running the risk of being disbarred.

His golden ticket to the senior partnership was ruined.

Leaning against the wall, he looked around at the place. Frank Rancini owned apartment complexes, condos, at least one RV Park... there had been no mention of elderly care centers.

Shit.

He took a deep breath and tried to think of what to do. He had to come clean and not continue with the case. Of course, if Frank were smart, and if he'd already signed the last set of documents, the case was already done.

His hand wiped his face and he knew he could be in serious trouble if he didn't give full disclosure. How would he define his relationship with Caroline? They had just met. One date. He only now found out about Avalon, so if this knowledge happened after the paperwork was signed, he should be okay.

Maybe.

Caroline walked down the hallway; her expression distant but upset. "Let's go," she said as she passed him and made her way to the control panel beside the exit door.

She punched in the number and left the building without a word.

"You were talking to that woman for quite a

while," Scott said once the two of them were back in his car. Caroline was quiet and buckled herself in without making eye contact.

"Are you okay?"

Her body slumped. "My grandmother can't stay her." A tear escaped and she brushed it off her cheek.

He leaned in and placed his hand on her shoulder. "What do you mean?"

"The director said my mother's funds are running out. I need to put her into a cheaper place."

He stared at the building. "Aren't retirement homes all the same?"

"No. She was first in a retirement home, then a nursing home, and now at memory care." She let out a sob and Scott caressed her shoulder, not knowing any other way to soothe her. "She's fading away quickly and there's nothing I can do about it."

He knew it probably wouldn't help, and possible would hurt the situation, but he said, "The woman is in her nineties."

Caroline took a tissue from her purse and wiped her wet cheeks. "I know I can't stop the inevitable, and she's lived a long life, but I at least want her to be comfortable the last few months—or years—she has left."

Scott doubted it would be years. "She looks very comfortable. Another place will be just as nice, even if it's cheaper." He heard the words as he said them, not really believing them.

"She pays thousands of dollars a month for this place already. If Medicare didn't help out, and if my grandfather hadn't fought in WWII, there's no way her money could have stretched out as long as it has." She blew her nose and added, "I put all of her money into an account for Avalon. I know it sounds crazy, but I didn't want..." she paused, and her body slumped more into the seat. "In case I ever got into trouble and debt collectors came after me, I put all of her money into a separate account that Avalon could access but would be difficult for me to withdraw from."

This was way too much information to process. Medicaid. WWII. Debt collectors? He took a calming breath and looked as reassuringly at her as possible. "Okay. The problem is that her money is running out?"

"She can only afford to stay here about another six months."

Scott took in the information. Did places like this really kick people out if they had nowhere to go and no one to care for them? He thought about what he knew of Frank Rancini's personality and knew that this place would.

"Medicaid will pay for everything once she has two-thousand dollars or less to her name."

"Two-thousand dollars? I don't follow you."

"My grandmother didn't have a lot of money, but when my grandfather died after knee surgery, she received a hefty insurance claim and settlement from the hospital. I also sold the house she owned."

That sounded awful. Everything that woman owned lay in that ten by ten-foot square room. Not that Scott believed material possessions were that important, but he couldn't fathom owning nothing. To not have money in the bank. To not know where or how you were going to live. It was a nightmare.

"She's been living the last few years on that settlement and house money, but now the money is almost gone. Avalon will kick her out. At that time, I'll have to move her elsewhere and pay out of my own pocket, or I could find someplace dirt cheap that may stretch out the money by a few months. After that, I'll still have to take care of her or declare her a ward of the state. Once she has no other options, the state can see to her needs."

He realized that wasn't ideal. An image of the state-run DMV came into his mind. He hated sitting and waiting for hours to get a new driver's license. The idea of living in such a cold and filthy place made him sick to his stomach.

"The state could have her move to Toledo or wherever there is a free bed. She'd be one of maybe twenty people in a ward of sick, dying, and mentally ill patients."

Locked away with the mentally ill. Nobody deserved that. Scott wanted to say something supportive, he just didn't know what that could be.

10

———

*C*aroline's scent still lingered on Scott's skin, and yet his body still hungered for her. Spending several nights at her place had left him well spent, dehydrated, and... still aching for her. Making her another breakfast in bed before she hurried off to her busy day, made him late for work.

But it was worth it.

Of course, they hadn't come up with a solution for her Grandmother.

Easily enough, he could just give her the money. But then he'd have to explain how he 'all of a sudden' had enough cash on hand to bankroll granny's housing costs.

Walking into the building, he noticed Ralph sitting in the lobby. He didn't have time to talk with the man, but Ralph stood and was making a bee-line towards him.

"Thanks for understanding your limitations and allowing a real lawyer to work the Landmark deal." Ralph's voice was filled with pride and he did a stupid little wink, a wink that made him look ridiculous.

Scott walked past him to the elevator, his pace a bit too fast for his sore foot. "Even a junkyard dog deserves a bone every once in a while."

Ralph glanced back at the exit doors and then hit the elevator button before Scott had a chance to. "I heard you RSVP'd to the company party with a guest."

Scott's plans weren't any of Ralph's business, although he had always taken a date. It was no newsflash.

"Joanna will be going with me."

His eyes quickly locked onto Ralph's, giving away his surprise. "That's fine," he said, as nonchalantly as possible and glancing back to the still closed elevator doors. "I wasn't planning on taking her. You're more than welcome to my hand-me-downs."

"She was your pity date last year."

"I guess she'll be your pity date this year." Scott's potential feelings for her during the months that they were dating disappeared once he caught her sleeping with an employee from accounting.

"She's gorgeous. Long legs. Beautiful smile. Killer body."

"Deceitful tongue. Black heart. The woman has many qualities." What was taking the elevator so long?

"How soon do you think an interior decorator could fix up that corner office for me? It's the holiday season, I might have to wait for the new year to spruce up the place."

"There's really no rush. Once I'm done serving as Senior Partner and retire, you can move in." That reminded him of his little side project of finding a home to buy. A good interior decorator would be hard to find during the holidays. He'd have to mention that to Beverly.

"That corner office is as good as mine." Ralph's head nodded slowly up and down. "I'll have to move everything out of it first."

"Tate isn't dead." Scott's voice bellowed down the hallway.

"Not yet."

Scott's jaw tightened and his body tightened. Tate was...*is* a good man. Vultures like Ralph always circled, showing just how ugly a human being could be.

"Doesn't matter. I never liked the guy."

The elevator ding sounded and gave Scott a perfect escape before belting the man.

"Anyway, I just wanted you to know that I'm taking the perfect date to the party."

Perfect date. Joanna was beautiful, intelligent, leggy, and could mold herself to fit any roll she needed to play. Scott stepped into the elevator and was grateful that Ralph didn't follow him.

As much as he didn't care for Joanna, she fit the corporate image. She knew how to schmooze the bigwigs and say exactly what they wanted and needed to hear. She had worked her charms on him, which is why they had vacationed in Mexico last summer.

But then, she was merely dating his wallet.

Once in his office, he set his briefcase down and stared out the big picture window. The building across the street reflected the morning sunrise and the light reflected into his office. His thought once again drifted to Caroline and her money problems, as they often had been doing over the last few days.

He had to come up with a plan to help her but to not let her know that he had money. Maybe she could win a radio show. Maybe he could come up with a way for her to conveniently find an envelope of money in a booth at her restaurant.

Knowing her, she'd turn the money into lost and found.

Whatever he decided to do, the plan had to be believable—and he had no time right now to really come up with something grand. After stepping down from the Landmark Leasing case, he picked up several smaller accounts. If he could close them out quickly enough, with good outcomes, it might make up for turning down Gilkrist's pet project.

He hated how busy he had become, and making a good impression on the directors kept him occupied more than he'd expected. He was mentally exhausted, and missing Caroline. He had done the right thing though. Conflicts of interest were taken very seriously, but it was odd trying to define his relationship with Caroline on paper since he didn't exactly know where it was, or where it was going.

Ralph had been in the limelight, having closed another case and picking up the Landmark Leasing deal.

Dammit.

He sat at his desk and brought up his computer. He should have been focusing on his daily schedule, but just couldn't bring himself to start his day. He continued with some private research for several minutes before a knock sounded on his door.

"You're late. You need to be at the partner break-fast in twenty minutes," Beverly said, her voice sounding professional and all-business as she walked, leaning on her cane, into Scott's office and closed the door.

He wanted to share with Beverly his newfound joy over finding Caroline, but as of late, the two of them were only obsessed with the workflow in the office—which was a shame. Beverly had been there when he graduated high school, when he received the letter about being accepted into law school, and every birthday and Christmas. He wanted to shout up and down the halls about how happy he was, but he didn't want to jinx his good fortune.

He also doubted that Beverly would find a waitress worthy of dating him. Sure, she had called him a snob, but she was one too. Caroline didn't have a formal education, none that he knew of anyway. She worked in the blue-collar world and probably wouldn't fit into his life of country clubs and high-class society filled with dull, snooty boring people.

But Caroline was full of surprises. And way more interesting than any of those people.

Right now, he was Google-ing 'cheap Chicago dates' for more ideas. There were many museums that allowed free admittance, as well as several inexpensive plays. Taking her to the opera was what he wanted to do, but these places sounded nice, too—in a charming sort of way.

He just had to build up his image and their dates from poor, to middle class, to doing well, to... I can buy you the world.

Beverly walked to his desk and, pointing at her watch, said with a firmer voice, "Breakfast. Fifteen minutes."

He shut down the browser.

The partner and division-head breakfast had quickly become a thorn in his workweek. Today, they would probably announce the new partner position. At least there was something to look forward to.

"I'll leave in a few minutes." His voice was unintentionally curt, nearly dismissive. He didn't want Bev to see him focused on a side project. Deep down, he knew she wouldn't approve of him dating Caroline or spending time researching cheap dating suggestions—especially not when a partnership was at stake.

"By the way, that shitty car was parked in your spot again. I called to have it towed."

Crap. There went his KIA Sportage.

He gathered his briefs and computer.

"What's wrong?"

He glanced up, keys in hand. "What?"

"You've surrendered the Landmark Leasing deal without telling me why and you've been distant for days. You're acting like that time in college when your..."

His hand motioned in the air dismissively, cutting her off. He didn't need to be reminded of the time his history professor had accused him of cheating and threatened to kick him out of school. He had been innocent then, and there was nothing he was guilty of now.

Other than lying by omission to Caroline and having her believe he was penniless when he could solve her financial problems and make her life so much easier.

He shrugged. "It's nothing."

Her hands went to her hips, and he felt the pressure of tension building in the room.

God. Not the dreaded lecture stance.

Not now.

"This *nothing* is going to cost you the partnership. Ralph took Gilkrist out to dinner last night. You need to up your game if you want to win."

Shit. Of course, Ralph would sprint the last mile of the race. Beverly was right. He needed to focus, but there were too many balls to juggle. Scott still had his caseload, wanted to spend time with Caroline, and had a lineup of asses to kiss. "A last-minute dinner isn't going to change the fact that Ralph's track record can't match mine—even with Gilkrist's special needs case."

He mostly believed that. But there was still a chance that the promotion could go to Ralph, and the idea twisted in his gut, making him sick to his stomach.

"This is the final stretch, and you need to make good impressions."

"All the years I've worked for this company should be enough for my *good impression.*

Schmoozing someone at dinner isn't going to change anything."

"The partners see you as a playboy." Her voice was concentrated and scornful as she eyed him. "You need to show them that you're a family man type of guy."

Determined and stern wrinkle lines formed on her face, which was always the expression she adopted when she needed him to just shut up and obey. It was a look he'd hated as a child, and now, as her employer, one he rarely tolerated.

"I'm not a playboy." He emphasized each word to convince her. Knowing his track record, even he didn't believe it. He just didn't want it to be true.

"The revolving door of your bedroom over the last decade says otherwise. Joanna was the longest dalliance you had." She shook her head. "She must have been good in the sack for you to put up with all of her shit."

Employees needed boundaries. He needed to give Bev a set for Christmas.

"I've made dinner reservations for you and Ms. Paster tonight," she said. "We need to prep her thoroughly, and I doubt you have time to schmooze Gilkrist before the party."

None of that sounded appealing. "Who is Ms. Paster?"

Bev placed her hands on her hips once again and

gave him an are-you-kidding-me stare. "The woman we hired."

"We? When did....?"

Her jaw tightened. "The other day when you told me you weren't working on the Landmark Leasing case. I told you then we needed to step up your game with a dead ringer of a date."

The conversation wasn't ringing any bells.

"You said, 'do what you think is best'."

Okay, it now sounded familiar. "I remember you twisting my arm just before *you* hired her."

Her eyes narrowed. If looks could kill, he'd be toast. "*I* did hire her. You need her expertise."

His face pinched in retaliation. "Expertise? Or skills as a hired escort?"

She stood taller, squaring off her shoulders. "I won't allow you to sabotage this promotion."

"I'm not going to..."

"Hush." Her voice had a way of backing up each word like a sledgehammer. "Who suggested that you change your major to law?"

He stared at her, not believing that they were going down this path once again. He knew she awaited an answer, so he said, "You did."

"Who told you it would be a good idea to move to Chicago and leave your little town of Decatur where you had no career advancement other than working for your rich father, which you didn't want to do?"

He gave her his coldest stare. "You did."

"Who told you to pursue MacMillan to hire you?"

Staring into her cold eyes, he wondered when she'd become his nagging work wife. "It was all you. You did all of that."

She slammed her hand onto the desktop and nodded. "I've been your career coach your entire life. So, when I tell you to take the woman to dinner tonight, you'll do it."

He clenched his jaw, knowing that it was always best to trust Beverly. "Fine. I'll meet with her." He reached into his desk drawer and pulled out a folded sheet of paper. "This will solve the other half of the equation."

"She unfolded it and took a good look. "Are you sure?"

"I need to do what I need to do. Just buy it."

*C*aroline didn't enjoy doing delivery duty, and absolutely hated lying to her coworkers—especially Maria since she was currently borrowing the woman's car—but a special delivery with a huge tip? That was hard to turn down.

Especially now that the garage mechanic had found even more work to do on her seventeen-year-old Chevy. She was lucky that it even worked half the time, but once one thing goes wrong with a car then more was always sure to follow. The timing belt needed replacing, there was a crack in something really important (but she couldn't remember what), her brakes needed work, and her four bald tires should be replaced. There was more, but those were the big ones. She couldn't afford anything, but had to get the timing belt, naturally the biggest ticket item, done. Right now, the mechanic had even said that *he* didn't feel right letting her drive the car.

The garage was waiting for a special part that was on order to be delivered. Special of course meaning expensive.

The smell of the breakfast burritos filled the car, reminding her that she hadn't eaten breakfast yet. Sometimes orders were returned at the restaurant—whether they were incorrectly prepared or some other mistake—which meant free food if she wrapped it up before her boss noticed.

God, she hated being this poor. She had eaten three meals this way over the last week. She was actually tired of eating Mexican food, but it was one of her favorites. Plus, the restaurant made the best burritos.

Her stomach growled.

She stopped at a red light and checked the name and address once more. 'Ralph Larimer' and the street was downtown just a few blocks from the library. She knew exactly where to go.

Caroline parked the car and began unloading the food. Her muscles tensed as she entered Westgate

Plaza, pulling a small cart behind her filled with breakfast burritos, drinks, and salsa. The sweet tea weighed the cart down and made walking on the ice on the walkway hard to manage.

The large building felt immediately warm and inviting, so she removed her hat and gloves and pushed them into her coat pocket. She had never been to this site before with an order, even though it was near the restaurant.

Caroline's shoes slid across the marble as she made her way to the elevator. It was early, but several people already stood by the lift and waited for a ride. She needed to go to the eighteenth floor, to an executive suite.

"Caroline?" a voice called from behind her.

Caroline turned and saw Ralph standing behind her.

"You're right on time." He reached down and took the handle of the little cart from her. "We'll walk you up."

She shouldn't have allowed him to do anything, but he was so polite and kind. "Thank you, sir."

"This breakfast is for our monthly partner and director's meeting." He gestured to the woman next to him. "Joanna is our Director of Research."

Caroline smiled and nodded to the impeccably dressed woman. She would have thought she was a lawyer in her suit. She held a bag of food so she nodded instead of shaking the woman's hand. "Nice to meet you."

The woman next to him sniffed the air heavily. "You're right, Ralph. These burritos do smell heavenly."

A buzzer on the elevator sounded and the crowd allowed them to get on first. When the lady held the door open with her hand, Ralph pressed the interior button. "I got it Joanna."

The people crowded in and Joanna helped push the cart more into the corner of the tiny space. "Your burritos, Caroline, are exactly what this board meeting needs."

*C*hatting with Beverly only gave Scott a few minutes to get to breakfast on time. And this was one breakfast meeting he couldn't miss.

He darted down the hallway to the conference room, his mind going over the meeting schedule and ignoring the pain from his throbbing ankle. A new partnership position would be announced at the start of the meeting. His name and Ralph's would follow.

A humble speech thanking the current partners and the board might be in order. Or, maybe just an appreciative smile.

Damn.

His shirt dampened with sweat, and his heart leapt into his throat.

He'd have to just wing it and see what Ralph did. Hopefully, Ralph was his only competition, and the man didn't have a long-winded speech prepared.

Scott straightened his tie as he hobbled down the corridor. The smell of food already lingered in the air. The fare wasn't what he normally ate. He could guess the menu contained bacon and sausage, and not the tofu or turkey kind. There'd be overly sweetened tea there, as well.

Not that he could eat. His stomach was tied in knots.

"There you are." Joanna stood, nearly blocking the conference room doors. Her smile—wild and wicked—was not what he needed.

"Not today, Joanna."

The evil smirk widened. It was the same one she used whenever she wanted something. It had worked until she'd used it last year when they traveled to Playa Del Carmen, and she tried to get him to propose to her. He found her naked with a coworker a week later in the copy room.

"I thought some breakfast burritos would be nice this morning," she said in a singsong voice. "I convinced the meeting organizer to order from an old favorite restaurant we haven't used in some time."

"Whatever." He tried to sidestep her, but his ankle boot made maneuvering difficult.

Her smile widened even more. "I made sure to order the breakfast with a side of Caroline."

At the mention of her name, Scott found it hard to breathe, and his chest tightened in a this-is-not-going-to-be-good type of way. He stood in front of the door, afraid to even peek inside. "What are you talking about?"

She hooked her arm around his. "Let's go in and find out."

His heart raced—loud and heavily—in his chest, ringing the beats in his ears.

She leaned in and said in a low whisper, "You really should have invited me to the Christmas party."

The bitch.

If what she said were true, Caroline was on the premises, most likely behind the doors and in the conference room. There was no turning back. He had to attend this meeting.

He slowly walked into the room with Joanna pushing him from behind.

"Let's get something to eat." She took a dramatic sniff of the air. "It all smells so good."

There she was. Caroline's back was to the door, but he'd recognize her beautiful feminine frame, her shapely bottom, and her soft, kissable neck anywhere.

Before she could turn around, he darted as quickly as he could to the back of the room—not that there was a sufficient place to hide.

The chair even squeaked as he sat.

Damn it.

He held up a sheet of paper in front of his face. *Please don't turn around, please don't turn around,* he thought repeatedly.

Caroline checked the lit canisters one last time and gathered the lids to the bins in her trolley, focusing on her tasks. The meeting would begin in mere minutes, as soon as the big wigs arrived. Scott glanced at his watch. The time was only eight-fifty-five.

"What is on the menu?" Ralph asked. The man sat three chairs down from Scott, a grin spread wide on his face.

Caroline's eyes wandered the room as she mechanically read off the prepared menu of breakfast burritos, sunrise sausage enchiladas, bacon tortilla breakfast bake, and chilaquiles. Her gaze narrowed, focusing on one person then the next, and Scott's heart nearly burst from his chest as she glanced at each of them in a series that circled the room.

That's when he dove under the table—to ostensibly tie his shoes.

Guilt coated him, slick and heavy, as he stared at her white Ked sneakers and long legs. She still rattled off the menu, finishing with the beverage cart.

He wasn't ready to have this type of discussion with Caroline, at least not yet. She would hate him for lying to her and probably cause a scene right here in the conference room. He didn't need that bad publicity.

"Are you all right, Scott?" Ralph asked.

Scott winced at the sound of his name. At the very least, Ralph hadn't mentioned his last name. But he knew that would be coming any second.

Like a coward, he crouched under the table and watched as Caroline's gorgeous legs turned and he could tell she was no longer facing the table. But that wasn't the only thing he saw. Joanna was now shifting her legs, allowing her skirt to ride up, and giving him a view of her upper thighs.

"Scott, is there something I can help you with?" Joanna asked.

He was between a rock and a hard place, with a room of coworkers and the board members. At least he didn't see the senior partners in the room, at least not yet.

"What's the heat level of the dishes?"

Joanna was preventing Caroline from leaving the room, and tying his shoes shouldn't be taking this long.

The coworker next to him leaned over and found him sitting on the floor. "You okay?"

He grunted something of a 'yes, I'm fine' and then lifted his head slightly over the top of the table so he could see more of the room. He watched as Caroline left. The food containers looked disposable, so she probably wouldn't be back.

Letting out a sigh of relief, he climbed back into his chair just as Gilkrist walked into the room.

## 11

"Tate isn't fairing too well," Gilkrist said as he began the meeting, his voice wavering. "He officially resigned a week ago and we thought it best make the announcement at our monthly department meeting." He glanced over to the other two remaining senior partners, MacMillan and Larimer. "We know that Tate's wife is...," he glanced away for a moment and cleared his throat, "...she's going through a rough time. We've helped her with some arrangements and when the time comes...." He rubbed the back of his neck and took in a deep breath. "Tate's in hospice right now and we'll let you know when the funeral is."

MacMillan lay his hand on Gilkrist's back. "Naturally, we want you take the time you need to personally grieve."

The three men stood at the head of the table, their faces paled and their expressions grim.

"We need to offer candidates to the board for our next senior partner," Larimer now said. "Tate wants us to continue striving for justice and he wishes his successor all the best."

The information hit Scott square in the chest and he felt choked up. Tate had devoted his entire life to this company. He was the founding member, finding only the best lawyers and growing the firm until what it was today.

Having the seniors talk about him was like hearing that your Grandfather wasn't doing well and then having the grandchildren fight over the will.

"Our first candidate for the opening senior partner position is Ralph Larimer," Larimer said as he gave a half-hearted smile and gestured to Ralph. Scott could tell that the expression on Larimer's face wasn't one of judgement over Ralph but one of sorrow for his friend Tate. The smile held a 'life goes on' sadness to it. The two men had worked closely together for decades and Scott could see the concern in his eyes for Tate and his family.

It brought the entire push for making senior partner into perspective for Scott. This company felt like a home, not just a job, and a family member was dying.

"Ralph's qualifications are numerous," Larimer began. He then continued with a list of credentials as to why Ralph had been chosen as a senior partner candidate. Ralph didn't give a speech but smiled at the team members. A speech wouldn't have been appropriate since everyone knew why a new seat was becoming available, and at least Ralph knew how to read a room.

Even Joanna seemed to have lost her thunder.

Larimer yielded the floor to MacMillan. "We also have Scott Hollister, who has been with the company since..."

Scott allowed MacMillan's words to fade into the background. He knew his track record and tried to look as humble as possible for the honor of even being considered. The one thing he did do however was lean over and shake Ralph's hand. That at least did seem appropriate.

"With Tate's passing, one of these fine gentlemen will continue on in Tate's place. The board of directors has been notified of our candidates and the formal announcement will be made shortly." MacMillan gave some slight head nods and looked as if he was trying to think if he had said everything that needed to be said. "Our monthly meeting will begin in a few minutes."

"Please help yourself to some breakfast and spend a few minutes letting this news settle in. Remember the company holiday party is just around the corner. We'd like to see everyone there. Tate would want us to celebrate our successful year and to toast the new one coming in."

Gilkrist's voice cracked as he concluded the meeting and then left the conference room. Scott realized that at this year's party Gilkrist would be saying the toast, not Tate. Gilkrist was now the most senior member of the company. The toast would fall upon him.

"I didn't know Tate was doing that poorly," one of the men at the table said.

"Hospice?" a woman sitting next to the man said, shaking her head. "That means there isn't much time left. His poor wife."

The meeting continued with a mix of feelings from discussions about how Tate's wife was doing mixed with questions about when the new senior position would be filled. The conference room resembled a wake but with hope of new blood taking the company in a new direction.

The atmosphere was eerie. Scott found himself half talking about the potential promotion and half explaining about his ankle and what had happened. There was only one thing Scott wanted to do—well two. He wanted to make sure Caroline hadn't seen him and he wanted to pay Tate one last visit.

Once the official monthly meeting had ended— and the food containers were bare—Scott made sure Ralph and Joanna were busy and not following him —and after grabbing his gym bag filled with secondhand clothes—Scott left to run two errands since his calendar was light this morning.

Scott drove over to Tate's house. He had called ahead and spoke with Donna, Tate's wife. She sounded distant and withdrawn. The emotional toll weighed heavily on her. He didn't know if his presence would console her or not, but she seemed pleased on the phone that he wanted to come over.

Scott just knew it would be hard to say goodbye.

---

"Remember, if there is anything you need, don't hesitate to ask." Scott gave Donna a hug goodbye before leaving. The visit had been brief. Tate was weak and merely nodded toward Scott when Scott spoke to him, but there had been closure.

The visit was one of the hardest things Scott had ever done. Seeing his once robust boss now laying helplessly in his hospital-style bed, his wife at his side doing her best to make him comfortable, tore into him.

The senior partner position just wasn't a title, it had been a man's life. Scott wanted to continue taking the company in the same direction Tate had done for decades. He wanted to expand upon the man's legacy. He wanted to be worthy of succeeding one of his life's heroes.

He was grateful when he got into the car and

could shed a tear in private. He didn't want to fall apart in front of Donna. She needed everyone's strength right now.

He wasn't in a frame of mind to visit with Caroline, but seeing Tate put everything into perspective. Life was too short and Scott needed to take care of what was important.

Of course, he had to swing by his gym first and change his clothes.

Just before noon, he walked into the diner, wearing a nice pair of jeans, a new button-down shirt, and a fitted jacket. The ensemble was some of the best clothes he could find at Goodwill, and looked nothing like the Armani suit he'd been wearing earlier in the day while he cowered under that table in the boardroom.

He'd never thought *"I'm worth millions"* would be a turnoff to a woman, but he knew that Caroline would be hurt by his lies. By slowly dressing better each time he saw Caroline, he might be able to tell her the truth before too long.

That is, if she hadn't already seen him earlier that day.

The diner was a madhouse, with customers pretty much at every table. He eyed one waitress, figuring it was Caroline's friend Maria. She flashed him what appeared to be a fake smile.

"Welcome to *The Patio*. Have a seat anywhere," she said without really looking at him.

Reading her nametag, he had guessed right. She was the person Caroline had mentioned to him that she liked at the restaurant, her only true friend. If he could get Maria on his side, he might have an ally.

Scott took one of the last seats at the counter, noticing a bouquet of flowers nearby. The bunch of roses looked new and freshly delivered. "Is Caroline around?" he asked as nonchalantly as he could.

Maria wore bright red lipstick, too much eye shadow, and was now inspecting him from head to toe. She stared at his medical boot and her expression was one of recognition, as though she now knew who he was.

"Caroline's around." She glanced down at the big black boot he wore. "Are you Scott?"

He didn't like the tone of her voice, but he answered. "Yes."

"You'd better not break her heart." Maria leaned in. "That girl has a lot on her plate, taking care of her grandmother. She doesn't need to be taking care of a man—"

He quickly deciphered the words. 'you'd better not break her heart.' That told him that either Caroline hadn't seen him earlier at the office, or perhaps hadn't shared with Maria her findings. Since the woman said Caroline was around, he hoped it was the former and not the latter. "I don't plan to break her heart."

Maria stiffened. "Men never *intend* to break a

woman's heart. They just do." She stared at him for a brief moment and then said, "Caroline will be right out." She set a napkin and fresh silverware down for him and noticed him staring once again at the flowers. "They're pretty, aren't they?"

He glanced down at the place setting, trying not to notice the arrangement, which was filled with red roses. They sat on the counter and stuck out like a sore thumb.

"Caroline gets a lot of flowers delivered here." She glanced at the tables. "She used her last bunch to decorate the tables. Seems like a lot of men have their eyes on her," she said, and then walked over to help another customer.

A card stuck out from the vase, but he couldn't read the name on it from where he sat, although it didn't look to be Caroline's name. She had poured her heart out to him about not wanting a relationship. Was there an ex? Someone who wanted her back? Or was Maria lying to distance him from Caroline?

It didn't matter. He didn't think flowers would work to get Caroline's attention. She was more into big gestures, something from the heart with a personal touch.

Which was why he was here.

He caught Maria's attention as she walked past with a coffeepot.

"Do you know how much longer she'll be?" he asked again.

She glanced at his clothing, sizing him up. "You two going for a walk in the park or something?"

Her tone was condescending and filled with judgment, and all he'd done was walk into the place. He looked into her judgmental eyes and saw something in them. Not pity. Not hatred. Something else.

And then it hit him.

Maria was a snob.

She thought she was better than him. If she believed he was homeless, he was worthless in her eyes. A pain filled his chest as he thought back to Beverly and her equal assessment of him. Did people see such an ugliness in him?

Maria thought he was homeless and beneath her. He wouldn't be able to change her mind, so he played along. "It's a beautiful day, no reason not to enjoy it with a walk in the park." When her eyes narrowed in on him, he added, "I'll just wait for Caroline at a booth." He got up and walked with his hurt foot to the corner of the restaurant, Maria's makeup-marred face and eyes rimmed with heavy eyeliner following him.

A sneer appeared on her face before she turned and walked away.

Caroline had only told him of how wonderful Maria had been, and what a good friend she was. He could only assume that her gruff treatment of him was just her way of protecting Caroline. He couldn't fault Maria for that.

And then he saw Caroline entering the main dining hall from the kitchen, her hair curling from beneath a warm cap and her coat and matching scarf clenched in her hand. She didn't look upset, just cold as though she had been doing deliveries all morning. Her cheeks were weather worn by the wintry air, but her eyes were not red and puffy from crying. She must not have seen him earlier as he cowered under the conference room table.

He let out the breath he didn't know he was holding, stood and approached her. "I thought I would surprise you." He looked at her outfit. She still wore her uniform, but no apron. "Are you off work?"

"Hey, you!" Her fresh, clean face held a smile that looked genuine. She wrapped her arms around him and leaned in.

He sniffed the air and took in her perfume. The scent of flowers mixed with the heavy smell of the fried food the cook had made earlier that day, but she still smelled wonderful.

Gently touching the nape of her neck, he kissed her waiting, soft lips. They were moist and sweet like berries with promises of passion.

She hadn't seen him earlier. A heavy weight lifted from his chest and a bubble of near giddiness filled him.

"I didn't think I'd see you today."

He glanced down at her coat. "Are you off work already?"

She smiled and nodded her head. "I pulled the morning delivery shift. Did you want to go out for lunch?"

An invite to another date. He was in the clear. "I was hoping you'd suggest that."

"I have an idea." She walked back to the counter filled with to-go orders and pulled a bag from beneath the cabinet. "I'm ready."

---

*C*aroline could feel Maria's eyes burning a hole in the back of her head as she headed out of the diner. Their talk earlier of aiming higher and finding a man with a bankroll was still etched in her mind.

Regardless, she had to admit that Scott cleaned up well. His jacket had a stain or two, but he looked perfectly acceptable for their date.

Scott was what she needed.

More importantly, who she wanted.

The cool air caressed her cheeks as they made their way outside. There wasn't a cloud in the sky, and the weather had warmed up since this morning. Crisp days like this where the weather was cool but not overly cold were the best winter could offer.

"I have some protein bars in my purse. We can

eat them by the lake. We should be safe as long as we don't fall in," she said, teasing him.

He limped to the path that led them to the center of the park with Caroline holding onto his arm.

"Is your foot feeling okay?"

"It's not going to keep me from our date." He walked her down the path to a quiet area with benches.

His soulful blue eyes and the smile he wore with his five-o'clock-shadowed face told her one thing. This was a man she could totally fall for.

She held up the small paper bag. "I collected some old tortillas from the restaurant. I thought we'd feed the ducks." Instantly, the fowl began swimming over in anticipation of a meal.

Caroline opened the bag and handed a slice of tortilla to Scott. It probably wasn't the best food to feed the birds, but she couldn't let food dropped to the floor or left in tortilla warmers go to waste.

They began feeding the ducks when Scott pulled out his phone. He snapped a picture of her feeding them, but then hit the button so the phone's camera lens rotated on them. "Let's take a selfie together."

She leaned in. It was too soon in their relationship, but she had always wanted to send out Christmas cards with a family portrait on them. Collect them all in a special scrapbook each year and then look through the book later to see your family grow up. To see her and her husband still in love over decades.

Scott showed her the image he had captured. Beautiful blue sky, snow-covered trees in the background, and the two of them perfectly centered in the picture—all smiles and truly happy.

"Now, that's definitely a keeper," he said, returning the phone to his pocket.

"Thanks for driving me to visit my grandmother the other day. I really appreciate it."

"No problem." Scott tore a piece of the tortilla and tossed it into the lake. "How often do you go there?"

*'Not often enough,'* she thought. "As often as I can." Shredding her own tortilla into thin strips, she added, "My grandmother took care of me after my mother was killed in a car accident."

She recognized the expression on Scott's face. It was the same one everyone gave her when they found her mother died. Shock mixed with pity mixed with concern.

She hated that look.

His hand touched her leg and gave her a reassuring pat. "And now your grandmother doesn't know who you are."

Looking into her grandmother's eyes and, somedays, knowing no one was home tore into her. No one prepares you for that. You see such things on television, in the movies, and in books, but to have it happen in real life...no one is really prepared for such a thing. Caroline shrugged. "Some days she remembers me."

"Do you have any brothers or sisters?"

"It's just me." She reached in her purse and pulled out the promised breakfast bars. She had been running delivery all morning, smelling the delicious food in her car, and she was quite hungry. "Chocolate and peanut butter."

He took the offering. His arm was already around her back, but now he pulled her in tightly. She leaned her head on his chest. The closeness of the hug felt reassuring, and she needed that.

"It's just sad to see my grandmother withering away. She never wanted to live like this."

He stroked her hair, his fingers running through, loosening her failing ponytail. "I'm sure she appreciates what you've done."

"It's just not enough." She resumed tearing up more tortillas and tossed them to the awaiting ducks. She didn't want to burden him with her problems, but needed to share. She had told Maria most of her issues, but not the one that lay heaviest on her mind. "My grandmother has the smallest room in the place, and her care costs nearly five thousand dollars a month."

"That's sixty thousand a year after taxes," he said after a brief pause. His soft voice filled with shock as it blew against her ear.

She straightened her back and pulled away enough to make eye contact with him. "Growing old in this country is hard on the ones who have to take care of the elderly."

His eyes held a concern for her that she rarely received from others. Maria would listen to her problems and wanted to help, but there was more from Scott—like he felt her pain. "I'd like to help."

She glanced at her watch. Her initial plan was to eat her protein bar on the subway as she went to job number two. She was going to be late but really needed a break. Sitting with Scott on the bench was the only reprieve she would have to a very long and tedious day. She turned and faced him. "That's sweet of you to offer, but how can you help?"

A half smile appeared and there was a glint in his eyes, like the one her grandmother would have on Christmas morning when she would hand Caroline her present and tell her to open it up. "I have some money set aside," he said. "It's yours if you want it."

They had never talked about money, or really about his job in the mailroom at a law firm. He probably struggled as much as she did to make ends meet. "No. That's very kind of you, but I can't take your money."

"I'd like to help." His face pinched for a moment, but then he said, "I have some odds and ends that need to be done. Maybe I could pay you for doing them?"

Odds and ends? She saw right through that, but it was sweet of him. "You don't need to make up something for me to do just so you can pay me…"

"But I really do need a few things taken care of." His voice sounded hopeful and his puppy-dog eyes looked pleading. "You'd be helping me out."

Even if she did believe him, which she didn't since he was the type of man who would do anything to help, she said, "I don't have any extra time to do another job."

"Well…," he said, as though fishing for an answer. "The job I need to have done won't take up much time and you don't have to go anywhere to do it."

"Sounds made up."

He chuckled. "I'm getting there. I need a minute to think of something."

She giggled and nestled more into him.

"I was wondering if you'd be free this Saturday night. There's a dinner party and…"

"This Saturday?" She glanced up at him with saddened eyes. "I just picked up some seasonal work. In fact, I was going to let you know that I was going to be extra busy soon and unable to see you—not that I don't want to spend time with you. I just…I have to work this Saturday night."

"It's fine. You're a busy woman." He looked as though he could appreciate someone who worked hard and had a good work ethic. She imagined he was the same way at his job. "What is this extra job you're picking up?

"It's a support bartender for a holiday party."

His smile spread across his face. "You bartend?"

"No, but they don't know that." She let out a nervous chuckle. "A friend set it up and swore that it was easy work with good pay."

"That will be something like your fourth job. I do have some money. Let me help."

He was adorable for wanting to ease her financial problems, but she couldn't be a burden to someone else. "You are helping. Just being yourself and comforting me is enough. You have no idea how good it feels to trust someone enough to share things with."

## 12

*S*cott drove away from the park, inwardly cursing at himself.

"I'm independently wealthy. Please let me help."

Just seven little words.

Why couldn't he have come clean and just tell her? He could solve all of her financial problems, be her knight in shining armor, and they could live in a castle if they wanted to.

He knew why he didn't confess the truth to her. She would hate him for lying to her, and he was a coward. She was hard-working and independent. The women he knew sponged off him and would consider it a perk for dating him.

Caroline had too much integrity.

Every time he saw her, held her, made love to her. He was lying to her. His plan to gradually build himself up to an employed, doing well financially person needed to go slower. It couldn't span days, it needed weeks. Weeks he didn't have.

And, damn it, he was about to invite her to the Christmas party. He had to go with Beverly's plan, no matter how much he hated hiring out a date.

He entered the five-star restaurant and walked past the hostess, all the while thinking of what type of super easy job he could employ Caroline to do for him that wouldn't seem too made up or give her an insight as to who he really was. It had to be something she could do at her home, something that wouldn't take too much time, and something that wouldn't distract her from anything else she was doing.

But, how much could he pay her? The rate couldn't be too much, but it had to be enough to help.

He was running late, and he knew Beverly and his 'date' were already here, so he'd have to think of something for Caroline to do later.

He saw them in the back of the restaurant, Beverly waiving her arms as though the task of finding them in the crowd would prove too difficult for someone with his IQ.

"Sorry I'm late."

"Scott, I'd like for you to meet Ms. Paster."

Ms. Paster was picture perfect, a size-two goddess with dark, long hair, and Mediterranean brown skin. Long, curly, brunette hair that framed her face and warm, brown eyes. She certainly fit the mold for being model pretty.

"Call me Ilene." She held out her hand and gave him a delicate handshake. Her manicured fingernails seemed too long for her to do any real work. How did she tie shoe laces? Type? Dial a phone?

Those nails were good for only one thing, and he enjoyed the sensation all too well. He just didn't want anyone other than Caroline digging those daggers at his back as he brought her, and only her, to climax.

He wasn't sure why that bothered him. After all, Ilene was just eye-candy, and supposedly they had been lovers for the past four months.

She twirled a brunette curl with her dainty fingers.

"We already ordered, and I took the liberty of ordering for you," Beverly said. Naturally, with a hefty hourly price tag, there was no reason to waste any time.

"Thanks, Bev." He sat next to Bev and studied his proposed girlfriend. "What kind of," he couldn't think of a better word, so he said, "services do you offer."

She smiled and let her business side come out, her face changing from a smiling porcelain doll to a money-savvy woman. "I can be whatever kind of woman you want me to be. Since the service mentioned a holiday party, I'm assuming it's a black-tie affair, expensive dining, and an A-game killer dress type of event."

Ilene was tall, leggy, and accommodating, in a plastic type of way.

"It is a premium affair. Posh and elegant," Bev said.

Ilene fell into the range of near supermodel status. Perfect hair, perfect nails, perfect teeth. He would never say she was a perfect ten because that would be downgrading her outer beauty.

He knew a high-priced hooker when he saw one.

The waitress arrived with their meals, setting each respectively in front of them. Ilene had ordered the most expensive meal on the menu, surf-n-turf with the steak served rare. He couldn't remember the last time he'd eaten red meat, preferring grilled fish instead.

In his past, he wouldn't have minded sharing a meal with such eye candy, and he wasn't sure when the change had occurred, but he felt as if Ilene sat too close. She cut into the flesh of her meal, and he watched her plate fill with blood.

It was enough to make him sick. But he smiled politely as she took a nibble of a bite. In between eating, she mentioned past jobs and her expertise. She did say that she had no references other than her five-star rating with the agency. The clientele there would certainly want to remain anonymous. He could understand that.

226

He wanted to be anywhere else, especially since Ilene's hand was now midway up his thigh and climbing steadily north.

Was it her job to rub herself all over him? Or was it genuine interest? Perhaps her attraction was due to the fact that she assumed his bank account could accommodate even her high standards?

"The party is this Saturday night at the Blaisdale Hotel, just north of the Midland Bridge. Cocktails will begin promptly at 7:00 p.m. followed by dinner at 8:00." Beverly sat the tickets on the white linen tablecloth. "I've already hired a limo that will pick up Scott thirty minutes ahead of time at the office."

Ilene leaned closer to Scott, her breath reeking of cigarettes. Her purple eye shadow and smoke eyeliner brought out her eyes, and she batted what he suspected were false eyelashes at him. "Should I be with Scott at that time?"

"Yes. No one will be at the office, so please be there on time for the pickup." Bev nodded and then glanced over at Scott. "I called the usual limo service."

He noticed a gleam in Ilene's eye as she took note of the fact that they had a *usual* limo service. She gazed at him, and her smile held a suggestive and seductive slant. It told him one thing. Money mattered.

"A limo. That'll be cozy and convenient." Her voice was pitched in a breathy, sexy kind of way, which made him wonder if any woman really talked like that.

He gazed into her brown eyes, and in the most matter-of-fact tone he could muster, he asked, "Ilene, will you be sucking my dick in the limo before the party, or would you prefer to do it afterward?"

She didn't even blink.

Her arm was already snaking around his, so she held him closer and leaned forward. "You're the client. It's whatever you want," she whispered in his ear so Bev couldn't hear.

And that was all the information he needed.

His caliber of women had never been high in the past, even he could admit that. But he had never stooped so low as to pay for sex.

Hell, he never had to.

"If you ladies will excuse me." He tried to untangle himself from Ilene and shift in the booth closer to Bev, but Bev made no effort to move out of his way.

"Ilene," Bev said in a nearly singsong voice, "would you mind giving me and Scott a few minutes alone?"

The woman left without issue and was barely out of earshot before Bev pointed her finger and jabbed him by the lapel of his suit jacket. "Listen. I don't know what's going on, but you'd better get on board with this plan."

Nodding in the direction Ilene had headed, Bev added, "Ilene is a professional. She'll get the job done and help you get the partnership. You just have to play ball."

"She's only interested in me because I'm paying her seven hundred dollars an hour."

"We're paying her *eight* hundred an hour, and I don't care if she sucks your dick or not. You will not come across as a playboy during this party."

Unbelievable. He wondered if Beverly was simply blinded by the possibility of the partner promotion, or if she truly didn't see the irony of the situation. "You want me to prove I'm not a player by playing this game and bringing someone like her to the party?"

"Ilene will say and do all the correct things. I'll make sure of that." Beverly grabbed her handbag from beside her and pulled out a huge folder. "I have examples to show her of how she should dress." Bev flipped through the notes. "I have suggested career options for her to embody, a list of suitable topics to discuss, and, of course, the story of how the two of you met."

Paper-doll perfect.

He was curious, so he had to ask, "How did we meet?"

"While on vacation last year in Playa Del Carmen."

He remembered that trip. Fun in the sun turned

out to be rainy and depressing. Two days into his weeklong vacation with Joanna, and he'd come back. Her constant complaining was too much in confined quarters.

"So, while I was vacationing with my last girl-friend, I met Ilene, got her phone number, and got together with her a few months ago?" He shook his head and gave Beverly a deadpan expression. "Player."

Beverly's eyes dropped down to the sheet of paper. "Good point. I can revise it so that the two of you met at a charity event four months ago."

"So now Ilene is going to pretend to be interested in charity work? The diamond necklace she's wearing could feed a family of five for a year, maybe two. I thought you wanted me to bring a woman of quality to the party."

"Believe me, eight-hundred an hour is quality."

"I think the partners would disagree."

His mind flooded with images of Caroline. The sweet way she smiled when she was happy, the lilt of her voice when she laughed, and the honest integrity she held in her heart. She was quality.

A pang of guilt stabbed him in the gut. Caroline's hair, no matter how clean it was, always smelled of the diner. Her fingernails were always unpolished and short. And she wouldn't be able to answer the question of where she'd gotten her degree and in what field was she working.

A blue-collar individual never impressed in the white-collar world, and he knew it.

Plus, what if someone from his company recognized her from the breakfast fiasco this morning?

No. It was too dangerous to bring her. His only choice was Ilene.

Beverly frowned and showed her frustration. "If it will make a difference, I'll dress Ilene in an apron and send her to your office with a handmade tuna fish sandwich for lunch the next day, making sure her hair is in curlers."

And that was the stereotype he wanted to avoid. "I hate tuna fish. Besides, I doubt she knows how to make a sack lunch."

Bev's eyes narrowed. "The point is, she's versatile and can be molded into whatever we need her to be."

Plastic usually was malleable.

He wanted a real marriage, with lots of kids and the white picket fence. If only Caroline weren't a waitress. Thinking about their past conversations, he remembered she had briefly mentioned dropping out of school, but had said she had no intentions of going back anytime soon. She'd never talked about work options, and he wondered if she had any career ambitions at all.

Even a socialite, like Lovey Howell, volunteering all the time would be better than someone who served the public at a restaurant.

"Time is running out on this promotion. We need

to work quickly. Ilene is all we have." Bev's formidable stare pierced him. It was the don't-hide-anything-from-me glare that had always forced him as a child to confess, even to things he wasn't guilty of. "Is there another woman you're seeing that we can work with?"

Someone more pliable and custom-fit to impress the bosses?

No.

"I don't think I really need to be here for the rest of the prep work. You seem to have the hang of arranging my life just fine." The booth was free on his right side, so he began scooting himself out, but Bev grabbed his arm.

"What the hell has gotten into you? Ilene is nothing more than a business contract. You sign contracts every day. If you don't like her for the part of your girlfriend, we can find someone else, but she's what we have for this Christmas party."

Caroline wasn't corporate material, she was busy the night of the party, and he didn't want to rush to tell her the truth. He scooted out of the booth. "Get Ilene ready. I'm sure she'll impress the company."

---

*C*aroline walked over to check her mailbox. Everyone else got Christmas cards or catalogs in the mail. She only got bills.

She opened the metal box and letters nearly fell out. She had checked the mail only yesterday but it seemed like every business wanted to send out some type of spammy postcard or flyer.

She glanced through the mail. Spam. Spam. Spend your money on this stupid product. Spam. New dentist in town. Come join our Synagogue?

Too many trees die for this crap every day.

A card from Avalon? Hopefully it was just Season's Greetings and not a bill, or worse. A notice insisting her grandmother move out before the holidays would not be appreciated right now.

The last letter was another card. No return address was written on it, but the envelope looked like a Christmas card. Someone actually sent her a card in the mail?

She placed all her mail in her bag and walked the short distance to the bus stop. The metal seat was dry on one end and it felt cold as she sat down. Since no one else sat with her, she figured she had a while to wait for the bus.

She had some time, so she took a deep breath and opened the card from Avalon. It had a wreath on the front and a generic 'Happy Holidays' sentiment. She opened it to find a lengthy letter.

Taking a deep breath to prepare herself for terrible news, she began reading the card with her eyes quickly scanning for the bad news.

'Congratulations' was the first word that caught

her attention. 'Raffle drawing' and 'free rent' were next. Her heart raced as she quickly read the letter. Evidently there was a holiday drawing and she had won first prize.

She felt the wind knocked out of her when she discovered she had won her grandmother a free month of rent! January would be paid for her and that meant thousands of dollars, that she didn't have, wouldn't have to be put on another credit card.

A tear escaped. This meant that not only would she save money, but Avalon wasn't kicking her grandmother out. At least, not this month.

She looked up at the sky and whispered, 'thank you'.

Today was a good day.

She now studied the second card. If she were on a roll, it too would be good news. But what if she were pressing her luck and the universe needed to balance out the good news from Avalon?

She opened the card anyway.

The image was of two cuddling snowbirds sitting in a snow-covered tree. The tree was decorated with bright colors and silver glitter. Her eyes immediately darted to the signature once she opened the card. Scott sent it to her. Her face flushed with warmth. He was thinking of her.

She opened the letter and five crisp one hundred-dollar bills were inside. She grabbed ahold of them before the wind could pick up, and before anyone could sit on the bench with her and see how much money she held.

*'My dearest Caroline,'* it began. Scott wrote about how much he missed her and wanted to see her. He didn't type it, he hand wrote the card. That was a nice touch. His beautiful penmanship swirled around and remained perfectly in the lines.

Everything about this man was gorgeous.

He then explained how he could get her some quick holiday cash. A lawyer at his company needed someone to monitor an app. The job was easy and all Caroline had to do was download an app to her phone, check it a few times a day, and anytime a stock with the company letter of SHP popped up she needed to text Scott the stock price. He then went on to say that the SHP company would probably only be listed once a day and she only needed to keep her phone handy and if a notification came in to let him know.

Holy shit.

She counted the bills again. Five hundred dollars?

Her heart raced. She really couldn't keep the money, but Scott wouldn't have sent her this job if he didn't want her to have it.

Scott should have kept this job for himself. This really was an easy gig and she was sure he could also use the money.

Who couldn't use hundreds of dollars literally just falling into your lap?

She placed the bills in her purse and read the instructions on downloading the app, making sure her push notifications, alerts, and location were set so she'd see any updates come in.

She wouldn't let him down. The lawyer that paid this kind of money for the stock info probably needed this info as soon as possible. She'd be on top of it.

She needed to give Scott a big 'thank you' the next time she saw him. She missed him terribly, but holiday business had picked up at the restaurant. People tended to be more generous during the gift-giving season and that meant bigger tips.

Not that she'd ever bring home five hundred dollars in tip money on any single day at the restaurant. But this stock money and what she was earning at her other temp job would probably be enough to pay for her car. Getting her car back, and having it actually run, would be so nice right now.

She had no idea how to bartend and felt completely out of her element. Fortunately, the Blaisdale Hotel—the party venue—sat at the intersection of the subway and a bus stop. Perfect since her car wouldn't be ready until tomorrow.

This Christmas party seemed important to the company sponsoring it. Big celebration. Big company. Big tips.

She needed big tips.

The bus arrived and took her to where she needed to go. She then entered the hotel and its brilliance amazed her. Many famous people tended to stay at the landmark hotel, which was built decades ago. Stars and rich businessmen liked staying here, that is, unless they wanted a glitzier place like Trump Tower. The elegant atmosphere of the Blaisdale oozed sophistication and class with its decadent furnishings and decorated interior. She had always wanted to stay in a place like this but would never be able to afford it.

The packed lobby held many people, but she managed her way through the crowd to the concierge desk. The hotel employee manning the desk became busy with a guest, so she quietly read the screen behind him. The monitor scrolled a list of parties and events the hotel currently hosted and their locations within the building.

After a minute the Tate Law firm name appeared. Holiday Party, Ballroom Sierra.

She just had to find that room now.

Glancing toward the elevators, she discovered a sign for Ballrooms Indigo and Topaz. The rooms looked small and the names weren't going in alphabetical order, so she wasn't sure where Sierra would be. The concierge was still busy, so she walked closer to the stairs and around the corner. There she finally found Sierra. Tightly tucked away and somewhat private, but it was the largest of the ballrooms judging by the two double sided doors that led into the room.

Taking a deep breath, she knew that half the effort of a pickup job like this was finding the place, dressing the part (her hand straightened the apron of her green uniform), and being on time. Check, check, and check.

She didn't have much experience in party hosting, but the pay was good—especially since Ralph had suggested she pick up the empty position of sub-bartender and help out at the last minute. She didn't even know that a title of sub-bartender even existed.

Thank goodness she'd only be serving soda, wine, and beer. If someone asked her to make a Bloody Mary or some other type of drink she had never even heard of, the head bartender, would fire her for sure.

A few hours remained until the party would begin, so she followed the instructions she had received over the phone and walked to some set-up tables and a beverage stand that were in the ballroom. Crates of alcohol stood behind the table and she wondered where everyone was.

A door opened behind her with a loud thunk and she saw two men walking in, each with a trolley of alcohol cases. They both wore the same green-aproned uniform, so she figured she had found the right place.

"You Caroline?" the taller of the two asked. When she shook her head, he put the trolley down and extended his hand. "I'm Dave. We spoke on the phone."

He looked nothing like he had sounded when he had called her. Wrinkles creased heavily in his face and he appeared to be much older than she had assumed. He did own the bar that was providing the alcohol for the event, so she should have assumed he'd be at least in his fifties.

Dave gave a set of car keys to the other man, who was blond and slim. The two talked briefly and Caroline realized the second man was autistic. He resembled Dave and was much younger, possibly his son. The man unloaded his trolley and then left, presumably to fetch more cases.

"Let me explain your duties." He went to a table and picked up a clipboard. "This room holds up to two-hundred people," he said, waving his hand to indicate the room. "Tables will be set up by my son in that corner and in this middle area."

So, she had been right. A family business. She always thought businesses where loved ones help each other were the best ones. She certainly didn't have a family business to work. Would never inherit a well-began startup or even millions from the hard work of ancestors. She could always dream, but, other than winning the lottery, she had to make it on her own.

Dave described her duties, where she would be working, and gave her advice on how to engage the customer without being intrusive. He also described how to work the machines, where the cooler was, and drink extras they had brought—such as olives—were and how to store them.

There were a lot of little details to remember. Dave's son finished the table setup and he and Dave disappeared to set up for a second location else-where—a hospitality suite upstairs—leaving her alone to finish up this room. A few other bartenders had arrived, but they too went upstairs with Dave.

Feeling a little claustrophobic in the vast ball-room, she became so nervous that she began sweating in the cool 65 degrees she figured the room was chilled at.

She plugged in the ice bath to keep the bottles and cans cold. The refrigerator was already plugged in and chilling. The first thing Dave told her to do was to find the bags of pre-sliced lemons, limes, pineapples, and cucumbers and put them into the fridge.

She wondered what type of drink the cucumbers were for. It really didn't sound at all appealing.

Next on her list was to open a case of olives, cocktail onions, and maraschino cherries, if she could find the boxes labeled as such. She never would have believed a temporary bar setup in a big hotel for a fancy Christmas party would be so detailed.

Finding another case of wine, she opened it and then set down the box cutter.

One by one, she lifted bottles of what she assumed were expensive wine out. She then sat them behind the bar, counting as she did to make sure that five were placed in the ice baths and another five lay behind the counter.

"Excuse me," a disembodied and gruff voice said.

Her heart jumped, and she nearly dropped a bottle. She turned and saw an elderly gentleman wearing a tuxedo standing in front of the bar. This was her first customer, and the bar didn't open for a while yet.

"I didn't mean to startle you, dear."

She held her hand to her chest. "I just wasn't expecting someone behind me." She set the bottle of wine down on the counter. "May I help you?"

The old man—gray-haired and fatherly looking —bellied up to the bar and stared at her. "Not too many people these days use the word *may*."

She grabbed two more bottles of wine from the case, not understanding what he was talking about. "Excuse me?"

He let out a slight chuckle and waved his hand toward the boxes of alcohol, which lay stacked on the floor. "Can you hand me a bottle of single-malt scotch?"

Shit.

She didn't know which crate held the scotch. She didn't know the brands the party organizers had ordered. She didn't even know what type of trouble —if any—she'd get into handing out hard liquor without a bartender's license. This was exactly why she was only allowed to hand out soda, beer, and wine.

"Sir, the bar isn't quite ready." She looked at her watch. "The party doesn't even start its cocktail hour for another two hours."

She had so much work left to do and had lied when Dave asked over the phone if she had any bartending experience. Ralph had said the job was hers if she wanted it, and she didn't expect the interview. If it hadn't been for Ralph's insistence that this was going to be one of the simplest, and easiest, ways for her to make a lot of holiday money she wouldn't have agreed to do so.

Lying was never a good idea, but she needed the fast cash to pay the mechanic tomorrow.

Not that that was a good excuse.

She grabbed a 12-pack of soda from a stack, put it on the bar, and opened it. "If you wouldn't mind coming back later sir, I'm sure the bartender can serve you then."

Giving him her best please-let-me-work smile, she tried to remember everything Dave had told her to do. Ice, wine, beer, soda. She searched for the large can of olives to open and put into the mini-fridge.

"My name is Bob." He gestured around the room with his hand. "I put on this shindig each year for my company."

He wasn't going to leave, even without a barstool to sit on, his feet were firmly planted at her station. Just like Mr. Sweeney at the restaurant, except this older man wore a tuxedo, had money, and had paid for her to be here.

His hand extended, so she wiped her hand clean on a bar cloth and shook it, knowing that her grandmother would insist that she show some manners. "I'm Caroline. Nice to meet you."

"Is someone setting up the hospitality suite upstairs?"

Bob must have been one of the big bosses Dave had told her not to talk to. Dave's would handle everything for the elite get-together upstairs since they were actually licensed.

There was no one nearby who was licensed or who knew the difference between single-malt and double-malt scotch.

Shit.

"The room upstairs will be set up very soon, sir."

His eyebrow rose in a manner that suggested he saw completely through her inexperience. "Is this your first-time tending bar?"

She glanced around at her station, which should

have been more set up by now. The man's soft smile and compassionate eyes convinced her to tell the truth. "Is it that obvious?"

He pointed to the machine behind her. "Did you put salt in the ice bath? It keeps the ice from melting too fast."

Crap. Dave had specifically told her to do that.

"Thanks." Her voice was a bit sheepish, and she grabbed the bag of salt. "A customer from a restaurant where I work set this up for me." She shrugged. "I need some extra cash to fix my car."

She wasn't sure why she'd shared that with him. He had a friendly face, but usually the bartender listened to the customers, not the other way around.

As she searched for the can opener, she asked, "Are you the boss of this company?"

A beam of pride crossed his face. "One of four," he said with a voice filled with a hint of humility. She liked that he didn't boast or take full credit. One person rarely built an empire, and, judging by the ritz of the party, the man's company was doing very well.

She gazed over at the box labeled scotch, still unopened. "The bartender just went to the van with his partner, and the wait staff won't be here for another twenty minutes." She'd have much rather been a member of the wait staff but Ralph said the hotel took care of that and he couldn't get her that position. Tending the beer and wine bar was more money per hour, but she didn't exactly know what to do.

"I know I'm early for the party. I like to inspect things. Make sure everything is running smoothly and set up for later."

"They're bringing in more cases of champagne for a toast later. I'm guessing that there is a big announcement tonight." She figured Bob wouldn't be able to tell her anything private about the company, but small talk was not one of her best suits.

"The Champaign is to toast the work of a man who is leaving the company soon."

His voice sounded sad, so she asked, "Retiring or just moving on?"

He took a deep breath and let it out slow and sad. "Dying. The toast is to his life and dedication as one of our senior partners."

She turned and looked into Bob's saddened eyes. "I'm so sorry. I guess he's one of the four, someone special and important to you."

He nodded and Caroline really wanted to help him, or, at least, make the night easier for him. "Dave will be back soon. I'm sure he can get you your scotch. I'm not licensed to hand out alcohol."

She couldn't find the can opener, and she knew Dave had brought three of them. As she kept searching, the man stared at her. His gaze made her uncomfortable. It was just like when Mr. Sweeney sat quietly on his counter stool, desperate for some company.

"Let me guess. You're a single mother with two jobs."

She felt a sweet smile, subtle and light, crossing her face. "No children, not yet. But I am single with *three* jobs. Plus," she said, motioning around the bar, "some pickup work here and there."

His smile widened, and there was a twinkle in his eye. "I admire women who work hard and get the job done."

It felt a bit eerie. Caroline wasn't sure if he was hitting on her or not. She knew that patrons typically hit on bartenders, but honestly, Caroline hadn't expected it with her first customer. "I just do what needs to be done," she said.

The dimples in his cheeks grew deeper as his smile widened. "You remind me of my mother. She was a petite blonde like you, hardworking and doing what needed to be done."

A heaviness in her chest lifted, knowing that he wasn't actually hitting on her. Small talk was good. "I'll take that as a compliment."

"Are you dating anyone? I imagine a beautiful woman like you has her dance card filled."

She felt a blush warm her cheeks. She was dating Scott and didn't want to hurt the old man's feelings; plus, as charming as he was, he was definitely not her type.

"If you were twenty years younger, you might turn my head," she said, flirting with the man. Maria had always told her that giving the impression of being sweet on the customers garnered bigger tips at the restaurant, and it worked. Being a bartender? She figured the alcohol would make the job easier. In any case, she figured she could handle Bob.

He waved his hand dismissively and looked like a young schoolboy asking a girl out on a date for the first time.

"Twenty years younger? I'm flattered, my dear. But it'd be more like forty years I think."

"MacMillan, there you are." A voice—low and booming—sounded from the opposite side of the room.

Another man, this one older and in a wheelchair, entered the bar. He was followed by the head bartender, Dave, pushing a trolley of linens for the tables.

Caroline quickly went back to work, making up for lost time, searching again for a can opener.

"Mr. MacMillan. Mr. Gilkrist. We'll have your suite ready in just a few minutes." Dave shook both of their hands and then went to the bar where he grabbed the box labeled *hospitality suite* and set it aside. He then found another one and placed it on top of the first.

He approached Caroline and whispered, "Those are the fat cats, and they're early. Look for all the boxes marked for the suite upstairs, and make sure the team takes them up."

She dropped what she was doing and began reading the sides of all the boxes, walking around the bar and searching while Dave opened a case of scotch and got out two glasses.

"Your man sounds reasonable," Gilkrist said, rubbing his chin, his thoughtful expression showing he was considering the option. "But you know Larimer wants his..." Gilkrist said, pausing. "His nephew in the position."

Caroline's ears perked up. Larimer was Ralph's last name. Did he have a nephew working with him at the company?

MacMillan leaned in; one eyebrow raised. "What's your honest opinion of Ralph?"

At the mention of her customer's name, Caroline listened more intently. They were talking about her friend. He was the nephew.

Gilkrist rubbed his forehead and shook his head. "The man is a mediocre lawyer, and spineless to boot." His face hardened. "Larimer has given the boy too many breaks."

Caroline worked quickly and efficiently, finding not only two more boxes but also a bag of lemons and olives in the refrigerator for the suite. Over the sound of Dave frantically working, she listened in on Bob's conversation.

"What we need is someone with gumption."

Gilkrist wheeled himself up to the bar just as Dave finished preparing two glasses of scotch for them. "No one is willing to take a stand these days and make a statement about how they really feel. Everyone is too damn worried about being politically correct and fitting in."

"Agreed," MacMillan said. "What we need is some new blood who is willing to take some risks."

The boys club left the room, still talking and ignoring her completely. People rarely noticed the help and talked absently in front of them. Patrons at the restaurant talked about their bad jobs, problem kids, and divorce settlements in front of her all the time.

Since he had gotten her this job, she owed Ralph the curtesy of spreading this little bit of gossip.

## 13

*S*cott could do without an evening in hell, but here he was anyway.

Sitting in the limo, he choked on the stench of perfume and cigarettes which radiated off his date. There was some hairspray mixed in which also mingled with the scent of his slight aftershave and cologne, so he needed to crack open a window to breath. Ilene sat next to him and adjusted the car vent to blow air directly on him. He stared out the window enjoying the fresh air.

He didn't like wearing rented clothes, and always thought renting a tuxedo was lower class, so he bought one and had it tailor made. His tuxedo was a perfect fit. It was the only thing that felt right tonight.

He knew after working her extra job that Caroline was most likely be at home, all alone. He could see her sitting at her computer, probably wearing her pajamas with her hair pulled back into a ponytail as she answered math problems until the wee hours of the night.

What he wouldn't give to be sitting on the couch next to her.

The fact that she could stomach doing Algebra and Geometry for hours each day impressed him. Those were classes from high school that he had long, and gratefully, forgotten.

Caroline worked too hard.

And he was sure there was no food in her refrigerator, which was why he had ordered a pre-paid pizza to be delivered later in the night. Her favorite was Canadian bacon and pineapple, but she usually ate cheese because the cost was cheaper—especially with a coupon.

He sent her a text to let her know to expect the food around midnight, but he hadn't heard back from her yet. There was one sure-fire way of getting her attention though.

It was time once again, so he pulled out his phone and opened up his fake stock app. He typed in SHP, a made-up stock that had his initials of Scott Phillip Hollister, and typed in a price. He had gotten the idea for the app from his monogrammed bathroom towel set, and a good friend in the IT department created it for him. Shire PLC held the real SHP label, but he doubted Caroline would notice that his made-up prices didn't match the company's real values on the stock market.

The fake stock was going to make an up-tick in the market and move up a quarter a share.

He hit send and a moment later he received a screenshot from Caroline and a message saying the price had just come in. There was also a note saying she was super busy but would talk with him later.

Her apron was probably tight around her waist and she was serving food somewhere.

Just thinking of her put a smile on his face.

If he were with her, he'd keep her up all night with something a hell of a lot more interesting than serving food. He thought of her luscious lips, her quivering thighs as he pleasured her, and her warm caresses.

On a cold night like this, he'd take her into the bathtub filled with bubbles. The two of them would either make love in the water or on the bathroom mat, too eager to move to the bed.

He shifted in his seat, trying to get more comfortable, but his lengthening dick wanted Caroline. It had been more than three days since the two of them had made love, and he missed her touch.

God, he wanted to be with her.

But, no. He was trapped in a limo with a gorgeous date, who had been ordered and pre-paid for by his ex-nanny.

Guilt, slick and syrupy, ate away at his gut. In so

many ways, he was cheating on Caroline. He didn't plan to touch Ilene. Wasn't planning on kissing her. And he sure as hell wouldn't do anything that involved clothes coming off...but it still felt weird. This was a date.

Ilene would impress the partners. Just by looking at her, any man would have a hard-on and wish they were Scott. Having a beauty such as her on your arm made every man notice you.

And, what ate at his gut the most, was that he wasn't completely unaffected by Ilene's charms. Beverly had been around long enough to know Scott's tastes in women, and she'd dressed up this Barbie doll to Scott's specific standards.

Her brunette hair was half up with tendrils swirling down, caressing her bare shoulders. The dress, with its tight-fitting bodice, nearly popped her breasts out, and the bottom slit almost went to her hip. The entire ensemble pivoted on five-inch 'fuck-me' pumps, which he normally loved, but not tonight.

He studied Ilene and her appearance. Beverly knew green was his favorite color, that he didn't like sequins, and couldn't stand pantyhose. Her emerald dress, bare legs, and high heels would turn any man's head.

A shiver ran up his spine.

It was like being set up on a date by his mother.

Scott wondered if Ilene had condoms in her beaded purse, courtesy of Bev.

He didn't want to think of that.

"I see you approve."

"Approve of what?"

She took a deep breath, heaving out her chest and flaunting it in his direction. "I spent the day at the spa, just for you."

Wiggling her fingers and playing with the strapless bodice of the dress, he realized her nails were painted and encrusted with what he hoped were fake diamonds since he was sure he paid for all of it.

"The clothes arrived last night by special delivery and were a perfect fit."

They were, not that he wanted to admit that he had noticed. "You look lovely." His voice sounded flat and as disinterested as he could make it.

A fake giggle and a pat on the arm came next.

"You're so sweet, Scott." She seductively licked her lower lip, showing off her bright red lipstick—the color he preferred, especially when lips surrounded his...he took in a deep breath and shifted in the seat. He had to avoid Ilene's temptations.

"I'm also completely waxed. I hope you approve of that, too."

His ears perked up. Completely waxed?

She inched up her dress, and Scott couldn't help but notice. "I'm also going commando."

He stared out the window and avoided the temptress. He had to admit, Ilene knew her job. She knew it well. But any paid escort would.

Ilene—if that was, in fact, her real name—didn't exist. She was made-up, hollow, and would look totally different if he were another man with different tastes.

Her name was probably Betsy Sue, and she'd grown up in a small town in the South with buckteeth, pigtails, and dreams. Only to end up here, waxed, made-up, and probably stitched together with plastic surgery.

"Scott." Ilene placed her hand on his knee and slowly caressed upward. Her eyes—smoky and sexy —locked onto his. "I know this is a job," she said, her voice low, breathy, and Marilyn Monroe sexy. "But you're exactly the type of man I'm looking for."

He knew it, too. Rich.

She leaned in. "Exactly my type."

She let out a Marlborough cough. He was sure Beverly had put into the contract that she couldn't smoke during the party, but judging by how strong the scent was, he felt certain she had burned a pack before heading to his office for the ride to the party.

She was probably the type of woman who smoked heavily to avoid eating but would always order the most expensive meal at a restaurant so she could pick at it and throw most of the food away.

Her hand found what it sought, and she cupped

his crotch firmly, massaging the tip of his manhood with her thumb, causing him to jump in his seat.

He removed her hand and shifted his legs away from her. His throbbing member was only hard because he had been thinking of Caroline.

"I was excited to take this job when the agency told me it was you." She licked her lips, closed the window between them and the driver, and stared at his crotch. "I'd like to show you how much I'm enjoying your company."

He had barely said anything to her since they entered the limo. She must be enjoying his radiant personality as he ignored her because he'd given her no signs that *he* was enjoying the evening.

Well, except for the hard-on he was certain she thought was for her.

She unclasped the seat belt and gave him a devilish grin.

He stopped her as she tried to get on the floor to kneel in front of him.

"Don't."

Pausing, she gazed at him, the bewildered look in her eyes telling him one thing—no one had ever rejected her before, and she wasn't sure how to process the rejection. She shook her head and took in a deep breath once she had wrapped her mind around his demand. "Let me please you. You look tense."

His eyes narrowed as he glared at her. "Get back in your seat and buckle yourself in."

Her face paled as though she had never been turned down before. With pouty lips, she sat next to him.

"Later, then," she whispered, leaning closer to him.

His virgin, seventeen-year-old self was mentally screaming in his ear. She was ready, she was willing, and the scene was porn perfect. Even in his twenties, he wouldn't have hesitated to be balls-deep in Ilene, pounding her on the floor of the car.

He wasn't sure when his tastes had changed. But over the last few years, he found he wanted the white picket fence, the rugrats, and the love of a faithful woman. Was that such a horrible thing?

What was the alternative? Women like Ilene, who wanted to date his wallet?

Dating a gold digger, plunging into debauchery with a string of loose women, trying to find someone of quality—only to discover he was dating a god digger, then plunging into debauchery,… it was a cycle he wanted to end.

Needed to end.

And it was all his fault.

He could barely breathe. He had never truly confessed this to himself before, let alone to another person. But he sought out women who would never make him happy. What was wrong with him?

He could probably tell Ilene to shut the fuck up, and she'd still want to suck his dick. Men who had money and prestige, like he did, could get away with that shit.

Ilene, with her spray-painted tan, wasn't worth it. He wouldn't mess up the best thing he'd ever had—Caroline—for something fake.

Ilene leaned in and kissed him. Her firm lips pressed against his and, opening her mouth eagerly, she invited him in even as he tried to pull away.

It was like kissing an ashtray.

The look in her eyes told him she was determined to land him.

He wiped his mouth, his hand now smeared with red lipstick.

"At least we got the first kiss out of the way." She tried to wipe some lipstick off his face, but he turned his head. "Now it won't be so awkward when we kiss at the party."

Awkward? That kiss was a near tragedy. One that the partners would surely have noticed.

Was kissing him ahead of time a directive given by Beverly? Or did Ilene have so much expertise at being a hired escort that she instinctively knew to do that so their skit at the party would run smoothly?

Either way, he didn't want to kiss her again, but he would probably have to.

"*I*'d like an Italian Martini."

Caroline looked up from her phone and noticed the party goer. He set down the list of available cocktails and said, "I'd like it dry."

She quickly put her phone away. She knew better than to do anything personal while on a job, but this stock app seemed so important. She wasn't sure what SHP was, why it would be critical to keep up-to-date with the stock price, but it had just gone up in price and the job was worth a lot of money. She didn't want to mess the job up. The stock quote had just arrived and she hoped another one wouldn't come until she was done with this bartending job.

She poured wine into the glasses she had arranged on a tray. She glanced toward Dave who took the man's order and expertly began mixing the drink. Caroline had no idea what went into an Italian Martini, and had no clue how to make any drink 'dry'.

Dave didn't seem to notice that she had been on her phone and not paying attention to her job. Coast was clear—this time. She should have been more careful.

"I'd like a black Russian," a man said. "My wife wants a Manhattan Iced Tea."

She could never be a bartender. Three men had already hit on her, the crates of alcohol were too heavy for her to lift, and she had no idea how Dave kept all the drink recipes in his head. She felt certain she'd jumble the orders up and serve some of the worst cocktails a party would ever have to choke down.

"There she is." A voice broke free from the crowd and she glanced up. "How are you enjoying being a bartender for an evening?"

Ralph's smile welcomed her, and even though she felt a little out of her element, she smiled back at him. Having a friend at the party, a friendly face in the crowd, was priceless. "I wasn't expecting such a big turnout."

"The Tate Law Firm knows how to throw a party. That's for sure." His hand snaked around the waste of the woman next to him, a woman that Caroline vaguely recognized. If she remembered correctly, the woman wasn't a lawyer but had an impressive title as Director of Research. "This is my date, Joanna."

She knew the woman looked familiar. The other day when she delivered food to Ralph's morning meeting, she had greeted her in the elevator. She had even showed her to the conference room and showed her where to set up.

The two of them made a lovely couple.

"It's nice to see you again." Relief washed over her. Ralph was just being a good friend and not hitting on her. She didn't need to reject any more men tonight, especially since she had already found her prince charming.

Joanna wore a stunning black dress and her hair and makeup must have been professionally done because she was a vision of beauty. She wondered why men were hitting on her when they had a coworker this lovely to see every day.

Of course, nobody should ever fish from the company pier.

"Please do me a favor, Caroline," Joanna asked. She reached into her beaded black purse, pulled out a five-dollar bill, and handed it to Caroline.

Caroline pocketed the money. "Anything, Joanna."

"I always get nervous during these parties." She lifted up her nearly full drink. "I stick to ginger ale to calm my stomach."

Caroline knew some people used soda pop to help with a sick stomach, the beverage never helped her though. "I'm sorry you're not feeling well."

Joanna gave a pffft sound and gestured with her hand. "It's nothing. But if you could please walk in a fresh ginger ale to me after the salad course, I'd really appreciate it."

Already with a twenty in his hand, Ralph said, "We'd both really appreciate it."

Glancing around, Caroline quickly took the money and placed it next to the other tips in her apron pocket. A tip of five dollars? Sure. But to toss twenty more on top of it? Felt more like a bribe.

She then reached under the bar and grabbed a cold can of Schweppes. "I can give you a fresh one now."

"Aren't you a dear." She gave Ralph a sideways glance, one that seemed a bit odd, but Caroline dismissed it. "I'd like a fresh, cold one later on." She set her current drink down. "If I have too much, the carbonation has the opposite effect."

Which was why Caroline rarely drank sodas. They always made her sick to her stomach.

"How will I find you in the dining hall?" Caroline filled a few more glasses with wine and set out some more beer.

Ralph smiled widely at her. "You won't be able to miss us. We're seated at the front and center table, with the senior partners."

She recognized the look of pride in his face. The partners had been talking about him when she over-heard their conversation. Feeling that her tray of drinks would survive a minute without her, and noting that Dave was busy with other guests, Caro-line leaned in and closed the gap between her and Ralph. "I didn't mean to eavesdrop, but I heard something interesting from the owners of the company."

His eyebrow disappeared behind his dark hair. "How so?"

She couldn't remember his name, so she said, "The one that sits in a wheelchair…"

"Gilkrist," Ralph said, filling in the name.

"Yes, Gilkrist. He said that the person they pick for the senior promotion thing needs to be someone who is willing to…," she quickly thought to his exact words, "take a stand."

His eyebrow dipped below his bangs. "Take a stand?"

Caroline's heart fluttered, so thankful that she could help someone who had helped her so much. "They want someone who isn't afraid to express himself," she said, trying her best to convey the exact message.

Ralph again gave a secretive nod to Joanna, who had also heard the entire conversation.

"Thank you, Caroline," Ralph's grin widened. "You've been very helpful."

Joanna's arm snaked around Ralph's arm and she seemed pleased by the news as well. "And please don't forget about the drink later."

"If I can help you feel better, then by all means. You can count on me."

"Trust me," Joanna said, "your presence later on will have the best effect."

## 14

*D*inner, hors d'oeuvres, and guilt—mixed with scotch—was a terrible combination.

Scott knew in his heart that he wasn't as bad as his ex-girlfriends had been to him in the fidelity department, but attending the event with a buxom brunette on his arm wasn't exactly being faithful to Caroline either. His indigestion created belches of fire in his gut, slowly eating away at him.

There was never an antacid when you needed one.

He exited the limo and held out his hand for Ilene, who immediately glued herself to the crook of his arm as she stepped onto the curb. The heavy scent of her perfume lifted on the cool breeze and wafted around him, causing his nose to wrinkle, and him to clear his throat.

So much was riding on this night, and the heavy

weight settling in his chest grew with every step he took.

It was show time.

He walked toward the entrance of the hotel. "We meet with the partners in their hospitality suite before mingling with the employees downstairs," he said, keeping his voice low and professional.

Ilene nodded, and her expression became more focused. It gave her more of an appearance of an employee than a date.

"Beverly filled me in." She took a deep breath and straightened her dress. "This is the big performance with the three partners—MacMillan, Larimer, and Gilkrist. The senior partnership in the company is up for grabs now that the founder Tate is dying."

For a brief moment, the sick feeling lifted. Ilene not only looked the part, but she had also studied up on her role. They just needed to get through the next three hours as the perfect power couple, and they were home free.

And then it occurred to him. Ilene had studied up on him, but he had no idea who she was pretending to be, what her background was, or anything. He only remembered that they had supposedly met a few months ago.

God. He couldn't even remember her fake last name.

He wanted to ask her for the details, but he just didn't care. She was here to serve him, and after the senior partner decision had been made, he could forget all about Ilene and pursue Caroline. He could tell Caroline the truth, and maybe have a future with her. He just needed to put on his A-game and get through the night.

"All the partners, junior and senior, are gathered in the private suite upstairs while the rest of the company enjoy cocktails in the ballroom on the first floor," he said, once they made their way into the hotel. "Dinner will be served in the main dining room for all employees."

She gazed into his eyes and gave a slight nod. "Beverly explained that. We are to be seated at the table with the three senior partners and their wives since there could be a major decision announced."

"Exactly."

"There are ten seats per table," she continued. "The senior partners and wives are six. You and I take that tally up to eight, so there is…"

"One other guest and his date are at that table."

"Mr. Ralph Larimer," she said, interrupting his train of thought. "He's your competition, and we must destroy him." She smiled at Scott, and there was a twinkle in her eye as though she were more than up to the challenge of torpedoing his fellow co-worker.

It gave Scott confidence that she could pull this off, and a smile crept across his face.

"You have a beautiful smile," she said as they

walked across the marble entrance. "Beverly is right, it makes you more approachable. You should smile more often."

In a flat tone, he said, "I'll take that under advisement." It was one of his buttons that Beverly always pushed. He didn't like people telling him that he should smile more often. He smiled when he was happy, not to please people.

He had been smiling a lot more with Caroline.

Laughing even.

He caught sight of Beverly standing near the concierge desk. It was subtle, and perhaps he was the only one who could tell since he had known her his whole life, but she was doing her best to hide a scowl on her face as people passed by. Her cane rested against the desk as she held her cell phone and was madly texting. It explained the vibrations coming from his phone in his pocket, so he chose not to answer.

She marched—well, quickly limped—over to them in her high heels, walking faster and more determinedly than usual. "You should answer your phone."

"We're here." He glanced at his watch. "And just a little late. You should have more patience."

The scowl returned. It was the look of a panicked and determined parent, worried about their child on the night of the big game. He knew she'd have indigestion all night, and wouldn't feel relieved until the moment of truth when everything worked out.

"Rumor has it that they will announce the new Senior Partner tonight." She studied the two of them. "You look like a believable couple." Looking at Scott's face, she added, "Smile."

He plastered on a cheesy, fake smile like a three-year-old, the same one that had ruined his early childhood pictures and made Beverly upset.

"Stop that." She straightened his tie and noticed a smudge of something on his face. Getting a tissue from her purse, she wiped his face. "Lipstick. At least it's Ilene's color."

He felt like a child, but at the very least she didn't spit on the Kleenex before wiping his face.

"I went through the receiving line and already got your tags," she said, handing them their badges so security would allow them into the rooms. "I'll be in the cocktail room on this floor while you impress the bosses upstairs." Giving Ilene a stern once over, she nodded. "The two of you are perfect together. I doubt anyone else here could hold a candle to you, Ilene."

*S*cott led Ilene from the elevator to the top floor of the hotel. The Starlight Lounge overlooked the city and held a reputation of being elite. The views from the restaurant had made it into many travel brochures of the city, as well as many newspapers and magazines.

Stars flocked here, as did CEOs and rich dignitaries.

Scott had dined here many times, and even had a favorite dish.

Following the sign, they walked through the crowd to a private room in the back where a man checked their badges and allowed them to enter.

Soft, elegant music played in the background and drinks and hors d'oeuvres lay on a serving platter on a table. Scott picked up a drink. Ilene on his arm, fake smile on her face, took one too.

Tonight's torture came with a side order of Ralph, who was already in the hospitality suite, schmoosing. He knew how to play the game and was running in the final stretch. He had cornered Gilkrist, and he was probably sharing the details of some boring story with him.

A woman stood with her back to Ralph. Long, curly honey-blonde hair—definitely not Gilkrist's wife. Mrs. Gilkrist had silver hair, and her style of dress had always been more mature than the high slitted one this woman wore. Mrs. Gilkrist also never hovered over her husband's wheelchair in what looked like spiked heels.

No, that woman was Ralph's date. The date that Ilene was supposed to not just match in professionalism but out do. Scott didn't like to be judged in such a way, and really didn't understand why their dates would undergo such an ordeal as well, but tonight was about getting a prize and he knew Ilene would be up to the challenge.

The woman pivoted on her heels and stood closer to Ralph.

It was Joanna.

He studied their hand gestures and body language, and it nearly made his stomach turn. But it wasn't until Ralph whispered in Joanna's ear, and she laughed, gripping his arm tightly and then kissing his cheek, that Scott almost felt pity for Ralph. Joanna was hedging her bets. She wanted to be the wife of a senior partner, and any potential partner would do, evidently.

Ralph let out a raucous laugh and, even with the man on the opposite side of the room, it grated against Scott's ear. Joanna's fake fit of laughter that followed was even worse.

He had heard that fake laugh before. Too many times really.

Hair highlights. Acrylic nails. Silicone boobs. Fake personality.

He realized his date wasn't much better, but at least Ilene was transparent. She wanted money for her services. A simple transaction. Not a ploy for a rich husband.

Scott pulled Ilene aside while Gilkrist finished

BACHELOR SOUL:

his conversation with the couple. "That," he said, his eyes shifting to the corner of the room, "is Ralph."

"Target acquired," she said, nodding.

"And that woman, Ralph's date for the evening?" he said, pointing at Joanna.

Ilene glanced around Scott's broad shoulders for a better look. "Bad bleach job at eleven o'clock, quickly heading our way, dragging Ralph with her?"

"Joanna is an opportunist who had her claws in me for a short time."

"The woman whom you vacationed with. The one that changed our backstory."

He needed to remember what the new backstory was. They supposedly met at a charity fundraiser, but he had no idea which one.

"They're grabbing more drinks, and a guest has stopped to talk with them. They will be here shortly," Ilene whispered in Scott's ear while his back was turned to them.

Seeing the backstabbing bitch wasn't a problem. Ralph was. The man had probably already regaled the partners with anti-Scottisms. He should have been doing the same backstabbing and smearing Ralph's name in the mud, but he had a feeling Ralph's failure on the Landmark Leasing case had already done that job for him. The failure wasn't Ralph's fault. That outcome would have befallen Scott as well.

Ilene's gaze stiffened as though studying something. "Do you have eyes on the other two partners?" Beverly had shown pictures of both MacMillan and Larimer to Ilene so she could spot them easily.

"No, I don't."

She still looked focused on something. "What is it?"

Her gaze stopped panning the room and she now looked at Scott. "What caused your breakup with Joanna?"

"It doesn't matter."

"It might if it can be ammunition for us. She was first with you, now with Ralph. Anyone else?"

He had caught Joanna sleeping with one other person in the office, but had Ralph also been in her bed? He wouldn't have put it past either of them.

"Maybe, but I don't know."

Before Ralph and Joanna made their way over, Scott added, "I'd like to keep the playing field only on the main players. If the fight focuses on our dates, I'd rather your true identity not be revealed."

"I can hold up my end." Her eyes narrowed. "I'm sure I can take her. She's an opportunist. My guess is that she has her claws into him because she believes he'll be the next Senior Partner."

He knew Ralph well. At least, well enough to know that if he was being played, he was playing someone too. "Let's just say that Ralph volunteered to be her next victim." Scott couldn't feel sorry for the man. The two deserved each other.

From behind them, he heard Ralph's grating voice.

"Nice of you to finally show up." He studied Ilene from her head to her toes and then backup to her D-cup boobs. "I don't believe I've had the pleasure."

His syrupy sweet tone wiped the smile off Joanna's face, giving Scott a glimpse of how their relationship was faring so far. Wishing that she were miserable didn't seem very charitable, but he hoped she was unhappy.

He actually hoped they both were.

And judging by Ralph's lust-filled eyes, Ilene was already earning her money.

"You must be Ralph. I've heard so much about you." Ilene's disdain-filled, cold stare held just the right amount of hatred that a real girlfriend would have for the man.

It was a nice touch.

"I didn't catch your name." Ralph held out his hand in an effort to shake hers, but Ilene didn't move. She stood and glared at him in a current-girlfriend manner.

Scott threw his arm around Ilene's shoulders. "This is Ilene."

Joanna's stance tightened. "I didn't know you were seeing anyone."

"Sleeping with my co-workers took you out of the loop regarding my personal life," Scott said, glancing at Ralph.

"I was just telling Gilkrist about the Landmark Leasing fiasco you left me with."

"You mean the case *you* lost."

"Only once you were done destroying it. You know, the man's business is now at stake. He's selling some of his properties to pay for damages to Prince Housing."

"Really?" Scott's eyes widened. "Which properties is he selling?"

His eyes narrowed in, giving him an even more weaselly appearance. "Let's cut to the chase. You set me up."

"Doubtful, you're just that bad of a lawyer."

"Why did you drop the case anyway?"

Scott wasn't going to share the reason; he was just grateful not to have spent more time with Frank Rancini or have the stigma of losing one of Gilkrist's special interest jobs.

"There you are," MacMillan's voice sounded behind Scott.

"Sir." Scott turned and held out his hand for a hearty handshake.

"Who is this lovely creature?"

Ilene's million-dollar smile showed off her veneers. She extended her hand in a dainty manner. "Ilene."

MacMillan took her hand and palmed it between both his hands as she curtseyed. The movement took Scott by surprise, but it was elegant and high-class. "It's good to meet you, Ilene. What do you do?"

"I'm in charge of the special programs for the Chicago Public Library," Ilene said, her voice confident and firm.

MacMillan's eyes lit up. "Gilkrist's wife contributes to many charities that help fight illiteracy. She is the co-founder of the Keep Kids Reading program here in Chicago."

"His wife is Kathleen Gilkrist?" she asked, her tone lifted with surprise that only Scott knew to be a lie.

MacMillan's smile widened and Scott could see Ilene's magic working. "Yes," he said, "she works at..."

Scott couldn't help but grin. Beverly had hand selected the perfect job for Ilene to endear her closer to Gilkrist, and MacMillan was eating right out of her hands. He had actually never seen the man look so happy.

"I've heard so much about you and this company." Gripping tighter onto Scott's arm, Ilene added, "Scott just goes on and on about this wonderful firm." Her hand playfully slapped Scott on the chest and she played with his tie.

MacMillan's eyes narrowed in on the shiny bling she sported. "Is that an engagement ring?"

Scott's gaze darted to her hand. "No," he said, louder than he would ever have intended. The expression on Ilene's face told him she was confused. This little piece of information had not been disclosed to him as part of their dating history, and he wasn't going to pretend to have a fiancée and keep Ilene around for longer than just tonight.

His heart was racing, but he smiled and let the heavy creases of his face relax. "Not yet, that is." He picked up her hand and kissed it playfully. "The ring was a six-month anniversary gift."

"He's so generous." She beamed a smile at him and seemed capable improvising and covering his blunder. Their cover story was for four months, not six.

"All in due time, I suppose." MacMillan's hand rested on Scott's shoulder. "Can I see you a minute?"

Scott couldn't breathe. Did MacMillan see through the charade? Or was this it? Were the next words out of MacMillan's mouth that he was the new senior partner, or would it be Ralph?

His mouth dried up, and he wasn't sure if he could even utter a word. He managed to get out, "Sure," before kissing Ilene on the cheek and saying, "give me a minute dear."

Pulling Scott aside, they walked to the corner of the room. "How's your ankle?"

"Healing." It still hurt like hell, but only because he'd been standing on it for quite some time now.

MacMillan raised his glass and his finger

uncurled from the drink to point at Scott's date. "Ilene's a keeper."

No, she really wasn't. He felt certain that Ilene had done her role well, and he'd have to confront Beverly about the blasted ring later. Hopefully his change of their dating history wouldn't mess up their story.

He wiped the sweat from his neck and nodded.

"We have to present our selection of senior partner to the board by the end of the year." He shook his head. "You know how it goes. We make the announcement and the board votes in our favor."

It wasn't news. It's how Larimer ascended to the throne eight years ago. He had been Tate's favored prospect, the then senior partners selected him to the board in nearly ceremonious fashion. The board would do their review, but basically come back with a unanimous decision to vote the new person in.

MacMillan's face turned ashen, and a pained expression appeared on his face. "Tate always made the decision, but this time it's different."

Of course, it would be. The company needed to replace its last founding member.

"The three of us need to present only one candidate to the board, and Gilkrist needs to make his decision between you or Ralph. He said he'd announce it during his memorial speech for Tate tonight, sometime after dinner during coffee and dessert."

That meant he already knew who he favored.

Scott's chest tightened, his heartbeats throbbing through him loudly, and he felt that what MacMillan wanted to share wouldn't be good news. "Do you know who he's leaning towards?"

His face saddened. "I'm not supposed to say anything, but it's Ralph."

## 15

$S$cott's gut ached, and his knees were giving way.

"I tried to sway Gilkrist in choosing you." MacMillan's eyes grew heavy and he looked more haggard than Scott had ever known. "I pleaded my case for you. Told him about your dedication, track record, and integrity."

Feeling numb, Scott just nodded dumbly.

"The two of you were neck-to-neck on so many criteria. There wasn't anything that really stood out... I mean, nothing that stood out in a character-building, better-man, sort of way. You know what I mean?"

Scott really didn't. In the eyes of Gilkrist, Scott was equal to Ralph. Equal...no, not equal. Worse. He wasn't the better man—Ralph was.

His stomach twisted and he thought he might vomit. "Thanks for letting me know."

"I didn't want you to be blind-sided," MacMillan said, his hand resting on Scott's shoulder. "The announcement is supposed to be kept secret until the big reveal tonight, so don't let the news slip out."

He managed a stoic smile and head nod to MacMillan before the man walked away, but what he really needed to do was to sit.

Sit and throw up.

Nothing was going his way.

All these years, all the long weekends, all the hard work. Worthless. All the senior partners were now between the ages of forty and sixty-five, years away from retiring. He wouldn't get another chance at making partner for at least another five to ten years, if that.

Ilene came up beside him. "Is everything all right?"

As far as he was concerned, she could pack up and leave. The farce was over. And they hadn't even sat down to dinner yet. He had to play out this charade to the end, cleaning up all the pieces and somehow saving some of his dignity.

"Time to eat." He strode out of the room, Ilene quickly following on his heels. He didn't make eye contact with her, or anyone else, as they crammed into the elevator and rode shoulder-to-shoulder down the twenty-three stories to where the main ballroom was.

The smell of dinner hit him as he forced his way through the gathering of coworkers who walked to the ballroom like a herd of cattle for slaughter.

"I'm guessing the talk didn't go well," Ilene said, as she caught up to him and placed her beaded clutch purse on the table. "We can work on this, regroup." She glanced around. "We should find Beverly."

He wanted to leave. Maybe he could pull a hamstring or throw up in the middle of the room. Anything to escape the torture of the night.

A few coworkers meandered into the room to find seats at the many dining tables. His seat was assigned to him. He would sit with the senior partners and Ralph, the next senior and his future boss. Dinner would begin in a few minutes and he had to sit and pretend that everything was all right.

It was anything but.

A man with a tray of drinks walked by, and Scott grabbed a glass of scotch from the selection. Slugging it back, he recognized it as poor quality, single-malt swill. Not the typical scotch he normally drank with MacMillan, but the cheaper party stuff that reminded him that he hated the taste of scotch.

He had only started to prefer this drink because he had read that aping the mannerisms of others endeared you to them. Who the hell was he?

"How'd it go?"

His heart skipped a beat, and he jumped at the sound of Beverly's voice. The woman looked out of breath, as if she saw him dash into the room and had to run to catch up.

"Don't sneak up on me like that." He held up the empty scotch glass. "This wasn't a celebratory drink."

Even with all the makeup she wore, he could tell the blood had drained out of her face. "Ilene, please powder your nose. I need to talk with Scott."

She pulled out two chairs once Ilene left. "Get off your ankle and tell me what happened." Her soft, motherly voice held the same level of compassion it had for him when he was a child. "Well?"

He took a seat and ran his hand through his hair. The crowd slowly came in, and he knew they only had a minute or two of privacy. He looked into her blue eyes and realized that he didn't want to disappoint her, but that's all he was—a disappointment. A second-place winner in the game of life. A collector of silver, not gold.

"Ralph won."

"Oh, no." Beverly's head drooped and she gazed toward the crowd. In her eyes, he could see the wheels spinning. He didn't need her games, didn't need her plots, and didn't need her sympathy. This wasn't the playground and a mean kid didn't want him to play on their team.

This was real life, and she couldn't take this pain away.

"It's over." When she placed her hand on his shoulder, he added, "I should have just listened to my heart and brought her anyway."

"Who?"

Not that he wanted to tell her, but he blurted out, "I'm seeing someone." He glanced at his co-workers who were now nearly within earshot. "I have feelings for Caroline." He swallowed the lump in his throat. "She's wonderful and caring and someone who means a great deal to me." His face pinched. "I should have brought her instead."

Beverly's face softened. "You never mentioned anything about her."

"No, I didn't." He took in a deep breath. "All I've been doing lately is playing games. I got exactly what I deserved. At least tonight can't get any worse."

---

*N*ow that dinner was being served, the ballroom had settled down, like being in the eye of the storm.

Scattered around the place were empty glasses, some still containing alcoholic beverages, some smeared with lipstick, and all her responsibility to clean up. Caroline grabbed a tray and started in on the work.

She carried another tray of dirty glassware to a rubber bin she had placed on one of the tables, careful not to spill anything on her uniform. The leftover hors d'oeuvres resting on dirty plates shocked her. So much food had only been nibbled at. Such a waste.

The smell of the hotel's catered meal had wafted into the room a good thirty minutes ago, and it smelled heavenly—causing her stomach to grumble. There had been no time to eat lunch and eating a protein bar before work had been less than satisfying.

She collected bins of dirty glassware, but left the tiny plates stacked on one table in the corner of the room. The plates were not her responsibility, but the tablecloths were, so she had to do double-time to get her job done since no one from the hotel had started cleaning up yet.

The small finger food looked tempting, but she didn't want to run the risk of tasting anything while on duty. She needed the money from this job. But, now that all the guests had left, and since Dave was not in the room, she helped herself to a serving tray of food that had been left out and not served. The crab cake in its cream sauce wasn't going to keep, and would only be thrown out anyway.

Maybe if there were any leftover in the kitchen, still refrigerated, the hotel could donate them to a homeless shelter. It'd be at least a kind act of charity during this holiday season.

Making sure not to forget her promise, she filled a new glass with ice and poured a freshly opened bottle of ginger ale into it. She made sure to grab a paper coaster and a drink napkin before walking to the dining hall.

She peeked inside. Ten people per table crowded the room. The waiters kept busy picking up the salad plates and she knew her timing was right.

Snaking her way around the tables and the servers, she made her way to the front of the room where the podium and speakers were set up. Ralph and Joanna had been so kind to her, and she was eager to help them out as well.

She saw her friend Bob with a woman she assumed was his wife, sitting next to them were Ralph and Joanna. She had found the correct table.

"Excuse me." She walked closer to the table and did her best not to spill the drink as she brushed up against purses that were on the backs of chairs.

She approached the table and did a double-take.

Her eyes widened and she looked again.

Was that Scott?

She studied the seated man talking with the curvy brunette, also seated at Bob and Ralph's table. Strong jaw line, dark blond hair, piercing blue eyes. He easily could be Scott's twin.

Her head tilted, her eyes narrowing to get a

better look at him. Her feet took a step closer to his end of the table.

Was it Scott?

The brunette leaned in and kissed the man, so it couldn't be him. Still, Caroline circled the table until she was a few feet from him.

The man glanced up, his eyes widening when he saw her. "Caroline?"

Her jaw slacked and she shook her head.

No.

She blinked several times and, with her free hand, rubbed her eyes.

Her chest tingled and there was a hardening in her stomach. The man—apparently on a date—that man *was* Scott.

Feeling lost, she held onto the drink, her lifeline for needing to be in the room and blending in.

She counted the people at the table. Ten people. Or, more to the point, five couples.

No. No. No.

Scott couldn't be on a date.

This was not happening.

It felt as if the air had been sucked out of the room. She could barely breathe even though her heart raced and she had begun rapidly breathing to keep from feeling light headed.

Ralph, Joanna, Bob, his wife, even whats-his-name in the wheelchair sat at the table next to a woman. Then another couple and Scott. Scott next to... Caroline cocked her head and stared at the woman. Scott next to a *date*.

Nothing added up, except that... Scott had lied to her.

He lied.

He had said he had a dinner to go to but he didn't say anything about this. He had said he worked in the mailroom, not hob-knobbing with the owners of the company. It felt as if the floor had given way, and her rubbery legs could barely hold her up, let alone allow her to walk.

"Ah, Caroline," Ralph said, catching her attention. "You're just in time."

Her head spun to look at him. "Wh-What?"

"You missed Scott the other day when you arrived with breakfast. It's only fair that you get to see him now." His hand gestured over to Scott. "You remember your little waitress friend, don't you?"

Oh, God. This wasn't real. This wasn't happening. Caroline again stared at Scott, who was getting out of his chair.

"I can explain," Scott said.

"Scott," Ralph said, letting out a slight chuckle, "you can't maintain your dating history like this and be a good representative for this company." Ralph let out a derisive snarl and took a stand. "I mean, talk about conduct unbefitting a senior partner."

Caroline felt numb, not knowing what to do next.

Ralph now gestured to Ilene. "How can you disrespect Ilene like this?" He now gestured toward Caroline. "Messing around with a nothing waitress? Where is it going to end, Scott? And, who's next? Some lowly maid in one of the rooms upstairs?"

Swallowing back the tears that threaten to spill, Caroline felt like a complete idiot. Not again. She'd be damned if she's going to allow Scott to get the best of her. No man was going to play her.

"Caroline," Scott pleaded, "it's not what you think."

She marched closer to him, her jaw tightening and her hand fisting around the glass she carried. "I have a special drink for you, it's called Lying Douche bag, and then you can chase it down with a shot of You Can Go Fuck Yourself." She threw the drink in his face, making sure the ginger ale hit him square on, before tossing it onto the table and storming off.

---

"*N*o, Caroline. Wait." Scott's heart raced and he felt a pitted sunkeness in his chest. He clumsily scooted his chair farther back, but it hooked around the chair next to him, causing him to fall over backwards. He and a waiter crashed to the floor. His ankle throbbed but he managed to upright his chair and stand with the use of his one good leg.

"I'm very sorry sir." The waiter, who was fortunately not carrying any dishes, got up and looked sheepishly at Scott and then the guests at the table.

Scott searched the room but only found the faces of his coworkers staring back at him. Caroline wore a green, button down shirt with black slacks and apron—with a scowl on her face that he had never seen before. Her outfit should have had her stand out in the crowd, but she was nowhere in sight.

Where was she?

"I can get you a towel, sir," a nervous voice sounded from behind him. The waiter wiped off his uniform as he dashed away, doing his best to avoid bumping into anyone else.

The senior Larimer now stood up, his nostrils flaring and his face reddening. He threw his napkin onto the table, and pointed at Ilene. "It's just like you to have *one* woman in your arms and *another* woman on the side." Now looking directly at Gilkrist, he added in a deepening tone, "This is exactly what I was talking about. A successful partner needs to be settled and keep his romances clean."

"A waitress?" Ralph scoffed; his sneering tone dismissive. He rolled his eyes. "What were you thinking Scott."

"Waitress?" Scott fumbled with the chair and untangled himself from Ilene's fingers, who had sought him out trying her best to remain the dutiful date.

Why was Caroline here? Wasn't she working tonight?

An emptiness hit him, mixed with a feeling of dread which gave him a sinking feeling. Caroline had been dressed as one of the upstairs bartenders, but it'd be odd that she'd be here. Why would she be here?

Cold eyes stared back at him, and Ralph's grin widened across his face as he seemed quite pleased with himself. "Seems to me that your dance card is full, my friend."

"Dance card?" Scott wiped the drink from his face, not even realizing how drenched he had become. He ignored the agony from his foot and now focused his hatred on his nemesis. Ralph knew something.

"You said 'waitress', not bartender." Scott felt the drink as it soaked into his white button-down shirt, but didn't care. "You brought Caroline in the other day for the breakfast meeting. You targeted her from the restaurant and brought her in, and that's how you know she's a waitress—not a delivery person or a bartender."

His mind raced, with him scrambling to come up with answers.

There were so many questions.

But one thing now seemed clear. "When the breakfast meeting didn't explode in my face, you thought you'd publicly embarrass her here." He glanced at the three senior partners who were now staring at him, their mouths agape. "You wanted to humiliate me in front of the company."

The senior Larimer put his hand on his nephew's shoulder. "I'm sure my nephew has no idea what you're talking about."

Spoken like a true lawyer.

"I can see why we never stood a chance," Joanna said, half in tears. "You always did have a roving eye. I thought you were done two-timing women after I found you cheating on me."

"What?" He glared at Joanna, not even fully understanding what she was saying. Their brief fling was mutually explosive, with *her* cheating on *him*.

"Scott, don't." Ilene grabbed Scott's hand and tugged at it in an effort for him to take his seat. She held up her napkin. "Dry yourself off and we can report that waiter later."

He narrowed his eyes and brushed aside the offering.

This wasn't right.

None of this was right.

And now he wouldn't be able to catch Caroline.

"That isn't just some waitress." He glared at Ralph and Joanna. "Caroline happens to be the woman I love. She's someone who deserves better than me, but, if I'm lucky, I'll be able to convince her to forgive me."

"Scott, what's going on here," Gilkrist said, his

voice authoritative and loud. He was the one man that Scott wanted to please, but at the moment just didn't care about. Not anymore.

Scott pointed to the back of the room, even though Caroline was long gone. "That woman is who I should have brought to this party but I felt..." He choked on the words and knew they were true. He took a deep breath, but was unable to fill his lungs completely. "I felt... I felt she wouldn't be good enough to impress you." He eyed each of the senior partners one-by-one. "I was stupid enough to think that Caroline—with her generous personality and beautiful spirit—wasn't enough to compete with the high brass and their dates at tonight's party."

"Scott, I forgive you for cheating on me. Now, please sit down," Ilene said, her voice wavering. She glanced at each of the men at the table, her face pale.

Scott's stomach tightened and he felt like he may throw up. He had wanted to stand out to the senior partners, but not like this. Not when so much depended on...

Depended on...

Everything was so loud in the ballroom, and his knees were growing weak.

This was wrong.

He was tired of playing games. Tired of being molded into what people wanted or needed him to be. His one shot at happiness was fading and he didn't need to impress these people. He didn't need their approval. Didn't need their pity. Didn't need their stupid senior partner position, especially since Gilkrist had already made up his mind.

All he needed was Caroline.

His hand gestured to Ilene. "This woman is only pretending to be my date so I could impress you people." His body tensed and he stood taller. "I was so worried that you wouldn't approve of me being engaged to a woman like Caroline that I've been lying to you all night."

"Wait," MacMillan said, his fingers touching his parted lips. "You've asked Caroline, that bartender, to be your wife?" he asked, his eyes wide.

"Unbelievable." Ralph placed his arm around Joanna's chair and leaned in. "You were actually going to marry that waitress?"

Scott's muscles quivered and he wanted to strike the sneer off Ralph's face. His body flushed with nervous heat. "I haven't proposed to her yet, but if you all will excuse me, I'd rather be a junior partner with the love of my life at my side than be a senior partner without her."

aroline punched in the security code and entered Avalon Memory Care. After five days of crying and avoiding Scott's calls, her dark sunglasses had done wonders hiding her reddened eyes, but she couldn't wear them in front of her grandmother. The poor woman already had difficulty identifying her granddaughter as it was.

Caroline removed her glasses and walked quickly past the office, glancing through the glass window to see if Ms. Rubinstein was about. Oddly enough, she didn't recognize the woman sitting behind the desk.

Most of the staff would have off on Christmas day though. The last person she wanted to see was the administrator. She had called and left a message twice over the last few days, but Caroline had managed to dodge the woman.

If Avalon were planning on evicting her grandmother, they wouldn't have placed Caroline's name in the raffle to win a month of free rent. But, if it were an accident and her name wasn't supposed to be drawn, would they take the money away?

Laying low and letting January's rent kick in seemed like the best idea. No waves, no worries.

She didn't want to see Ms. Rubinstein, didn't want any of her coworkers to see her like this, and certainly would rather be at home. But it was Christmas, and her grandmother was going to have a visitor and a gift to open.

Holding tightly to the small package, she walked to the dining area. Several people sat at the family-style tables drinking warm beverages and Caroline could smell the sweet aroma of hot cocoa. The lit Christmas tree looked cheery and holiday music played in the background. Gone was the near feeling of this being akin to a hospital. Instead, the place now resembled a home. A warm one that her grandmother would have to leave once it was February.

And then what?

"Hello, Ms. Caroline," a familiar voice sounded from behind her. She turned to find the cook George smiling back at her. He wasn't part of the administration, wasn't a mean-spirited person, and probably was the only friendly face she knew in the entire place. Plastering a cheery smile on her face, she managed to say a weak, "Merry Christmas."

"Merry Christmas to you, too." The man's smile

became infectious, and, even though she didn't have much holiday joy in her heart, she returned a genuine smile to him. She was fortunate not to have to work today, but, of course, a cook at this type of facility would be here—even though the family Christmas party with relatives was held a few days ago. Turkey, ham, stuffing, and the green bean casserole had tasted delicious. Sniffing the air, she figured the residents would be getting leftovers or something similar for dinner tonight.

A man walked past the kitchen who wore the same green apron as George. That made another person that Caroline didn't recognize. "Do you have holiday staff working?"

George glanced at his partner in the kitchen and then back at her. "We've had a lot of turnover this past week."

"Because of the holidays?"

His eyes widened, and his head did a swivel from side-to-side to check for anyone nearby. "You haven't heard?" he whispered.

Glancing around, the place looked lovely and she didn't need any bad news. Ms. Rubinstein still wasn't around, so Caroline felt safe to talk with George a little while longer. "Heard what?"

He leaned in. "I don't have all the details, but we're under new management come the first of the year," he said in a hushed tone.

"New management?" she whispered back.

"The place was sold. Many of the employees left."

Like rats leaving a sinking ship. Caroline had seen this happen before. The second-to-last care center her grandmother was at had been sold. The transition was hard on the staff, and even worse on the residents. Meals and medicine were still given out daily, but, other than that, the routine completely changed—causing many residents to worry or become confused.

"Everything is kind-of on hold right now." He began counting on his fingers. "Special programs, our health network, the computer system we're buying and migrating our records to." He shook his head and Caroline could see the frustration in his eyes. "I mean, new management might be better, but it could be worse. At least we know that the place isn't closing down."

Closing down? Caroline had to find her grandmother a new place to live, and she didn't care what became of Avalon, but she didn't want George and the other staff that she liked to hurt and lose their jobs. "How do you know the place isn't closing down?"

"We're meeting our new boss the first of the year."

It wasn't much, but Caroline assumed that meant a ray of hope. Her grandmother would be gone soon after that, not the Caroline knew where she may end up.

"I'm sure everything will work out," she said as pleasantly as possible. "I hope the new management will honor the raffle drawing." She wasn't sure why they wouldn't. The card wasn't a binding contract but she'd hold them to it.

"What raffle?"

"The free January rent."

His face pinched and his eyes narrowed in on her. "We had a raffle for free rent?"

Caroline hadn't even known about the raffle until she had won, but it seemed odd that an employee wouldn't have known about it. Of course, he wasn't part of the administration team. He was the cook.

"My grandmother won a free month's rent," she said, her voice cheery and happy.

A smile spread across George's face. "I had no idea. Congratulations."

"Thank you." She held up a small paper sack with tissue sticking out the top. "Free rent is a great gift from Avalon, but I also have a present for my grandmother."

George pointed to a sitting area near the small parlor, behind the double-sided fireplace. "Our salon was shut down a few days ago, but some of Grandma Frankie's granddaughters were here this morning and volunteered to paint everyone's nails."

Caroline knew Grandma Frankie. She was a good ten years younger than her grandmother and carried a doll around all day, saying it was her baby. The doll's hair was a mess, the rubber face was scratched up, and the soft body had stains on it. Overall, it was a terrible sight but it comforted the old woman.

"Your grandmother had a manicure this morning. She's enjoying the warmth of the fire."

Caroline looked past the double-sided fireplace and saw her grandmother. Her hair was pinned back into a bun and she was wearing a sweatshirt, soft sweats, and the oversized cloth bib that all residents wore while eating or drinking anything. Her grandmother carefully lifted a small coffee cup to her lips and took a sip. The woman was a complete teetotaler, and Caroline knew there'd be no coffee in that mug. Although, she did love chocolate and there was a good chance it was cocoa. "She's awake. The last few times I've been here she was sound asleep."

"Your grandmother slept well the last two nights. She usually sleeps in front of the television for hours during the day, but she laid in her own bed and got really good rest the past few days."

"She looks great."

He grabbed a mug from the kitchen counter and poured some cocoa from a pitcher in it. "Here's a hot chocolate. Enjoy your visit with her."

"Thanks." She walked over and sat next to her

grandmother, placing the mug of cocoa on the table in front of them. "Hi, Grandma."

She barely looked up. "Gone."

Her voice was soft, but Caroline figured she heard it correctly. "What's gone?"

Her aged finger pointed inside her cup. "White bumps."

"Here." Caroline took the mug from her grandmother and replaced it with the new cup which was filled with marshmallows. "You can have this one."

Caroline wanted to help her grandmother pick up the mug and take a sip, but she knew the more things her grandmother could do on her own the better. Besides, the cocoa wasn't that hot.

"I like chocolate."

"I know." The woman used to be a self-professed chocoholic, and Caroline always could find the treats at her grandmother's home, especially when she was younger and the woman wanted to spoil her.

Knowing that Ms. Rubinstein wasn't around, or at least not that Caroline could see, she allowed herself to relax. Her grandmother wasn't being kicked out today. Not on Christmas day. She could worry about what was going to happen tomorrow.

"Merry Christmas." Caroline set the gift bag in front of her grandmother. "I got you something."

She eyed the gift and a slight recognition glinted

in her eyes, almost as if she knew the colored bag has something good but she didn't remember why. She reached for the present and fumbled to hold it. Her fingers struggled to open it, so Caroline pulled the gift out. "Dark chocolate Hershey kisses. Your favorite." She opened the candy bag and unwrapped a treat for her grandmother. The small size was perfect and she knew she wouldn't choke on it.

But that didn't mean the chocolate wouldn't ooze from her mouth and get all over the bib.

She cleaned up her grandmother with some napkins she found on the table and then sat the bag of candy aside. "I like your nail polish." Caroline hated small talk, but somehow talking about the obvious stuff in the room helped keep her grandmother engaged. They talked about the beautiful lights on the tree, the music that filled the air, and how good the cocoa tasted.

They spent a lot of time talking about the cocoa.

"I've been seeing someone." She had hoped for some sort of response from her grandmother, but saw none. No glint of recognition in her eyes, no nodding of her head, no comment about what Caroline had just shared with her.

Caroline glanced around the room. There weren't too many visitors here today but she figured they'd trickle in throughout the holiday. She watched as another family spent time with their elderly relative, their small children coloring in coloring books at the table. The elderly man seemed just as engaged as her grandmother was.

"I've been seeing this man for a couple of weeks. And the entire time he was lying to me, Grandma." Caroline held her grandmother's hand and held back the tears. She needed to talk about what was truly bothering her, even if her grandmother couldn't understand.

Her 'go to' person was still here. God willing, she'd be here for a while longer.

"I started to care for this man, but he's a filthy liar, just like the rest of them." An image of her high school boyfriend came to mind. He had lied to her for years. God, she was such an idiot. She had learned nothing from the past. But she would learn her lesson this time. Men should be avoided. Avoided like the plague.

Noticing her grandmother wasn't responding, she added, "I guess we all can't land a good man like Grandpa."

An aching grew in her heart. She missed him dearly.

She stared into the distant eyes of the only family she had left. Her grandmother needed another place to live and had no money. She had other problems right now other than a man that she believed just a few weeks ago was a filthy, homeless, bum.

Caroline nodded as she wiped away a tear.

"Filthy. Yeah, he's filthy rich," she said, emphasizing the word 'rich'. "Has more money than God." Her jaw tightened. "He was at the party dressed up in a tuxedo, Grandma. He was in a tux, sitting with the owners of the company."

"Who?" Grandma's hand waved in a stopping motion to get Caroline to slow down. "You're not making any sense."

Not sure who her grandmother thought she was, Caroline put her face directly in front of her. "It's me, Grandma."

"I know who you are." A sweet smile appeared, and for a moment Caroline caught a glimpse of recognition in her eyes."

"Do you know my name?" She smiled and hoped for the correct answer, but her grandmother stared past her. She asked about her name again, but her grandmother just shook her head.

"It's me, Caroline."

Her grandmother took a sip of cocoa, her hand shaking as she put the cup to her mouth. Cocoa dribbled from her mouth and was caught by the bib she wore.

The conversation ended there, so Caroline continued, "I googled his name. And you know what I found out?" Knowing her grandmother wouldn't answer, she said, "He's mega rich. I'm borrowing a five-year-old computer to find the truth out about him and he's rich enough to wipe his butt with hundred-dollar bills."

And to think she had given him a free piece of pie the day she met him. Her phone buzzed and she barely gave it a cursory glance. It was him again. He had called three times already today, leaving voice messages.

She really needed to block his number and forget about him.

Hopefully, he wouldn't show up at her doorstep again. She didn't need him banging on the door and giving her neighbors a reason to complain. Thankfully, she had been at work when he had done so. She didn't know how she could ever face him again.

Another tear threatened to escape, and she used the sleeve of her sweater to dry her eyes. "He was the first person I've really liked in a long time. I thought he was someone I could...," her voice trailed off and she didn't want to say what she was feeling in her heart. Her grandmother didn't need a weepy, teary eyed person on her hands. She needed to be the strong one now and take care of her grandmother, not the other way around. Besides, it was Christmas.

She let out a deep sigh. Cocoa had spilt from the cup and Caroline used the paper napkin on the table to wipe her grandmother's chin and then the table. Glancing at the empty mug, she said, "Looks like you're done."

Grandma's eyelids lowered, and she turned her head toward her granddaughter. "Caroline?"

"Yes, Grandma." Hope bubbled up within her and a tear of joy escaped and rolled down her cheek. "It's me, Caroline."

"Sounds like you love this man."

here wasn't a lot of traffic as Scott made his way downtown to his office building. Most people were still on holiday vacation, and he got to the office in record time.

He walked down the hallway to his office, at least, the office he had before the holiday. The place was empty with just a few people about. The place felt eerie.

Several messages came over the last few days from the company. The senior partners needed to speak with him. He just wasn't in a rush to speak to them. He was certain the talk would involve human resources for some sort of backlash over the spectacle he made of himself.

He really did look like an idiot at the party. He didn't care about the mess with Ilene, he didn't even care about how silly he looked in front of the company. The senior partners probably thought he was worthless. But that didn't matter.

Caroline mattered.

But she didn't want anything to do with him.

And life had to go on.

He couldn't hide any longer and claim that the holiday was the reason for his absence. Santa had come and gone, presents had been given, and relatives were already traveling back home. Soon most of the company staff would return from vacation and life would return to normal at the Tate Law firm.

Go on with Ralph in charge.

Gritting his teeth, Scott figured it was for the best that he move on. The Ellington-Weston law firm had called him over the holiday and, even though the position wasn't exactly the fit he had been looking for, it would do.

His office door was open so he shuffled in, his ankle nearly healed but still stinging with every step.

"Where have you been?" Beverly stopped packing up a box, dashed over with the help of her cane, and hugged him. The bear hug nearly squeezed the stuffing out of him.

"Skiing."

Her hands went to her hips and she glanced down at his hurt foot. She then made eye contact with him, her eyes looking sternly at him. "Don't lie to me."

His excuse really wasn't a lie, but he thought about the trip and answered, "Actually, sitting in a ski lodge drinking. Drinking a lot."

His office sat in boxes. It made sense. Ralph was the senior partner, and Scott had been let go. Even if the three older senior partners were willing to excuse Scott's behavior, they now had a fourth senior partner to deal with—and Ralph hated him. His first act was probably to get rid of Scott.

"You look pale." Her hand went to his forehead and she brushed his hair aside. "When was the last time you ate anything?"

Who keeps track of something like that? Life didn't matter anymore, besides, he hadn't been hungry in days. His only answer was a half shrug.

"And you couldn't answer the phone?" Her eyes narrowed and her hand touched his scruffy start of a beard.

Scott didn't want to hear about his appearance. After Beverly would chastise him about his facial hair, she certainly would mention his casual jeans and sweater. He never showed up to work without a suit and tie, but he had no clients. No one to impress, at least, not any more.

"I needed some space. I did get the message that Tate had passed away." The call had come from Tate's secretary, and it was the only office call he took. Tate's family had him for one more Christmas, which was nice, but not for the start of a new year.

Scott had drunk a toast to the man once he heard the news of his death. That was when he realized he needed to come back and attend the funeral.

Beverly walked around the desk, picked up his name plate and paper blotter to set them in a box. "The funeral is tomorrow."

"It's why I came back." Regardless of his standing in the company, he owed it to Tate to pay the man his respects. It would be Scott's last act as an employee.

Hell, not just an employee. Scott was a junior partner. Even if he didn't work here anymore, he had to make a good impression to the other employees.

"I know Tate meant a lot to you, but I've never seen you like this before." Beverly crossed the room and closed the office door, nearly tripping over some boxes in the center of the room.

He waved his hands around the office. "None of this matters." He then glanced at his empty row of bookcases. The sight of them looked haunting to him. "You packed all my books."

"Of course."

"Thank you." He would need them at his next job. A lawyer's library was important. Those books were his domain. He definitely didn't want Ralph laying claim to any of them, especially since many of them Scott had bought while in college.

The mini bar was stocked, but she went to the

Keurig and selected a K-cup. "Come and sit." After a minute the smell of Texas Pecan roast filled the office. That blend was his favorite, and Beverly knew it.

She placed the mug on the coffee table. "Tell me what's going on."

The coffee did smell nice, even though he would rather have a shot of scotch.

"It's this woman, Caroline, isn't it?"

He took a seat on the couch and picked up the coffee. Taking a sip, he weighed the pros and cons of opening up the deep wound in his heart.

"I'm not going anywhere, Scott." She sat back on the couch and dug in. "I can be here all day if needed."

Seeing the concern in her eyes, he said, "Caroline won't return my calls." He filled Beverly in on how the two met, how he had deceived her, and how much she meant to him. For a woman who constantly had her two cents to pay, Beverly sat and listened. She listened to every word and every unsaid desire he had.

When he began repeating himself as to how much Caroline meant to him and how much he had hurt her, Beverly asked, "So Caroline is the one?"

Her voice was soft and determined, as though she had always expected Caroline to come into Scott's life. "I knew one day you'd find her."

Beverly had always believed in true love and soul

mates. It had never been his thing though, that is, until he had met Caroline.

"I didn't get to see her, or see the drink get thrown in your face. I just heard the commotion after she had left the party."

"Everyone had heard it." He was sure the company gossip over the last week was nothing but how he had made a fool of himself at the party.

"You should have told me about her." Just as he was about to protest, she added, "I know you mentioned her name to me after we had hired Ilene..."

"*You* hired Ilene." That was such a stupid mistake. If he could go back in time and fix one mistake... well, he'd go back and not lie to Caroline. That was what he was guilty of. Being honest with her would have led him to ask Caroline to the party earlier, make sure she couldn't be hired as a bartender, and they'd still be together.

"You should have taken Caroline to the party, and I should have made it easier for you to do so."

Motherly advice from Beverly after the fact wasn't helpful. "I was a fool. She won't even answer my calls." He reached into his back pocket. "I really just came in to get this notarized."

"What is it?" She took the envelope from him.

He didn't want to get into all the details. Ten minutes. It was all he needed to get a signature on a piece of paper. "Some property I'm buying."

She opened up the paperwork. "Not another house. You know, I closed on the Essex Manor home on Christmas Eve. Good thing you gave me a temporary power of attorney to do so before you took off."

He hadn't even seen the home. Beverly had handled everything, including bringing in a decorator and paying him twice his salary to get the home fixed up as soon as possible. Not that it mattered anymore. He had wanted to surprise Caroline with it, well, once he had had the courage to tell her he was rich and could make all her dreams come true.

She flipped through the paperwork for the new property. "Is this a home?"

"It's not a house, not really."

"Landmark Leasing?" Her eyes widened as she read the information. "Wasn't that the pet project for Gilkrist?"

"Yep."

"The case Ralph lost?"

It still bothered Scott that Ralph could lose as many cases as he did, brought in as few new clients as he did, and could even botch up a favored case and STILL make senior partner. How is life fair?

"I excused myself as the lawyer on that case. Frank Rancini was selling some of his holdings…," Scott's voice trailed off. "I offered to buy this property."

Beverly shook her head and looked deep in thought. "I guess there isn't any conflict of interest now that the case is over with. And, you certainly have the money to buy it."

Scott shook his head and let out a heavy sigh. "I just need a notary public to watch me sign it."

Beverly pointed to the west side wall of the office, where the hallway was. "Mr. MacMillan's secretary is here. She's not on vacation anymore and can help you." She placed the envelope on the desk.

He glanced around the room. His personal belongings, as well as the painting which had hung on the wall, were all gone. "Thanks for packing me up. Two different law firms have made me an offer. I'm not exactly happy with either of them, but they're both respectable and a good friend of mine is the CEO of one of them. If I take my friend up on his offer, I wouldn't have to answer to Ralph or see Joanna anymore."

"What?"

He could guess that the confusion in Beverly's eyes was about what their next move would be. "Don't worry," he said, "You'll always have a job as my assistant, no matter where we end up."

Beverly's eyes widened and she leaned closer to him. "I'm not packing your stuff for you to leave." Her head tilted to one side and her eyes narrowed. "Have you spoken with MacMillan or one of the other senior partners since the party?"

Scott slumped into the soft cushion of the couch, letting out a groan from the back of his throat. "That is my next stop. They've been trying to reach me, but I didn't have cell service at the ski lodge," he said, lying. In truth, he just didn't bother to pick up the phone.

"Scott," her voice sounded energetic with a bubble of excitement. "I'm packing up so you can move into the corner office. *You're* the new senior partner."

Scott's heart stopped. He spun his head around and leaned toward her. "What did you say?"

"I thought you knew."

He gulped some air, finding it hard to breathe. There was no way. Ralph had synched up the deal.

"There was a big commotion at your table during the party, and then you stormed out on your bad ankle." She glanced down evidently taking inventory on his bad limb, but deciding not to ask since he still wore the black boot.

"You hopped into a taxi and took off. I had followed you outside, but once you left, I returned to the party. Her eyes narrowed sternly. "I called several times to see…"

His heart beats echoed so loudly in his chest that he could feel them pulsing in the arteries of his neck. "Skip to the end," he said in a rushed tone.

"Originally the new senior partner was going to be announced after dessert and a tribute to Mr. Tate, but then you left. I think people thought you'd be back. The seniors said they needed to discuss a few things." She gave Scott a look as though he was supposed to guess the rest. He wasn't up to playing games.

"And then...?"

She shrugged and added, "rumor has it that the senior partner position was still under negotiation even during the party. The partners had a mini-pow-wow to finalize everything." Her eyes widened and she stared at him. "Meaning, they left the party for a good fifteen minutes. After they came back, Gilkrist gave the announcement. He said you were the new senior partner."

Senior partner.

Top Dog.

He caught his breath. He had joined the three partners... a giddiness filled him, there were, once again, *four* partners. A smile—big and wide—spread across his face. *He* was the youngest senior partner. There were four of them.

He did it.

He took in several deep breaths to steady himself and to let it sink in.

"You had no idea?" Beverly came and sat next to him.

He perched on the couch, his body tensing. "I was told Ralph had been favored." Cold sweat beaded on his temple. "Gilkrist had chosen Ralph... I can't understand why he named me as senior partner."

"His speech was lovely," she said. "I wish you could have heard all the nice things Gilkrist said about you."

Gilkrist? The man probably hated him. "I made an ass of myself at the table, in front of him."

"All I heard was that a waitress got upset, you yelled at the partners, and then left." She scratched her head and looked confused. "I called you several times. The rumors that circulated sounded crazy."

"More rumors?"

Her face pinched as if trying to collect them all in her head. "Something like you wanted to get married but worried about the company image..." She gave him a stern glance. "I know that can't be true because you being married wouldn't hurt the company image." Beverly slumped on the couch. "Ilene was upset. Before she left, she must have said something toward Joanna because she showed her true colors."

"What do you mean?"

"Joanna attacked her."

Scott's jaw dropped.

"I heard it was a slap. I heard it was a hair pull. Doesn't really matter. The thing is, Ralph broke the two apart and let slip out that the 'plan' wouldn't work with Joanna acting the way she did." Bev waved her hand through the air as though brushing aside the unnecessary details. "Bottom line, I think the partners believed both of you were playing games to win but you were the only one who confessed. MacMillan also didn't like how Ralph dismissed Caroline and as being only a waitress."

Guilt coated Scott and his chest felt heavy. It was his first thoughts about Caroline as well, not that he thought of her like that now. "What exactly did Gilkrist say?"

"New blood. Something about... gumption?" She shook her head. "His speech sounded disjointed, like he didn't have time to polish and practice it." She looked thoughtful for a second. "I guess if he had chosen Ralph initially, and then changed his mind, it would make sense that he wouldn't have had time to work out his speech."

Something had turned the tide. Deep down he knew what it was. He declared his love for Caroline and didn't give a damn about anything else. Gilkrist must have seen that. He must have appreciated a man who knew what he wanted and was willing to sacrifice everything to get it.

Scott knew what he wanted.

More importantly, he knew *who* he wanted.

"I need your help to win Caroline back."

$\mathcal{I}$t was a crazy idea, but they were on a mission.

A mission to win Caroline back.

"I can't believe you came up with this idea." The wind picked up, and Scott wrapped his coat closer to his body as they got out of the car and headed toward the restaurant. "It's never going to work."

"Oh, hush." Beverly weaved her way around the cars parked in the handicap section of the parking lot and approached the large front window of The Patio. "She's not answering your calls, and she won't open the door to her apartment and talk to you." A couple walked past them on the sidewalk leading to the front door, and Beverly nodded and tried not to look stalkerish. "It's been days. I'm tired of seeing you so depressed."

He had been down. Everything and everyone reminded him of Caroline. His first thoughts in the morning, and his last at night, were of her. What was she doing? Who was she with? How was dealing with his betrayal? Did she even miss him?

His gut twisted again at the memory of seeing her hurt and angry face during the party. He couldn't blame her for not wanting to see him. But she'd need a court order to keep him away.

"Are you sure she's working today?" Beverly asked, once again glancing through the window at the huge crowd inside the diner.

"She was off the last three days." He shook his head, knowing that he really wasn't privy to her schedule. "At least," he said sheepishly, "that's what one of the busboys told me." He then took out his phone and pulled up his fake stock app. He hit a few buttons and a map showed up. It zeroed in on their location. "My IT friend made an app for me. It's a long story, but I noticed that Caroline shared her location with the app. I know she's at the restaurant today. My guess is that she's working if she's here."

Scott noticed several cars circling the tiny parking lot. More people were filing into the diner every minute. The crowd would make for a great cover, but it could foil their plan if Beverly couldn't get Caroline alone.

He put his phone away knowing that—even as

mad as Caroline was at him—she was probably so busy she didn't even realize she still had his app on her phone. "None of the waitresses will talk to me, let alone share her work schedule with me." He gazed through the window, but didn't see her. "They won't even let me into this place. Not even when I offered them money."

"Sounds like Caroline has some protective friends." She placed her gloved hand on his shoulder. "That's a good sign. It says a lot about someone's character when they have people who care that much about them."

Caroline was wonderful. Anyone spending even five minutes with her would know that. She was the girl next door, the sexy neighbor who didn't know how special she was, and the woman you brought home to meet your mother.

Scott's heart ached knowing what was at stake. He stared at Beverly, his life-line for the solution. He wanted her to know Caroline. Beverly's approval had always meant so much to him, but in this moment, he realized just how much he appreciated having Beverly, and her crazy schemes, in his life.

Only a true friend would do something as half-assed as this.

Beverly wore sunglasses, a hat, and was covered from head to toe in her winter coat. She looked like a housewife turned spy from a B-rated movie, the one who does anything—crazy as it may be—to get the job done. He was lucky she was on his side.

"Good God, this place is busy." She took a deep breath and let it out slowly. "Who would have guessed breakfast burritos and enchiladas were so high in demand."

His eyebrow rose. "You've eaten their food, you know how good their queso is."

"Very true." She tilted her head in agreement. "All these years of ordering for your office meetings and I've never actually been inside the restaurant."

"My first time was when Caroline rescued me and my foot." He shifted his stance once again, still feeling the slight pain of his sprain. Caroline had saved more than his foot that day. She had saved his soul.

"Why aren't you wearing your boot?" Beverly's chiding voice was full of motherly scorn, her face reflecting the same emotion.

"I'm fine."

"Uh-huh." Beverly grimaced but allowed the topic to drop.

"This place is kind of a hole-in-the-wall dive filled with history, loyal customers, and not too much glamour." She looked up at the old marquee, worn with age. "It reminds me of a place where Morty and I used to eat."

For a moment, her face saddened. It had been

well over a decade since her husband died, but he'd been like a father to Scott. Scott placed his hand on Beverly's shoulder, but she stood straighter and put on a proud face. He knew how lonely she was; after all, it wasn't like all personal assistants were eager to meet with their boss at five in the morning and work until midnight.

She once again turned to the window. "The flowers spruce up the place, though," she said in an obvious attempt to change the subject.

He had noticed that there was an excessive amount of blooms on each table. They were from the bouquets he had sent Caroline, the roses now dispersed around the room in tiny bud vases. He didn't remember how many arrangements he had sent her but figured they were all torn apart, unwanted.

"Is that her?" Beverly pointed to a Latina woman busy at a table.

"Look for a blonde—beautiful, and curvy." Beverly had sat at another table at the Christmas party, one in the back, and had missed seeing the show from a front-row perspective.

The crowd parted, and then he saw Caroline at the counter. It had been a week since he saw her face, and he stood mesmerized by her beauty. Her hair was up in a tight bun, and her eyes were slightly puffy. She had been crying. Weeping over what he had done.

She opened the cash register, and a concentrated expression appeared on her face as she counted out change for a customer. He watched her as a wave of people crossed between them and momentarily blocked his view. She then picked up some dishes and set them in a bucket for a busboy.

"That's her." His voice wavered and he swallowed the lump in his throat.

Beverly grabbed a hold of the strap of her purse and walked determinedly to the door. "Wish me luck."

---

*T*he restaurant was a madhouse.

A waitress had called in sick and, even though Caroline had asked for a few more days off, her unexpected vacation had gotten shortened.

At least she had something to keep her mind off Scott and all of his lies. Plus, she had a place to take the three bunches of flowers to. Her apartment was beginning to smell like a florist's shop.

Not that she minded the beautiful aroma, she just didn't need a reminder of what he had done.

She bussed the recently vacated counter spot, and then grabbed a clean, wet rag, knowing that another customer would soon take the seat.

"Caroline, another cup please."

Mr. Sweeney's breakfast was long gone. He had

sat at the counter for the past two hours, drinking coffee and bending her ear every chance he got. He'd probably stay until lunch, which was fine by her, but she needed more tips, and he was taking up a choice position at the counter.

She set the towel down and picked up the coffeepot.

"Like I was saying earlier, Caroline..." he began once she had refilled his mug.

Focusing on her job, she smiled at him and began wiping down the counter as he continued his tale. She didn't remember what he'd been saying earlier and, once again, just bobbed her head and said "uh-huh" every once in a while.

He and Maria were the only two who had asked her how she was doing after the breakup. They were also the only two she felt comfortable sharing her sadness with.

She needed to be nicer to Mr. Sweeney.

Even though she only saw him at work, and only paid him half of her attention, he was important to her. His father-like humor and advice tended to brighten her day—just not lately.

She didn't want to be here. Everyone was either in a rush for breakfast or eating with their families. All she wanted to do was scream and tell them to leave her alone. She didn't want to get their coffee, didn't want to serve them their eggs, and didn't want to listen to their problems.

Didn't anyone understand that she was dying inside?

"Is this seat free?" An elderly woman stood at the counter, sunglasses and hat in hand.

Mr. Sweeney turned toward the voice behind him. "By all means," he said and nodded to the barstool.

The woman removed her gloves and took a seat. "It's crowded in here today."

"It's crowded every Sunday morning." Mr. Sweeney grabbed a menu from farther down on the bar and handed it to the woman. "Huevos Rancheros is the special on the weekends, but I always prefer the Heuvito en Salsa."

Caroline couldn't help but smile. If anyone knew the menu by heart, it'd be Mr. Sweeney. In fact, getting him a job at the restaurant wasn't a bad idea, but Caroline suspected he was retired with a nest egg. Probably a cache of money he had saved over his entire life so he and his wife could travel, or at least take it easy in their old age.

Life wasn't fair.

Instead of traveling with his late wife, he was spending his retirement years here. But, at least, Mr. Sweeney had found someone special. Someone he could trust, who was worthy of walking down the aisle with all those years ago. It had only been a few weeks that she had been seeing Scott, but she had hoped to truly introduce Scott to her grandmother when she was awake and could remember him. Maybe even one day, sometime in the future, eventually hear wedding bells. But his lies, and the other woman...

No.

She forced back the tears.

She wouldn't fall apart at work.

She flashed her best fake smile at the customer now seated in her station at the counter. At least now, Mr. Sweeney had someone else to talk to.

"You sound as though you're a regular," the woman said.

He held up his coffee mug. "Best coffee in town."

His eyes had lit up, and Caroline noticed him sitting straighter on his stool. His button-down shirt, neatly tucked into his khaki trousers—*pants* didn't sum up his outfit, the man always wore pressed trousers—gave him an air of dignity.

In fact, he was perfectly dressed for a date. The two were roughly the same age, and the woman wasn't wearing a wedding ring.

Just because Caroline was lonely and likely to die alone didn't mean that Mr. Sweeney had to. Besides, a project would be a good way of getting her mind off Scott and his lies.

A genuine smile crossed her lips. "Mr. Sweeney is one of my regulars. He's here most mornings."

"Is he really?" The woman didn't glance over but kept looking at Caroline.

"You couldn't have chosen a better person to sit next to." Caroline made sure her voice was cheery and pleasant as she could. "He's a true gentleman."

She noticed a half-blush from the woman as she smiled at Mr. Sweeney. "I'm Beverly," she said, half to Mr. Sweeney and half to Caroline.

"My name is Jonathan."

Caroline's eyebrow rose. All of these months, and she had never known his first name.

"It's nice to meet you, Beverly," he said and then gave her a charming smile as she shook his hand.

For the first time in a week, Caroline felt thin strands of happiness spinning a web around her. The two made a nice couple. Everyone deserved to be happy, even if she weren't destined to find true love.

She bit her lower lip and took in a deep breath.

Not here. This was a tear-free zone.

Coffee cup. Silverware.

Caroline placed each item down in front of Beverly, focusing on her job. "Huevos Rancheros and Mexican Omelets are the special today." Caroline pointed at the menu. "Let me know when you're ready."

Beverly didn't touch the menu, merely tapped her finger on the counter. "I'd like to place a to-go order." She reached into her purse and pulled out a sheet of paper with a long list.

So much for getting Mr. Sweeney some company.

Caroline was lucky to have pulled the "to go" order shift. She had to deal with the customers at the counter, but taking phone and internet orders was easy. "Yes, ma'am." Caroline pulled out her order pad from her apron. "What's your zip code?"

"I live in Oak Brook. Zip code 60523"

Caroline's eyebrow rose and she held the pencil so it hovered over the pad. She loved that area of town. She had jogged her way through most of the winding roads of the neighborhood over the last few months. Oak Brook was the elite neighborhood on the outskirts of the city with the million-dollar homes. The gated community was a haven for the richest people in Chicago.

The one she had shared with Scott on their way to Avalon Memory Care.

She studied the woman. Diamond ring on her right hand, fur collar on the leather coat, and a handbag from…was that Gucci? The bag alone could easily cost several hundred dollars. She probably had a Rolls Royce with a driver parked outside.

Whoever she was, she was slumming it in this area of town. And by the way she clutched her purse, she knew it.

A frown settled on Caroline's face. "I'm sorry. We don't deliver that far out."

Beverly's face showed no concern, and she leaned in. "I'm prepared to pay extra for the delivery."

Money made the world go around, but there were some things it couldn't buy. Maybe a few weeks ago Caroline would have felt otherwise, but right now, she wasn't in the mood to deal with a rich, privileged person.

Beverly took a deep breath, and a smile crept up on her face—a smile that said, *'I'm used to getting what I want, dear'.* "I read about your policy online."

Why was this woman wasting her time then? There were other patrons in the place, ones who she could wait on and get tips from. "If you know about the policy…?"

"The food is for my best friend." Beverly quickly explained, her face flushing with a hint of excitement—or was it worry? Caroline couldn't be sure. "He met the love of his life at this restaurant, and it's a special New Year's party for the couple."

*Love of his life.*

Caroline wasn't sure if she believed in 'true loves' anymore. She had thought what she had found with Scott was love, but it was nothing more than deceit and lies. Her gaze wandered to Mr. Sweeney—Jonathan—who smiled and had a gleam in his eye as sat and studied the woman from head to toe. Love had worked out for him, at least for a while until he became a widower. She wanted him to be happy, but she didn't care about some rich stranger. The snarky words of, "how wonderful for your friend, Beverly,"

nearly escaped. Instead, the manners her grandmother had instilled within her prevailed. "I'm
sorry," she said, and she put her order pad away.

She didn't need to hear about someone meeting
the love of his life. Didn't need to hear about any
holiday party. And especially didn't need to hear her
boss yelling about any orders outside the delivery
zone.

"The order is easily over a hundred dollars in
food." Beverly reached into her purse and pulled out
cash. She began placing twenty-dollar bills on the
counter.

Caroline glared at the woman. Rich people.
Flashing cash and getting whatever they wanted in
life. Like everyone and everything had a price.

In the back of her mind, Caroline had tallied up
the money with each bill laid on the counter. She
hated that she knew the total amount, even before
Beverly had announced the complete sum.

It was like a dog salivating when a steak is
cooked.

The dog would, at best, only get the bone.

Looking at the money, Caroline could understand that feeling.

"I'm not allowed to place orders to be delivered
out that far," she said, her voice flat with a hint of
disinterest. She shook her head and ignored all the
money on the counter. "I'm very sorry."

Beverly leaned in. "I'll double the cost of the

order as a tip if you can deliver it personally this Saturday night. I'd need the food by 7:00 p.m." She placed another hundred dollars on the counter.

Beverly's voice sounded determined, and it caused Caroline to glance down once again at all the green on the laminate. A tip of that kind would be worth the extra trip, if her car could get her there.

"I work Saturday night until eleven."

Mr. Sweeney tapped the counter, his smile nice and wide. "Didn't you say earlier that you were covering another waitress's shift today?" He looked down at the money. "That is a fantastic tip for you, honey."

It *was* fantastic.

Pretty damn great.

Caroline bit her lower lip. The place was crowded and the person seated next on the counter had noticed the money on the counter. She didn't need a scene, plus the wait staff was always switching work shifts.

"You're covering for that new waitress right now. Can't she cover for you after 6:00 p.m. next Saturday?" Mr. Sweeney asked. "She owes you a favor."

"I like the way you think," Beverly said, tapping a manicured nail on the cash and smiling at Jonathan.

Mr. Sweeney gave Caroline a boyish grin back. "Just trying to help." He added in a whispered tone, "You didn't get paid for the bartending job that you walked out on. You should do this delivery."

Caroline glanced around, and no other employee was around to overhear their conversation, and the customer was no longer interested in their conversation. Once again, she pulled out her order pad and leaned in. "What would you like to order?"

## 19

"Thanks for the drive, Mr. Sweeney." Caroline shifted the bag of food on her lap and balanced the two that rested on the floor by her feet. The last thing she wanted was to spill food on the leather interior of his town car. "I'm sorry I'm taking up so much of your time tonight. I hope you can get to whatever party or outing you have planned for New Year's."

"I'm happy to help. And you were right not to drive out here alone, you never know what to expect. A home delivery?" His eyebrow lifted and a questionable expression showed on his face. "A young woman shouldn't do something like this alone. I doubt there is any cause for alarm, but you never know. Driving out here alone isn't safe." He gave her a gentlemanly smile as they exited the highway to Essex Manor.

"Well, besides the safety issue, my car won't be ready until tomorrow." It was actually ready, but the garage wouldn't let it go until she paid them what was due. In truth, she had the money but wasn't about to spend the five-hundred dollars that Scott had slyly given her. She'd have to find a way of returning it to him.

Which reminded her. She still had the stupid app on her phone. She'd have to remove that later when she didn't have a lap full of food.

"You need a reliable car, honey." He leaned forward and studied a street sign before turning left on the road, his car's tires sloshing in the slush of the cold streets. "I'd hate to think of you stranded on the road, especially in a bad neighborhood."

This house was definitely not in a bad neighborhood. Her running path went right past this home, and it was the one she had showed to Scott.

Dang. She almost made it the entire day without thinking of him. Inwardly cursing herself, she glanced at the car's clock. Almost seven o'clock. Her resolve was better than most days. Usually she was reminiscing about him and crying by noon.

"I have a friend down at Nationwide Auto," Sweeney said. "He's nice and would be able to get you into a good car at a good price."

She did need a good car. The money from this delivery would go straight to her mechanic, but what she really needed was a new mode of transportation—and taking the bus wasn't what she had in mind, even if that were the next step that she could afford. "I might just take you up on that offer, Mr. Sweeney."

"Honey, you can call me Jonathan."

For some reason, with his age and choice of clothing, it always felt right to call him so formally, but she smiled and said, "Of course, Jonathan."

Mr. Sweeney slowed the car and turned on a street in front of the school. Caroline glanced down the path they didn't take as they passed. If he had continued straight, she'd be at her grandmother's place in a few minutes. Thankfully, since the management at Avalon was in a mess, her grandmother could stay a little longer—hopefully, she could just stay. Of course, new management didn't mean cheaper rates, probably just the opposite.

She took in a deep breath. One problem at a time.

"That lady sure does live in a nice area."

Caroline glanced at the bag of hot food resting on the floor and read the name off the receipt, "Her name is Beverly."

"I remember," he said, smiling. "Sure, is a pretty name."

Suspecting that Mr. Sweeney gave her a ride for more than just to be helpful, Caroline said, "Beverly seemed nice. Very pretty too."

His smile deepened and curled on his lips, his cheeks slightly flushing. "And she's ordering plenty of food, probably for a husband and some kids..." He shrugged, "well, maybe grandkids."

"I don't recall seeing a wedding band on her finger." She caught a glimpse of his reaction. "A woman like that would wear a ring if she were married."

His face reddened, and he looked guilty. "I noticed her bare finger myself."

Dating someone with a family wouldn't be a bad idea, but not if Beverly was already spoken for. Caroline could see Mr. Sweeney being a sweet grandfather, but he never mentioned having kids, just a late wife.

Some people were meant to be parents.

One day, hopefully, she would be one too. Of course, one step at a time.

The car turned down a Logan Street and she could see her dream home.

Could it be?

The 'for sale' sign was gone, and now a white picket fence encircled the yard. Gazing at the porch, she saw a sofa rocker meant for two.

They were nice touches for such a perfect home.

Beverly had moved into her dream home. What were the odds?

Caroline may never be able to afford such a place, but she would be able to get a peek inside to see the entryway and maybe a little of the living

336

room. If she were lucky, Beverly would ask her to carry the food to the kitchen.

The kitchen certainly would have the latest appliances and, probably, hard wood floors throughout. She loved hard wood floors.

Mr. Sweeney whistled as he studied the house. "This is it." The two sat looking at the home, which was easily the largest one in the community. "Beverly must do very well for herself."

Judging by his car, Mr. Sweeney wasn't hurting for money. He was in what she guessed was reasonable health, was charming, and quite a looker for a mature man. He was also lonely.

"You should ask Beverly out. She was totally flirting with you at the restaurant. I'm sure she'll say yes."

For a mature man, he suddenly looked like a school boy. "I don't know."

"Worst case scenario, she tells you she's married. But you'd probably make her day." She patted him on the shoulder. "A handsome man like you asking her out. She'd likely love to have the compliment."

He turned off the engine and faced her. "Maybe."

Caroline didn't want to scare him away from a great opportunity, but it was like approaching a wounded bird that you wanted to help. "I'm thinking coffee. Maybe dinner." When he didn't answer, she added, "Love can be so wonderful."

He grimaced and his forehead furrowed. "Love can also hurt you deeply."

She knew that was true. She had felt so close to Scott and had really thought he was the one. But most men lied. She glanced over at Mr. Sweeney, who sat focused on the front door of the house. He certainly wasn't a scoundrel and liar. Maybe it was his generation, and the younger men she dated just didn't know how to treat a woman right.

"Love is worth the risk," she said in a hopeful, dreamy way.

"Do you really feel that way?"

His tone sounded sad, sad in a way that made her turn and look into his deep blue eyes. "I do believe that true love is important, and should be fought for."

"Now, that is interesting," he said with a pause in his voice. "You were happy when you were dating your young man. But now," his voice trailed off. "Now it seems like you're so sad and lonely. Like something in your life is missing."

A tingling of anger raced up her spine, and her body tightened in a way that makes it feel like your heart will explode. "It's different with Scott. He isn't a 'forever' type of man." The words stung her deeply and she pinched her lips together while she opened her eyes wide. The tears were coming, but she fought them off.

His hand gently touched hers. "I didn't mean to upset you."

"There's nothing to be upset over." She wanted to sound determined and strong, but her voice cracked.

"You're putting on a brave face, but if you really care for that young man, why don't you fight for him?"

Mr. Sweeney didn't know the entire story, and she wasn't interested in telling him—at least not all the details. He was like her father in so many ways—someone whose shoulder was there to cry on, but not someone you wanted to share any intimate bedroom details with. "I don't want to date a liar. He's dripping with money but pretended he was homeless."

"You said he had a job, and a cell phone. Doesn't sound as though he presented himself as being homeless."

True. But he never said he was rich.

"Did he ever tell you that he was poor?" Mr. Sweeney's gentle voice filled the car with fatherly concern and wisdom.

"We never went to his house, he never told me where he lived…"

"You've never been to my house. Do you know where I live?" Mr. Sweeney asked.

This was so different. She wasn't sleeping with Mr. Sweeney. Hadn't, at least in her heart, settled down with him and wanted a lifetime together. "That doesn't matter."

She stared out the window at the front door of the house once again. Just before she was able to say that they should take the food inside, Mr. Sweeney asked, "Did Scott ever tell you what he did for a living?"

She slumped back in her seat, her right elbow perching on the car armrest. "He said he was a clerk at a law firm." Or, did he say he worked in the mailroom? She thought back. He only said he worked at a law firm, not exactly what he did. "It doesn't matter. He led me to believe he was someone else."

"And he did this by telling you a false name?"

She didn't want to justify her rage, but Scott had told her his real name. "That was the only true thing he told me."

"Scott. Scott Hollister." Mr. Sweeney said the name clearly and distinctly. "He's some big shot heir to a hotel chain or something, right?" When she didn't answer, he added, "from the Hollister hotel chain?"

Sure, she should have recognized the last name of Hollister, but, honestly, you never think the person you just met is a rich millionaire.

"Everyone in the world, including me, knows how to use Google, Caroline. It didn't occur to you to do an internet search on him?"

She had thought to do it, but Googling him

seemed like an invasion of privacy and so cold natured. Her gut twisted. She had been a fool and knew it. She certainly would use Google the next time she started dating someone.

A pain twisted in her gut. She didn't want to date another man. Never wanted to date again.

"Is there anything wrong with a man working a family business and inheriting wealth?" His eyes held concern and wisdom. She suspected Mr. Sweeney had worked hard for decades before retirement, saved every penny he could, and lived comfortably. No one handed him his wealth, he was a self-made man. The expression in his eyes told Caroline that having a rich family, as long as you didn't become spoiled, wasn't inherently evil. And, she knew it wasn't. Family business—at least good and reputable ones—were always enviable. Just because she wasn't handed an easy life didn't mean she should hastily judge those lucky few who never had to work hard a day in their life.

But that was beside the point. Scott had lied to her. And, now after having Googled the name "Scott Hollister" after the party, she understood him to be quite the playboy. He had attended a good school and worked hard as a lawyer, keeping his name out of the tabloids, but not the social rags and social blogs. They showed that Scott had a new beauty on his arm every year.

"Well, is there anything wrong with a man inheriting wealth?"

The food was going to get cold if they didn't take it in, plus she hadn't eaten all day. The smell of the Mexican food had filled the car and she wanted to 'anger eat' the entire meal. "Inheriting wealth is fine. I just shouldn't have to Google someone's name to find out if they're telling me the truth or not."

"Not giving you full disclosure about his money isn't the worst thing a man can do. It's not like he was funding terrorism or something."

She didn't want to talk about it. A lie, whether deliberate, by omission, or by misleading someone, was still a lie. "I'm done with him." Her jaw tightened and she was desperate to switch topics. She pointed to the front door. "Are you going to ask Beverly out?" The tone of her voice was vindictive in a 'don't throw stones in a glass house' type of way.

His pain-filled eyes locked onto hers, making her wish she could take back her sharp words. "I had my one great romance. I doubt I'd find anyone to take her place."

Caroline took a deep breath and let it out slowly. It wasn't Mr. Sweeney's fault Scott had lied to her, no need to take it out on a friend who was spending New Year's Eve with her so that *she* could earn extra money. "No one can replace your late wife. But someone can fill the void her death left behind.

Besides,"—she glanced down at the sack in her lap —"I'll need help taking the food in."

*E*ven the doorbell's tone sounded rich.

"Hello," Beverly said, opening the door and greeting them. Alarm chimes sounded from an alarm unit and announced that a door had been opened. She wore a classy, church-going type of dress, fresh makeup, and looked ready to go to a charity dinner rather than entertaining at home. A perfect match for Mr. Sweeney and his daily khaki trousers and button-down shirts.

"Hello Beverly," Mr. Sweeney said. If the man had been wearing a hat, and not carrying in the majority of the food, Caroline was sure he would have tipped it with his greeting.

"Jonathan, I wasn't expecting you." Her smile led Caroline to believe him being here was an unexpecting surprise, one that she liked—especially since she remembered his name.

"Come in." She opened the door wider. Two rottweilers stood at attention behind her and kept an eye on them.

If ever a breed belonged to the rich, rottweilers was it. They sat like pristine marble statues with ears perked up and snarls on their faces.

"Don't mind them. The girls won't give you any

trouble." Beverly stepped aside and allowed them in, even though the dogs looked like they were poised to attack if given a command word. Again, the entry chimes sounded announcing a door had been closed.

Alarm chimes would drive Caroline crazy. In the summer she enjoyed a cool breeze in, and didn't need an electronic guard to beep every time she opened a window.

She juggled the tea in her hand and the bag of tortillas and chips as she walked in, her shoes clicking against the marble entryway. The pictures she had seen in the 'for sale' brochure did not do the home justice. Of course, the home was now exquisitely furnished with no tell-tale signs that Beverly had just moved in. No boxes stood in the corner needing to be unpacked, no crushed boxes in the corner for recycling...nothing. Picture perfect from the homes of the Lifestyles of the Rich and Famous.

"Please follow me."

The kitchen, with its marble countertops and top of the line appliances, accentuated the very best. It wasn't that everything matched. No, that would just be a sign of being rich. All the appliances were built in, custom jobs—the sign of someone being *super* rich.

There was no reason Mr. Sweeney couldn't fall in love with a rich person.

At least someone should be happy.

Beverly pointed to an empty spot on the large

center island and Mr. Sweeney placed the heavy bags onto it.

"Please put the drinks in the refrigerator, Caroline."

Caroline followed Beverly's request and placed the ice tea away. Inside the refrigerator she found some wine chilling, but not much more. Since the house had just been sold, Beverly probably hadn't had a chance to cook a real meal in her new kitchen yet. Or, maybe she was the 'ordering-in' type of person who had a personal chef—unable to even boil water—type of a person.

The house alarm bells went off again, followed by the sound of two rottweilers on a barking mission.

"That'll be my friend," Beverly said, handing her a stack of twenty-dollar bills. "Thank you for delivering this yourself."

Caroline's heart raced. This was the easiest money Caroline had ever made. Plus, she had time to stop off at her grandmother's place if Mr. Sweeney didn't mind a quick stopover.

She gazed into the adjoining family room. Leather sofa and chairs, wood tables, and a fireplace. Nice and cozy.

Her eyes narrowed in on the picture over the mantle.

What?

She blinked and involuntarily took a step closer to the room.

How did…?

Her mouth fell open and she walked from the kitchen to the family room, her feet nearly tripping over one another once she crossed from the hard wood to the carpet.

How did that picture get hung above the fireplace?

Her heart stopped. The room lost all the air. She could barely breath.

Why was the picture she and Scott had taken while feeding the ducks in the park hanging over the fireplace?

"Hello," a male voice sounded from behind her.

The voice sounded familiar.

It sounded too familiar.

She put the money in her pocket and her body stiffened.

"It's good to see you, Caroline."

No.

Her head craned around and she caught a glimpse of his blond hair.

No. No. No.

"It's been a while."

She reminded herself to breathe as she turned her body around and laid her eyes square onto him.

"You!"

She scanned the room, her gaze moving from his face to Mr. Sweeney's to Beverly's, then back to his. He wore casual blue jeans and a t-shirt today, not a tuxedo. Taking a step back, she glared at Beverly. The woman was smiling. Not a pleasant smile, but an evil scientist about to cry out eureka type of a smile.

She couldn't breathe.

"Wh...What the hell is going on?" Her voice cracked and she pointed accusingly at him.

Scott's hands went up innocently. "I wanted to see you, but you wouldn't answer your phone."

This was... he was... No. She wasn't going to be trapped like this.

Pulling the money from her pocket she threw it at him. "What kind of game are you playing?" She gulped some air. "You can't just..." her hand gestured around the room, "you can't...No!" She pointed a finger at him. "We're done."

She strode past him, lifting her arm and avoiding his touch as he tried to stop her. "Mr. Sweeney, we're leaving."

"I'm afraid my car is blocking the driveway," Scott said.

Her hands balled into fists and she turned and got into his face. "You can't just pay your friend," her hand waived in Beverly's direction, "or whoever this is, to... I don't even know what your plan was. Bring me here and win me over with more lies?"

The dogs, who stood at attention at his Scott's side, growled in unison—baring their fangs and looking like the fierce guard dogs the breed was known for.

"Meffie. Modie. Ruhig."

The dogs calmed down with that command, with one yawning and laying at his feet.

He may be able to command his dogs like that, but he wasn't Caroline's master. She wouldn't lay down and obey.

"I'm not going to lie to you, Caroline."

She crossed her arms. "That'd be different for you." She stood taller and studied him. He was the master of this house—her dream house—with a friend to do his bidding, his brunette model date probably somewhere lurking in the home, and two razor blades in fur coats at his feet.

Not to mention he had more money than God.

"Did you think I'd swoon and forget what you did?"

His face softened and he gave her a look of regret. "You're right. I shouldn't have lied to you like I did."

"Damn straight." She poked her finger and hit his strong, muscular chest. "You can't treat me like this." Tears threatened to spill, but she wasn't about to show weakness. "You made a fool out of me, pretending to care about me while dating that brunette…." She closed her eyes and wiped a tear away.

"Bev, can you and this gentleman please give us a minute," Scott said.

"If Caroline wants to leave, I think it's best that we go." Mr. Sweeney took a protective step closer to Caroline. He knew the right thing to say, and she'd thank him later for it. At least one person was on her side.

"Jonathan," Beverly said, her voice pleasant and calm, "let's give them a minute."

Mr. Sweeney's gaze darted over to Caroline, concern filled them. He puffed up his chest, even though Caroline knew he was no match for Scott. "What do you want to do?"

She took in a deep breath. It would be best to end everything right here right now. She needed to speak her mind, and Scott needed to hear it. "I'll be fine."

"We'll be in the library." Beverly ushered Mr. Sweeney out and began to close the kitchen door. The two dogs took an interest and began to follow them.

"Beverly," Scott called to her. "Please take Meffie and Modie with you."

Caroline watched as the dogs pranced out. Meffie and Modie. His killer dogs had baby kitten names. Everything was deceptive in this house.

"Please," he said, gesturing to the adjoining living room once they were alone. "Please have a seat."

She glanced at the sofa he pointed to, the one

facing the fireplace and their picture. "You have one minute. After that, I don't care if you sic your dogs on me. I'm out of here."

———

*A*t the very least she had agreed to stay for a minute.

"Please, have a seat." He gestured toward the leather sofa. His mind, once again, recited his prepared speech but he found it difficult to concentrate with his heart racing.

She gave him a cold stare, her stiffened body walking past him where she remained standing in front of the fireplace, studying the picture of the two of them. "This house was up for sale two weeks ago. It looks like you've lived her for quite some time."

"I…" His gaze shifted to the fully furnished room. "The interior decorator just finished. This is the first time I've been inside the place."

"Just like that?"

He took a deep breath, pausing his apology momentarily. "What do you mean?"

Glaring at him, her facial muscles hardened and a look of disgust, one that tore into his heart, bore into him. "I like this home so poof," her hands moved as if he had done some magic, "the house is now yours."

He had hoped to please her with the home, but, evidently, the home just made her hate him even more. "We don't have to live here if you don't want to."

"Live here?" Her eyes narrowed and a snarl crossed her lips. "You sure have some balls to say that to me."

"I never lied to you." His voice raised slightly and he chided himself on his lack of restraint. Getting angry and yelling would only make the situation worse.

"You never told me the truth." She wore a cross-over small bag and she opened it and took out the money he had given her. "All five-hundred dollars." She placed the stack on the side table. "I'm insulted that you played me with it."

"I wanted you to have the money but you wouldn't let me give it to you."

"I'm such an idiot. No one would pay that kind of money just to have someone watch a stock for them."

He did find it hard to believe she fell for it, but she did such a good job. "You earned that money."

"Really?" Her frosty tone cut into him. "I don't need your money."

He locked eyes with her, matching her intensity and passion. After a brief pause, he said, "And if I had said I'm worth millions, would you still have gone out with me?"

"We'll never know now, will we?"

"You would have seen me differently, and you

know it." He knew she wasn't a gold digger, not someone who would date him solely for his riches. But everyone saw you differently when they knew you had inherited millions of dollars.

"I'm seeing you differently right now." She took a deep breath and bit her upper lip as she eyed him from head to toe. "You're not the same Scott I fell in love with."

He couldn't help but smile. She loved him. She hadn't run out of the room crying—or screaming—and she confessed her love for him. There was hope.

He limped closer to her, his ankle barely giving him pause. "I'm in love with you, Caroline."

She turned and looked out the window, not responding to what he had just confessed. "Leather furniture. Custom fitted curtains. Naturally, only the best." She shook her head. "There's probably a Monet hanging in the bathroom."

"Having money isn't a crime."

She didn't look at him. "I thought you were a homeless person who needed help."

Gently touching her arm, he spun her around. "I did need help. But I'm not homeless. You assumed I was. I really did fall in the lake that cold day." He glanced down at his foot. "I really did hurt my ankle, and you took care of me."

A single tear escaped, and she wiped it away. "You had no money, no phone, and had to borrow my cell phone."

"My money was in my car, my phone had been damaged, and you were gracious to allow me to use your phone." He took a step closer. "You also gave me ice and...," the back of his hand brushed away a second tear that had fallen to her cheek. "And you were so kind to me."

"Anyone would have helped you."

"Not anyone. *You* helped me, even when you thought I was homeless and penniless. That's a rare quality."

She took a deep breath and stood straighter, filling her body with more fight. "At any time, you could have told me that you were rich. Instead, you took me to the park, you took me on dates that..."

"That I thought you'd enjoy."

"No," she said pausing. "You took me on dates you thought a poor girl like me would expect and appreciate."

His mind rapidly repeated that sentence, trying to understand her anger. "I liked the picnic. I liked..."

Her hand gestured toward her outfit. "No fancy operas for me, no fancy plays. What was I? Some sort of experiment?"

"My feelings for you are genuine, not..." A bubbling of frustration and anger rushed him and choked his words.

"Not some pity for the poor girl?" She said, completing his sentence.

"No." His defiant voice filled the room. "I continued to let you believe I was poor because I had never had a woman fall in love with just me before."

She stared coldly at him.

"You fell in love with me when you thought I was poor, when you thought I lived on the street." His chest tightened and he found it hard to breathe. "I fell in love with you because you loved me, not my wallet. Even after I told you my name, and you could have Googled who I was, but no, you only saw *me*." His hand beat on his chest. "Me and only me."

"But *you* didn't *just* see me." Another tear dripped down her cheek. "Who is the brunette?"

Guilt coated him and he needed to clear the air. "A mistake."

Her head slowly nodded and her expression hardened. "What? You accidentally fell and your dick landed on her?"

"What?" His muscles tightened and he felt flushed. He had always been faithful in his relationships and never thought he'd be on this side of such an argument. "I didn't sleep with Ilene."

Caroline crossed her arms. "Oh, so the slut has a name."

Damn it to hell. "I didn't sleep with her!" His hand raked through his hair and he began pacing. "Beverly," his head nodded toward the library, "hired a date for me so I could impress the founders of the company."

Caroline pointed to the closed door. "I don't know who that woman is. You may also be sleeping with her too for all I know."

His eyes widened and his jaw went slack. "She is my ex-nanny. I've known her my entire life." He added, "She's my personal assistant now. She takes care of me," his arm gestured around the home, "and my house."

Caroline looked away, studying the room and then eyeing Scott in a way that told him there was still fight left in her. "When?"

She stared defiantly at him, but he didn't know what she wanted.

"When what?" he asked.

"When did the date with the that woman get arranged? Was it a month ago?" Her jaw tightened. "A Christmas party would have been on your calendar for probably... I don't know... a year since the last one. When did your ex-nanny arrange this date?"

A knot twisted in his gut. She had every right to be angry about Ilene, and she needed to know the truth. "Beverly..." No, he had to be honest. It had been Beverly's idea but he went along with the plan and had shelled out the money. He had to own up to what he had done. "I hired her a week before the party."

Caroline's eyes narrowed again, a vein popping

out of her neck. "So, while we were dating you go and hire yourself a paid escort."

"It wasn't..."

"So, I'm good to sleep with but not to get dressed up and be taken somewhere fancy." She turned to leave. "I'm sorry you thought me and my poverty would have embarrassed you."

Before she could walk to the door, he grabbed her arm. "It was wrong to do, but you thought I was poor. I didn't see how I could tell you the truth in such a short amount of time. I needed a date for the party, and I wanted to take you, but I couldn't. I wish I had." He gazed longingly at her eyes. So much rode on her understanding how desperately sorry he was. "I don't want to lose you."

She stood still, so he added, "If I had told you before Christmas that I was rich, would you have gone to the party with me?"

"Well," she said stiffly, "you should have given me the chance to decide, but you didn't."

"You made the assumption I was poor. You even told me to go to a shelter for help, and a free clinic to have my foot looked at. I never told you a lie, I just let you believe what you wanted so I could get to know you. So, you could know me and not my money. Even if you would have been ready to know about my riches back then, I wasn't ready. I needed to..." his voice cracked and he took a deep breath. "I needed to tell you I was rich in a way that wouldn't scare you away, make you hate me, or... make you just want my money."

"And the brunette..."

"The brunette was eye candy for the company. Not as pretty as you. Not as charming as you. And definitely not as captivating to me as you are. I just needed a date for the party."

"You didn't have sex with her?" Her eyes softened, as though she were willing to believe him.

"No. I paid her as an employee to charm the bosses. But it didn't matter." He lifted her chin. "MacMillan told me that you had already charmed him. The single waitress working three jobs. *You* impressed him, and he said that a man who could win the heart of a lady of such quality was worthy of his company."

"What does that mean?" Her eyes held a brief moment of recognition. "You mean Bob?"

He explained about MacMillan being one of the senior partners. He also told her how Ralph and he had been fighting for the position of senior partner, and how Ralph had set her up. But Scott didn't want to dwell on that. He only wanted to talk about Caroline and their future together. She had moved from a standing position to a seated one on the couch. She seemed to listen to his every word. He took that as a good sign.

"They announced my senior partnership just before Christmas. I went out of town for a few days."

He shifted his weight on the couch and faced her more. "I just needed a few days to clear my head."

She studied him. "You don't seem overly excited to be the new senior partner."

He had wanted the promotion for so long. Now that he had the position, he discovered it was merely a stepping stone in his career. It's not what he really wanted in life. What he wanted sat next to him on this couch—her hands crisscrossed in front of her and leaning away.

In a softened tone, she said, "I need to think things over."

Fear gripped him, choking him. "To think what things over." He inched closer to her.

She unfolder her arms and rubbed her thighs. It was hotter in this room than he had realized and his hands were also moist with nervous sweat.

"I need to go." She moved to stand but he placed his hand on her knee.

"Here." He reached for an envelope on the coffee table. "I had some lawyer friends check everything out, and Beverly had an inspector at the place. The foundation is strong, but I feel that the management could use some adjusting."

She sat back down and settled into the couch. "What is this?"

He handed her the envelope, an excitement tingling within him and breaking out in a huge smile across his face. "Your Christmas present."

She opened the package and began scanning the many pages of the paperwork. "Avalon?" She flipped through the pages and stared at the last one. "What does Avalon Memory Care and this property sheet mean?"

Whether they ended up together, he wanted to ease her burdens. "You're now the owner of your Grandmother's facility. There's a brand new management staff ready to run the place the right way."

She flipped back to page one, her eyes flitting across the legal-speak. As she turned the pages, her eyes grew wider and wider.

"I don't want you to worry about your only living relative. I see how stressed you are about her care, and the financial problems you're having. Let me ease your worries."

"You're giving me a retirement home?" She stared blankly at him.

"No. I'm giving you peace of mind so you don't have to work three jobs."

She looked away, but not before a tear escaped. "You bought Avalon." She made eye contact with him, her lips pursing. "You bought Avalon...for me."

She wasn't smiling, but he thought he heard some happiness in her voice. "Not the entire chain, just the one your grandmother lives in."

A chuckle escaped and her lips pulled upward

into a smile. "I don't need an entire chain of elderly care places."

"I figured you could manage this one. The salary is good, probably more than what you'd earn as a waitress. Plus, you'd be with your grandmother the entire day, and she could stay there for free." He needed her to know one more thing. "Which is why she won the fake raffle and got January's month free."

She flung her arms around him and planted a kiss—passionate and loving—on his lips. The warmth of her mouth engulfed him, and he eagerly returned the passion. He closed the gap between them and held her close, finally holding her with all his might, never wanting to let her go.

"Can you forgive me?" he whispered in her ear.

She pulled away and beamed a smile at him. "I forgave you when you said you loved me."

## THE END

ALSO BY REGINA MORRIS

**Christmas in Newbury: A Billionaire Dad & Nanny Romance**

ISBN: 978–1–948997–47–8 (EPub Ebook)

ISBN: 978–1–948997–48–5 (MOBI Ebook)

ISBN: 978–1–948997–49–2 (Paperback)

Audio as well

Billionaire James Nielson plans to close many of his business's installations, including the original factory started by his grandfather in the small town of Newbury, when a woman—whom he had a sexual fling with over a year ago—abandons her baby at his company's headquarters claiming he is the father.

He and his baby daughter visit Newbury during the holidays where he hires a local woman, Melanie Frank, to be his nanny. She has been furloughed from her job at his factory, and, like everyone in the town, relies on the company for her livelihood. She wants to be an artist, but is financially trapped in the town by the company.

It is obvious to Melanie that James is uneasy around his daughter, isn't finding the town charming, and doesn't feel any Christmas spirit. She's plenty attracted to James, but will this city mouse really be interested in a country mouse? As James discovers lost family members, the warmth of a small community spirit, and the compassion from his daughter's nanny, he develops a stronger sense of family and his romantic feelings for Melanie grow.

He decides he must keep the factory running, and after buying Melanie's artwork at the local Christmas auction, she has renewed interest in her studies. The two search for the perfect Christmas gift for each other while trying to save the factory, which leads to a Christmas miracle.

## Contemporary Sweet Romance Short Stories

### Taking Chances

978–0–9966192–9–5 (ebook)

Available as an audio book

Broken engagement, a disappointed father, an emotional mother, what else could a wounded soldier ask for? Tommy has no idea that his sweet nurse remembers him prior to his injuries. Always professional, Abby treats Tommy no differently because of their awkward past. Once the truth is out, what will become of their friendship and budding romance?

* * *

### Christmas Joy

978–1–948997–18–8 (MOBI)

978–1–948997–19–5 (ePub)

978–1–948997–20–1 (Paperback)

Jake needs to clear out his father's old cabin and sell it. He's prepared to deal with the freezing cold weather and the remote location, but not with the sexy woman, who was once his late father's nurse, still living in the place.

\* \* \*

## More Than Puppy Love

978–1–948997–01–0 (MOBI)

978–1–948997–02–7 (ePub)

978–1–948997–03–4 (Paperback)

Ex-wallflower, now veterinarian, Kacie Preston is eager to go to her ten-year high school reunion where she can meet up with the boy she crushed on for years. But then his dog, her patient, shows up at the event mistreated. How well does Kacie really know her old heart throb?

\* \* \*

## FANASY / TIME TRAVEL BOOKS

### Just in Time (Short Story - Prequel to Time Historian)

ISBN: 978–0–9966192–5–7 (ebook)

ISBN: 978–0–9966192–6–4 (paperback)

Managing teams to send recorders back in history is stressful enough, but when the government makes a play for proprietary technology from the Historical Preservation Agency, Caleb must rely upon a well-connected, and sexy, developer at a government agency for help. Can the two of them keep time travel in the hands of historians?

\* \* \*

### Time Historian

ISBN: 978–0–9966192–8–8 (Print)

ISBN: 978–0–9966192–7–1 (ebook)

Also available as an audio book

Hank McConnell's is having a bad day at the office. First, he just destroyed history. He finds himself living in the Confederate States of America, Lincoln was convicted as a war criminal, and slavery existed for another fifty years. Secondly, his blunder erased his family from existence and his alternate self works as a lonely tenured professor instead of at the Historical Preservation Agency.

He doesn't have much time. He travels back to Lincoln's presidency to right what went wrong. Unfortunately, correcting time is like herding cats and one fix leads to more and more changes.

Is he willing to do the unthinkable to make the world whole again?

## PARANORMAL (VAMPIRE) ROMANCES

### COLONY Series Books

Vampires exist among us. They can be our neighbor, our best friend, our child's teacher...

They alter their aged appearance based upon the amount of blood they consume. They move to a new area, drink a lot of blood, and appear young. Slowly they limit their intake of blood and age, right in front of our unsuspecting eyes. After decades, they fake their death, move, and do it over and over again.

Most live quiet lives in an effort to blend in.

Some, however, want power and control.

The COLONY is an elite group of vampires sworn to protect the President of the United States from these rogue vampires. Few humans are privileged to this knowledge.

\* \* \*

**Eternal Service (Book #1)**

Top 100 Bestseller

978–0–9888222–0–7 (ebook)

978–0–9888222–1–4 (paperback)

Available as an audio book

Vampire Raymond Metcalf has too many balls to juggle and life is getting more complicated by the minute. As if working with a covert team of sexy vampires to protect the President isn't enough, he has to deal with his rebellious half-breed son, save the President from a crazed vampire, and break in a new director for his team since the last one, his best friend and the only human he trusts, has decided to retire. Why does his friend's replacement have to be the most beautiful human woman Raymond has ever seen?

Career military woman, Alex Brennan, is being offered the promotion of a lifetime, and with it a romance that she has desperately been seeking. Does she dare accept the position as Director of the COLONY, an elite group of deadly creatures of the night and risk a dangerous romance with a man who isn't even human? Together, can they save the President?

\* \* \*

**United Service (Book #2)**

Top 100 Bestseller

978–0–9888222–6–9 (ebook)

978–0–9888222–7–6 (paperback)

Available as an audio book

Sterling Metcalf is a modern–day vampire who clashes with his father's antiquated ideals. Being the half–breed of the COLONY group, Sterling hates being the team's weakest link. He jumps at an opportunity to do some fieldwork rescuing kidnapped vampire children and is accompanied by Kate Spencer, the nanny of one of the children.

Kate is a purebred vampire with a secret of her own. Can Sterling put aside his bad–boy ways and woo the lovely Kate? Will Kate accept the advances of a half–breed? Together, can they save the children from a religious cult who wants to kill them?

\* \* \*

**Enduring Service (Book #3)**

Top 100 Bestseller

978–0–9914034–0–0 (ebook)

978–0–9914034–1–7 (paperback)

Available as an audio book

Colony Agent Sulie Metcalf, the President's private physician, has been in love with the same human man for nearly thirty years. She refuses to allow herself the joy of true love because her feelings are unrequited by her human boss, Jonathan Dixon. As Dixon's retirement looms near, and his memories of Sulie and the last thirty years of his life are about to be erased, does she confront her fear of intimacy and take a leap of faith before it's too late?

Dixon has decided to retire and enjoy what time he has left. When his best friend Sulie, a vampire team member, is kidnapped during a medical emergency, Dixon realizes that retirement means giving up everything, and everyone, he's known for the last three decades. Will he risk his life, and his heart, to save her?

\* \* \*

### Equality of Service (Book #4)

978–1–948997–07–2 (MOBI)

978–1–948997–08–9 (ePub)

978–1–948997–09–6 (paperback)

Available as an audio book

Fifteen years ago, COLONY Agent William Wardell met his future wife Jackie Pearlman. She's sexy, opinionated, and finds him to be a mockery of the American dream of equality for all.

Can a past Freedom Rider and racial activist from the 1960s, now turned vampire, prove to the love of his life that he's not a political puppet?

\* \* \*

### Reliant Service (Book #5)

978–0–9914034–2–4 (ebook)

978–0–9914034–3–1 (paperback)

Available as an audio book

After faking his death from an assassination attempt on

the President, and retiring his first and only alias with the COLONY, Daniel Brighton discovers the mandatory sabbatical to be less than exciting. He chooses to do a favor and act as a security guard for a fading pop–singer, Lori Austin, whose career is winding down. He travels across Europe with her and discovers her past to be one of deception and intrigue with a history leading directly back to the COLONY itself.

Lori Austin is struggling to keep her career alive, and is willing to do what is necessary to save it. From bad press and scandalous stories, she travels across Europe on a relief tour to revitalize her career, but doesn't realize she is traveling with a vampire. Discovering a hidden family secret, she realizes that the one man who can save her is the handsome security guard she fought so hard not to hire.

\* \* \*

### Echo of Service (Book #6)

ISBN: 978-1-948997-31-7 (EPub Ebook)

ISBN: 978-1-948997-32-4 (MOBI Ebook)

ISBN: 978-1-948997-33-1 (Paperback)

Also available as an audio book

After the President of the United States is poisoned, Vampire COLONY agent Mason Warner steps in as the man's double. He manages the President's hectic schedule just fine until the political party sends in a public relations expert to clean up the President's image. She is the one woman from Mason's past whom he has never forgotten —the woman who is the measuring stick he compares all other women too—but he compelled her decades ago to forget their one night together.

Nicole Banner is assigned by the party to do a makeover on the one man from her past she despises the most. Years ago, her short-lived secret fling with the Senator of Massachusetts, now President of the United States, left her with a son to raise on her own.

Mason can't risk her remembering their tryst from decades ago since she believes him to be the President. Nicole has always hidden her affair from prying eyes, until now.

He still desires her. All she wants is revenge.

## COLONY World Series Books

These vampire romances feature vampires from the COLONY world, but these vampires do not work for the government.

\* \* \*

## Winter Wishes (Book #1)

ISBN: 978-0-9981866-0-3 (ebook)

ISBN: 978-0-9981866-1-0 (paperback)

Available as an audio book

Sammy needs a holiday miracle. The Vampire Council is after him, he's falling in love with his best friend's mother-in-law, and there's artwork hanging on the wall that was stolen by the Nazis. Life is spiraling out of control for this Jewish vampire as he spends the Christmas holiday baking cookies and wrapping gifts for the needy.

Louise is busy with her charities and hosting her annual Christmas party. Putting a smile on her face proves difficult when her soon to be ex–husband arrives with a bimbo on her arm, her proposed divorce settlement is far from fair, and the sexy stranger she's starting to fall for believes she's a Nazi.

\* \* \*

## Destined Desire (Book #2)

ISBN: 978–1–948997–16–4 (EPub ebook)

ISBN: 978–1–948997–15–7 (MOBI ebook)

ISBN: 978–1–948997–17–1 (paperback)

Available as an audio book

After a car accident nearly kills his immortal father, Alexander rushes to his father's side only to discover that his parents want him to marry and stay closer to home. He's already been down this path once before with a less than desirable outcome, so he refuses. He's steadfast in his decision until his parents threaten to financially cut him off and he's forced to approach the Vampire Council for a new marriage contract.

Dionora is enjoying her new job at the Vampire Council Marriage Office. The holidays take an exciting turn for her when she discovers the next match she does is for her ex–fiancé.

Revenge is sweet with this sensual romantic comedy.

# ACKNOWLEDGMENTS

Special thanks to my husband and our children for their love and support; to my sister for believing in me and encouraging me to follow my dreams; to my critique partners, Jean and Pennie, for being with me every step of the way; to my editor Chelle (Literally Addicted to Detail); and my proof reader team. I also want to thank my beta readers, and street team. This book would not be possible without the support I have had from all of you.

# ABOUT THE AUTHOR

*Dear Readers,*

*I hope you enjoyed reading my novel, Bachelor Soul (Book 2 of the 'Rich Indulgence' series). Please leave a review on the retailer site where you purchased the book.*

*You can find a link to all retailers at: reginamorris. com/bachelor-soul.*

*Please visit my website (http://www. reginamorris.com) for more information about my other novels and short stories. A list of my books and descriptions are below.*

*Please feel free to contact me through my website, through my many social media sites (see my website for the a list) or by email at mailto:regina@reginamorris. com?subject=Email from fan.*

*I like to play games and have fun in my quarterly electronic newsletters. Please sign up at newsletter.reginamorris.com*

*By day, I work in a small cubicle as a computer programmer, but at night I write about vampires, billionaires, and other romance combinations. I capture my creativity on the pages of my passionate stories. I write* about second chance romances, mature romances (where the characters are 40+ years of age), and about vampires.

My contemporary romances are mostly sweet romances (please check descriptions to confirm). The romances build a connection between two people with happily-ever-afters. No cliff-hangers, but complete stories.

The books in my series are all stand-alone novels that can be read in any order.

My COLONY series is about vampires who can alter their aged appearances by the amount of blood they consume. The series is about a covert team of sexy vampires who protect the President of the United States. This series' success prompted me to launch another series ("COLONY World") that involves the same world, but about civilian vampires who live among unsuspecting humans.

The heat level differs from mild to hot in my books. My stories involving the Historical Preservation Agency and time travel are mild. My COLONY series, COLONY World series, and some of my contemporary romances are hot. These hot stories have an age warning of 18+ on them. My contemporary short stories are mild. My contemporary novels vary.

I live in Austin, Texas with my husband and two children. I graduated high school in Germany and I attended the University of Texas at Austin, where I received a degree in Computer Science with a minor in math. After enjoying a career in software engineering, I discovered that writing is in my blood, and had to put pen to paper!

www.ingramcontent.com/pod-product-compliance
Lightning Source LLC
Chambersburg PA
CBHW021431240626
47153CB00001B/106